The Cost Of The Coat

Published by Darbie Hamilton
Copywrite © 2025 by Darbie Hamilton

Cover design by Mike Mulcahy
(www.blackironcreative.com)
Editing by Robert and Melanie Hamilton

Paperback ISBN:979-8-9999504-1-3

To Mama and my mermaids.
For believing this was possible even when I doubted.
Without you this dream would not have become a reality.

Prologue

The woman leaned on the doorframe as she studied her husband. He was not an exceptionally tall man, yet tall enough to make her tilt her head back to look him in the eye when standing at his side. Broad shouldered and strong, many had thought twice before matching him in a fight. However, as he braced himself against the railing of the upper deck of their house, violence was the last thing you would find in his eyes. Eyes which were, at this moment, honed onto the small child playing down on the shore below them.

Pushing out of the doorway, the woman moved forward and tangled her arms around him from behind, laying her head against his back. "She moves like you." she murmured gazing down at the young girl with him. A low chuckle, more felt than heard, rumbled through him.

"I was thinking she looked just like you. That mess of hair all over the place." The woman gave him a playful swat on the arm and joined in his laughter.

Their daughter, all of six years old, was racing the ebb and flow of the tide crashing on the sands under her bare feet. Carefully edging her way further onto the wet sand as the current pulled back, then jumping and dashing forward to beat the wave ashore. All the while the icy water nipped at her heels driving her on. Pure joy and delight painted itself across every aspect of her small face. As the water drove her forward again, a smile, which would have been laughter were she capable of such a sound, became the crowning jewel of this precious moment.

"I will miss this the most." The soft words held a hint of an Irish lilt to them, but at the same time, was completely unique to him. "When I return, she'll be nearly grown. I'll have missed so much. Will she even remember me, Annie? She's so young." Annie hugged him tighter, and the man clung to his wife.

"I won't allow her to forget." A heavy sigh broke free at her words, firm and confident. He knew without any doubt he could believe her. Turning so he could look her in the eye, he forged ahead to a subject neither of them cared for.

"You remember your promise? She will be much safer here with you, but she must never find it."

Annie released a sigh of her own, looking back into those stubborn eyes she loved so much. This was an argument they had had on many occasions. While she did not want to spoil these last few moments she had left with him, she had to ask one more time. Give him a final opportunity to change his mind.

"I gave it to my mother to hide. That way not even I will know where it is. But are you sure Eoin? She is your daughter after all. It's a part of her. Without it, she may never have the chance to speak. Be what she is...What you both are." Eoin gently placed his hands on Annie's cheeks to frame her face.

"You're right, without it she will not speak. Yet better for her to be silent, and retain her freedom, than to have her voice and be trapped. When she is older she can make the choice for herself. Until then, I say we give her as carefree a childhood as we can." Somewhat reluctantly Annie nodded in agreement.

"Then it will stay hidden as long as it needs to be."

Pressing a gentle kiss to his wife's lips, Eoin made his way down the long, wooden staircase of the deck, to the beach. At the bottom, he sat down on the steps and laced his long fingers together, propping his elbows on his bent knees.

"Shannon lass!" he called over the brisk wind. "Come over here, please."

Abandoning her game at her father's call, the child barreled over to where Eoin perched, stumbling a few times along the way due to the shifting sand. Flushed and panting slightly from her mighty dash,

Shannon came to a halt and gazed up into soft hazel eyes, such a contrast to her own, a striking blue so like her mother's. Her tangle of chestnut curls whipped around her slender shoulders in the salty air.

The young girl's hands, small and fragile looking, began to move in practiced but clumsy motions, as only a child could, in order to speak to Eoin. "*Want to play Daddy? I made a new game.*" Eoin's hands moved in the same sign language at the same time he spoke, his fingers more precise.

"I can't, Dear One. I have to go away for a while." Eoin's heart, already strained with grief from what he knew came next, nearly shattered at the look of confusion and pain that flashed across his daughter's face.

"*I don't understand.*" she signed. "*Where are you going?*"

"Somewhere far away. It will be a while until you see me again." His hand motions turned firmer than before. "But you will see me again. I promise." Reaching into his pocket, Eoin pulled out a simple leather strung necklace with a single pearl threaded into its center. Two small knots held it in place. Eoin's hands remained tightly clasped on the small piece of jewelry, but he continued to speak.

"You can use this to mark time. Mama will help you remember. Every year I'm gone put a new knot on one of the sides." Moving his collar aside he pulled out a matching band of leather. This one however, sported a small oyster shell held secure in a web of thin twined strips around the twin halves. "I'll do the same with mine. When I come back, we'll untie the knots together and it will be like time has not passed."

Shannon grinned slightly as her father draped the long cord over her head. Then without warning the girl flung her tiny arms around his neck. She clung so tight it became a bit hard to breathe, but Eoin did not care. He closed his eyes and desperately tried to commit every second to memory. Another set of arms enclosed around the pair on the steps.

Silent tears were not spared from anyone's eyes as the small family remained on the stairs. Unwilling to release the time and step into their new future.

Finally handing their daughter over to his wife, Eoin brushed the faces of his girls. With a pained smile he whispered, "My Treasures." Then he turned and walked up the beach, leaving his whole world behind him.

Eleven years later

Eoin Rowle sat in the crowded cafe as he waited. The bitter aroma of the coffee that sat on the table in front of him allowed him to focus on something other than springing out of his chair. Nolan already had him on a short leash. Making a scene in the middle of a restaurant may very well anger him enough to revoke Eoin's shore leave permanently. That was one thing Eoin simply could not risk.

His memories of living in this small town with his wife and daughter were more like a pleasant dream these days. He was able to see his precious Annie whenever he came back, but Shannon, she was another matter entirely.

Shannon was the reason Eoin found himself in the cafe at all. This was one task involving his family Eoin absolutely refused to hand off to another, no matter how much Nolan protested. Their protection was his responsibility, one he happily took on. So here he sat, drinking lukewarm coffee, and nearly vibrating with tension.

Finally, when the bell attached to the front door announced another customer had entered the building the man he had been waiting on answered the chime. A short hostess with a pixie cut and a contagious smile walked over to the young man. He was somewhat tall, reaching a height not quite six feet; lean and sturdy; built like a runner. When the hostess asked if he would be dining alone, he flashed her an easy smile and simply said, "I'm actually meeting someone." Making a show of glancing around the room, although knowing him he had already taken in as much detail the small establishment had to offer, he pointed over to where Eoin hunched in his corner table and gave the young woman another grin. "I see him over there; thank you though." The hostess almost looked disappointed as he made his way over to the older gentleman; but another group of customers were coming up to the counter to pay for their meal and the young man was pushed to the back of her mind.

Tristan McKenny dropped down into the seat across from Eoin and relaxed back in his chair. "Apologies for my tardiness, sir." He leaned forward to place his arms on the table between them, interlacing his fingers. "It's been a while since I've been up here. Had to find my way around." The words bore the same lilt as Eoin which would lead most to mistakenly believe they were from Ireland.

"You will certainly have enough time for that if all goes well today." Eoin grumbled taking a sip from his coffee. Tristan's eyebrows turned down slightly.

"Sir?"

Eoin did not get the chance to answer however, as this was the moment the waitress decided to come over and ask for Tristan's order. After a second coffee had been brought, and Eoin's topped off, they returned to the topic at hand.

"Heard you have been settling nicely in your current posting." Eoin said. Tristan gave a slight shrug at the comment as he poured sugar and creamer into the black liquid.

"Well enough I suppose. I certainly practice enough. I would hope there would be...some improvement."

"According to Angus, you're one of the best students he's ever had," the younger of the two men let out a harsh snort.

"Never took Angus for a flatterer."

"He's not, which is why I paid attention when he said it. Made sure to keep an eye on you after that."

"And what exactly did you find?" Tristan asked, wondering where this conversation was going. Eoin set his coffee aside, making a point of looking Tristan in the eye as he said his next words. If nothing else, he had the young man's full attention.

"Angus as usual was spot on in his evaluation of you. You have a natural talent for combat, one of the best I have seen in a long time. Weapons seem to come easy to you as well as hand-to-hand. Would certainly give a lot of us older veterans a run for our money if you wanted; and that is before you even get in the water. What I'm most interested in, is the fact you don't let brute strength dictate your actions." Eoin tapped the table. "You're a thinker, a planner. You take in everything you can about a situation before you act, and you do so within seconds." The older gentleman eased away from the table, and let his gaze rove the bustling cafe. Too many times he caught himself looking at one table in particular.

Without looking back at Tristan, Eoin continued to speak. "There is one more thing I noticed about you, which made me ask you to come out here today." Tristan decided it was most likely best to let his superior move at his own pace. Something was different with him. Tristan had never seen Eoin Rowle distracted before. Most of the time he was so intense it was hard to hold any kind of prolonged conversation with the man, but obviously now was not the case.

Finally, Eoin turned back to again focus on Tristan. "From what I can tell, you don't seem to be incredibly interested in moving up the ranks, despite your ability to do so." Absently Tristan ran his finger around the rim of his mug.

"I serve where I am needed. If I'm needed in a higher rank, I will be. Until then, I am content to stay where I am." Eoin closed his eyes for a brief moment in what appeared to be relief.

"Over to our right, sitting in the third booth, there are two girls. Do you see them?" Tristan took a beat to scan the room once more and quickly found the young girls he was talking about. Each had a milkshake in front of them and what looked like textbooks strewn all across the tabletop. They were waving their hands around all over the place and laughing. A bit confused Tristan turned back to Eoin. The older man just stared back. "The brunette... is my daughter."

This floored Tristan. He was pretty sure his mouth was hanging open as well. Everyone knew the Lann had a family on the mainland. But they were treated more as a sort of rumor than anything else. Very few had ever seen them, let alone met them. Even their names were mixed up on quite a few occasions. This never seemed to bother Eoin Rowle, at least not so anyone could tell.

"Sir, if I may, why exactly did you ask me here today?" It was Eoin's turn to fold his hands on the table.

"As most know, I am currently not permitted to live here on the mainland . This leaves my family vulnerable. There are at least two enemy strongholds in the territory, and while they are not aware of who they are, my wife and daughter still need to have a competent guard placed for their protection."

"Understandable. I'm assuming you are wanting me to take over this position?" Eoin nodded.

"You would be well paid. I have set up a small house along the shore with everything you would need there. It's a fairly simple assignment. It would be for a year, minimum."

"Sir, forgive me for being blunt." Tristan hesitated for a moment, but Eoin waved his hand for the young man to keep going. "From the little you've said they're not exactly targets, at least not yet, and hopefully never. That being said, they are your family. I would assume this would go to a much more experienced person. Not a green, twenty-year-old grunt." He scoffed at himself and spread his hand in front of him. "What's the catch?"

Eoin gave a chuckle with no humor attached to the sound. "I would think that would be obvious. It is a guard position. Not only that, but a guard position of a teenage girl. You would be watching her go to school, work, or to the mall. This is probably the most boring assignment I could give you. To add to it, you would be here full time, completely separated from the clan. It wears on a man. The longest I have ever been able to keep a guard here is two years. The men I place here get tired very quickly of not being on the front lines."

Eoin used a wooden stick to stir his coffee into a whirlpool, then just watched it spin. "My brother insisted this only be a volunteer assignment, so there was nothing I could do on the matter." His eyes shifted back to meet Tristan's, who was focused on his every word. "All I am asking for is one year. That's all. One year. After such time, if you want to go back to regular duties, I will transfer you back and find someone else. Will you do it?" His tone was even, yet Tristan could hear the strain behind it. All the man was trying to do was find someone to protect his family when he could not. Still, Tristan had never been separated from the clan for that long a time and he wasn't sure he was mentally prepared for the ache the distance would bring.

He looked back at the two girls sitting in the booth. They had settled into their studying, which Tristan assumed had brought them to the cafe in the first place. The blonde girl sitting with Eoin's daughter apparently said something funny, which set the two off to giggling again. There was something off about the scene that Tristan couldn't put his finger on.

It hit him like a brick wall. It wasn't possible, but his ears told him otherwise. Tristan could only make out one audible laugh coming from the booth, even though both girls were enjoying the mirth of whatever they were talking about.

Tristan's eyes landed on Eoin in questioning horror. However, he saw the truth in the older man's face. Tristan's heart began to hurt for the girl who was, most likely, not aware of what she had lost.

He refocused on the pair in the booth. They had managed to calm down enough to make an attempt at studying once more. A determination, which surprised even him, filled Tristan. In the end he only had one question for his superior.

"What's her name?"

"Shannon, her name is Shannon.

Chapter One

Six years later

The town of Shelter Bay was as unexciting as any town could possibly be. To call it small would be so gross an understatement, it would be along the same lines as calling the ocean wet. What the demure town lacked in size, however, it made up for in pure character. In most cases this statement would be regarded as a local's desperate attempt to defend the town's honor against its more developed neighbors. Though along the upper coast of Maine, those cities could barely claim such a title themselves.

Bustle or not, Shelter Bay certainly had its own personality. It was the kind of place where everyone knew everyone. A place where your friend's grandparents had grown up with your grandparents. They in turn had raised their own children here, who then raised you. The best comparison one could make was having a town-sized family; complete with crazy relations everywhere you looked.

At times it was an odd place to live, yet Shannon Rowle loved every brightly painted house, unevenly paved street, and eccentric store owner Shelter Bay had to offer. It was her home, in every sense of the word. Every memory she had, whether good or bad, had been made within its limits.

Today was simply another ordinary day. Shannon made her way along the boardwalk, taking her time on her way to work. She had a car of course, but Shannon had always preferred to be outdoors whenever she was given the opportunity. Her joy was strolling through town, or hiking in the woodlands around the township, or most often, ambling down by the coastline, barefoot and striding through the clear waves, despite the chill of the northern waters.

While she had opted for her usual mode of transportation, Shannon knew this was no time for a leisurely walk on the beach. Field trip season was starting today. In such a small town, teachers had limited choices that did not include several hours in a bus crammed to the seams with elementary-aged kids.

The Shelter Bay Marine Center was a local option yet was not exactly the most impressive place to go. Originally built to be a state-of-the-art aquarium with the intent to bring in tourists from larger cities, it devolved into a fancy research station and animal rescue. The fourth and fifth grade teachers, whose predecessors had stolen the Natural History Museum in Bar Harbor one too many times, liked it as a fun alternative for their students.

All employees were encouraged to park along the back of the building to leave as much room as possible for guests, so it was a barren parking lot Shannon trotted across, to a set of double doors. The stylized symbol of two dolphins chasing each other in a circle was frosted across the glass, along with the words Shelter Bay Marine Center in thick bold lettering.

Tugging her lanyard from the side pocket of her backpack slung onto one shoulder, Shannon snatched the chime of keys dangling from its end, selected the correct one and jammed it into the slot. There was always a minor battle first thing in the morning when attempting to coax the latch to do the job it was designed for. The door had to be in precisely the right position, and key at exactly the right angle, and the perfect amount of pressure applied before the lock would release and allow the would-be intruder entrance. To most of the staff it was an incredible annoyance, and many had petitioned the office manager to change the temperamental contraption, to no avail. "The door can still be locked and unlocked. As long as it does that, there is no need to change it out," was the only response.

After a few seconds of struggle the door relinquished the fight and unlocked with a solid thunk. Swinging the glass wide, a wave of air blew past

Shannon carrying scents of lemon cleaner, salt, and somewhat burnt lint from vacuuming the carpets the night before.

Hurrying over to the small wall-mounted security panel she methodically punched the code into the faded keypad. The war with the door always made getting to the panel in time a bit of a challenge. Any day not having to endure the growly tempers of deputies sent down to investigate the alarm was a good one. It was early enough in the morning without adding that nuisance.

Potential inconvenience avoided, Shannon re-adjusted her backpack and started toward the break room at the back of the building. Most of the lights were still off, but the sun was beginning to peak over the trees providing plenty of light for someone who in all likelihood could maneuver the entire facility blind-folded.

Despite her familiarity, upon reaching the de-sired space, Shannon made a swipe at the panel coming in, throwing all the switches on. Florescent light flooded the area, forcing her to take a moment to allow her eyes to adjust from the dimness of the lobby.

The room was a good size for its purpose. There were not many who worked at the marine center, so they did not require much space. Tucked in the corner, rested a small couch and a couple of chairs, faded and worn, but still comfortable and kept clean. A table ringed with folding chairs occupied the center of the room. Cabinets, a fridge, and a tiny microwave oven made up what the staff called "the kitchen" along the far wall. Unslinging her bag Shannon walked to the final adornment of the room. Nine sets of tall lockers stood in the opposite corner of the furniture. Rolling through her combination, the padlock popped off into her hand and she deposited her backpack on the hook in the back of the metal box. An extra pair of clothes and socks were folded neatly on the tiny shelf at the top, along with a spare swimsuit. Working with all the animals as well as their food could at times get messy. Even some of the front desk employees kept spare essentials in their lockers in case of emergency.

Shannon was strapping on the walkie-talkie all crew members were required to have on them at all times, when a voice from the front of the room startled her.

"Getting an early start to the day as usual Miss. Rowle?" Shannon spun and stumbled backward into her locker door slamming it shut with a metallic crash. With it now firmly closed, she leaned against the lockers and forced her breathing to go back to normal.

"Goodness! Are you alright?" said the petite woman in the doorway.

A somewhat sarcastic smile touched Shannon's lips as she touched the tips of her fingers of her flat right hand from the edge of her chin to slap against her left palm, then brought her right arm around her horizontal left arm. One of the signs everyone had come to know, even the most hopeless in learning the language, "Good morning."

More than half of understanding sign language was reading body language and facial expression. Conveying what you felt as well as what you were trying to say was simply par for the course. As such, despite knowing next to nothing of American Sign Language, Alice Lennot, manager of the Shelter Bay Marine Center, had no trouble at all understanding Shannon.

"Sorry for scaring you, that was not my intention" Mrs. Lennot said walking fully into the room. Immaculately dressed in a navy-blue skirt and blazer, ruffled cream shirt ironed and neatly tucked, and white-streaked blonde hair perfectly tucked into a French twist. She was the picture of office pro-fessionalism. A fact she was teased quite often about by the more laid-back staff.

Mrs. Lennot was not a harsh woman, schoolmarm attire aside, she simply had an idea of how things should be and led by example, both in attitude and appearance. Perhaps choosing an establishment where those who worked there on a regular basis handled raw fish, cleaned out algae slicked tanks, and were routinely soaked in tank water, was not the best audience for such an effort. Yet she attempted the feat anyway, which ironically just made the staff love her all the more.

"I know today will be quite busy with so many schools scheduled for tours, but if you could remind Mr. Timmons to drop by my office this afternoon, I would be most appreciative. There are some things I would like to go over with him about the new exhibit." While speaking she unconsciously smoothed her skirt. Shannon gave her a thumbs up and nodded. Sometimes the simplest forms of communication were best.

"Thank you," she replied turning and heading for her office. Shannon bent down to pick up the walkie-talkie from where it had dropped when Mrs. Lennot had manifested. Shannon quickly checked the device over for damage. Satisfied, she strapped it to her belt while she made her way to the prep room.

The prep room was where most of the people who worked directly with the animals started their day. Essentially, it was a large kitchen. Multiple full-size refrigerators lined one wall. These housed the majority of the food supply for the aquatic residents of the marine center for that particular day. Two long stainless-steel tables provided plenty of working space. The dull concrete and drains on the floor made it so they were able to keep the prep room near spotless.

Shannon snagged the handle of the first fridge and threw her weight back in order to haul the heavy, sealed door open. The snap of the cool interior dashed away what little drowsiness was left over from the morning. Hooking her fingers on the top bin down from the shelf, Shannon let gravity and momentum aid her in shifting the awkward tub to the counter. The sardines piled in their plastic container shifted when jerked free from their frosted storage, throwing Shannon's balance off kilter. The bin, instead of being gently placed on the prep table as intended, crashed on the metal surface. Shannon winced as the sound echoed around the empty room.

At least what she thought was an empty room. A deep chuckle accompanied the entrance of a tall, broad-shouldered man. Dark skinned with his hair cut short to his scalp, and a jagged scar along his forearm made him look more like someone who belonged in a biker gang rather than the marine biologist he truly was.

"*Graceful as always. Good morning, Shannon.*" Instead of speaking, his hands conveyed the amusement playing in his eyes. Ezekiel Timmons was one of the few people outside of her immediate family who had taken the time to learn Shannon's way of communicating in its entirety. His large hands sometimes made it difficult to sign quickly, yet at the same time it was not an issue at all. The almost drowsy way he signed made it seem as though he had all the time in the world to say what he wanted. Mirroring his southern drawl, it calmed you without even knowing you were stressed to begin with.

"Morning Zeke, no coffee this morning?" Shannon answered the greeting with a smile that always came easy when Zeke was around.

"Just about to go make a pot. You want some?"

"No thanks. I have to get the buckets started and it would just start tasting like fish" she signed making him laugh. "Oh, Mrs. Lennot wanted to see you in her office later today." Zeke nodded his thanks then went in search of liquid energy.

Ducking underneath the counter Shannon pulled up several white plastic buckets each written with the name of a tank or specific animal and the feeding times so everyone could keep track of who had been fed already and who was still waiting. The eraser board by the double doors leading to the backstage network for all the tanks sported the same schedule. With both systems working together, it was rare for any of the animals to miss their supper.

Tying back her thick, brown curls, Shannon snapped on a pair of gloves, threw on an apron, placed the first bucket on a scale, and began the monotonous task of cleaning and sorting all the fish for the day.

About halfway through the first bin, Zeke returned, steaming mug grasped contentedly in his hand. After pulling a swig of the sharp drink, he set the cup aside and pulled out his own bin to start sorting alongside Shannon. The two worked in comfortable silence for a good portion of the morning. This was one of the few times of the day when there weren't dozens of people buzzing around, and both preferred to preserve the moment of peace.

Hands buried in scales and fins; Zeke chose to speak. "During morning exercises this morning, I want you to spend a bit of extra time with Romeo." Shannon shot him a questioning look. Accustomed to interpreting her various expressions, Zeke answered the unspoken query without missing a step. "He's been getting a bit too aggressive for my liking, especially with Juliet's pups coming soon. He likes you a lot more than me; I'm hoping you can burn off some excess energy so he won't cause as much of a problem." Shannon nodded in understanding.

Three bins sorted and ready for the day, people began trickling in as they continued with the rest. The extra hands walking in the door joined in and made the rest of the task fly by.

After all the cleaning had been done, Shannon grabbed one of the rolling carts and stacked the scaly breakfast on top, then set out to do the morning rounds.

While the marine center was a modest facility, the backstage workings could at times become a maze if you were not familiar with the building. Cries for help over the walkie from an unsuspecting new employee was not completely uncommon and wonderful source of entertainment for the veterans who remembered the confusion of their first days. Having worked at the marine center in some form or another since she was a teenager, the place had become as much her home as the house she shared with her mother.

Making quick work of the larger tanks housing the majority of the sharks and stingrays, Shannon guided the cart toward the mammal enclosures. Before reaching the door, loud barks and yips echoed back through the halls to her ears and made her smile. Falling against the door, Shannon pulled the cart through into the raucous chorus.

The tenants of the spacious room were at first too occupied watching a pair of males showing off for them to notice they had a visitor. Placing two fingers at the front of her mouth, Shannon released a shrill whistle which caught the attention of all, including those in the heat of battle. Three sea lions and two harbor seals hurled themselves out of the massive pool and onto the smooth concrete. The first to reach her as always were the trio of sea lions, who, being able to somewhat walk on their fore-flippers, were much faster than the seals with their shuffle-scoot across the slick floor.

By far these were Shannon's favorite inhabitants of the center. Always playful, always cheerful, each with their own distinct personality, and far too smart for their own good at times. They all gathered around her like excited puppies when their owners returned home. Unable to speak to her flippered friends, Shannon clicked her tongue to the roof of her mouth, one of the few audible sounds she was able to make, as she knelt and petted a few of their silky heads.

Knowing she had to continue on with her task, Shannon held up her palm and loudly clicked once. Immediately they all backed up and got into a semi strait line. There was never complete uniformity when dealing with wild animals, yet at least when Shannon was in the room it was very close. For some unknown reason the barking quintet always behaved themselves around her. Most of the animals did but the seals and sea lions especially loved her. They must have known the feeling was mutual.

Bringing over one of the buckets, Shannon stood and divided out the variety of fish. The seals each trying to inch closer to get more of the coveted treats without her seeing and reprimanding them. Swallowing the fish whole one by one they all finished their breakfast and began to bump and nudge Shannon in an attempt to get her to play.

Shannon gave the creatures a long side look. *"Well, I was asked to wear them out a bit,"* she thought going over to the box on the wall containing the collection of toys, much to the excitement of her audience. The eager barks rose as all five seals converged on their friend, fighting for her attention. Laughing silently, Shannon selected two of the multi-colored balls and tossed them as far into the pool as she could.

Darbie Hamilton

It was as though someone had fired the starters gun at a track meet, with a slap of blubber and fur the race was on. The three sea lions easily took the lead getting to the edge of the pool. Shannon knew, however, that once they all were in the water the playing field would be instantly leveled. As awkward as the harbor seals could be on land, they moved like dancers in the water.

Romeo and Bosco, two of the sea lions, were the first to reach the fluorescent, floating ball. A minor skirmish as to who would drag it to a watery death ensued, Romeo being the ultimate victor. A fact he chose to taunt an annoyed Bosco with. A sharp whistle put an end to that.

Shannon observing all this thought, "I see what Zeke meant. If Romeo keeps that kind of behavior up, Bosco is gonna start a real fight." Shannon did a quick scan of the water and found Juliet relaxing on one of the rocks at the far end. She was one of three females they had at SBMC and was the only one currently pregnant. The vet was scheduled to come and see her today to check on the pups. It was almost time for them to be born. It was possible Romeo was guarding them.

Still can't have them injuring each other. Another whistle and Shannon pointed at Romeo then drew her hand back in a 'come here' gesture. He understood. Diving down further into the pool, Shannon lost sight of him for a moment before he reappeared at the edge nearest her, shedding water as he slipped over the side.

Snatching one of the smaller containers of fish Shannon ran Romeo through most of the tricks he had been trained on. Rewarding him with a sardine for his trouble. The sea lion had been living in captivity for more than half his life after an injury made it so he would not do well in the wild. As a result, the training he had received gave him an impressive number of skills. Ones he thoroughly enjoyed showcasing.

Not wanting to tire him completely, out Shannon released him and allowed him to go back to the group. Collecting the toys from the pool, despite the avid protest of its occupants, Shannon set everything to rights, made sure the gate was locked shut, and began pushing the now empty cart back to the prep room.

Depositing it back in the now bustling kitchen, Shannon then went in search of her mentor.

Chapter Two

The day's activity was gradually rising to its full momentum. Most nights they set everything so the morning crew could simply walk in and begin working straight away. Only simple things, like setting out the fan of folded maps and event schedules on the front counter and sorting out tour responsibilities had to be seen to. A task the group in polo shirts ringing the front desk were engaged in. One of which was a young woman of medium height, with straw blond hair tied high on her head in a ponytail. She stood in the semi-circle of crew members listening to Mary, the senior guide, lay out how they wanted the rotation to flow for the day.

Mandy Luis was a spunky, exuberant, and overly sarcastic girl that had been attached to Shannon's hip since both were in grade school. A fateful playground meeting had welded them together. The fearless, "new girl", Mandy, had come to the rescue of a shy and reserved, Shannon, who had caught the attention of the school bully. Flinging wood chips and insults that were pure genius for a seven-year-old, Mandy made certain anyone would think twice before messing with her new friend again. She, like Zeke, had learned American Sign Language to perfection. A skill she used often to get away with teasing those who had no idea what was going on.

The tour guides began to disperse, and Shannon took the opportunity to step up beside her friend. Mandy stood leaning her hip against the front counter, arms crossed, smiling and chatting with the reception-ists cloistered behind the line of outdated computer monitors. She still had a few minutes until the first buses would arrive.

Shannon knocked against Mandy, pushing her slightly off balance. Mandy smirked as she teetered back onto stable footing and began signing, her slender hands quick and sharp. "*Morning! Any miscreants today?*"

"*Nothing a few bouncy balls and sardines can't fix.*" Shannon answered.

Chuckling, Mandy returned to bracing her arms on the counter, and for the benefit of Mary and the young girl trapped behind the barrier, began speaking aloud while her hands continued to dart through the air.

"Rebecka, this is Shannon," Mandy said to the teenager wearing one of the Center's logo T-shirts and a volunteer name tag. On occasion, when college application time rolled around, the center would have a stream of eager-faced teenagers wander through their doors in search of volunteer hours. Shannon would have been shocked if the fidgety brunette was older than seventeen. This must have been one of her first solo jobs because Rebecka's gaze was locked onto Mandy like a lifeline as she talked. "Shannon's basically the apprentice of Dr. T. You'll meet him eventually. He's one of the marine biologists and trainers here. Anything you need to know about this place," Mandy pointed at Shannon and clicked her tongue. "She's the girl to ask. Shannon has been here longer than most of us."

Shannon propped her elbows next to Mandy's and gave the girl an easy smile and a wave. Shannon signed a few words and Mandy interpreted automatically. "Nice to meet you, Rebecka. Hope you have fun while you're here."

A hesitant look came across Rebecka's face as she glanced between Mary and Mandy, then back to Shannon. A sense of mild dread washed over Shannon. She knew what was coming but could not do anything to stop it. Rebecka had come to the same conclusion as everyone else in her life when they were first introduced. Rebecka also decided to do the single most annoying thing possible. She began to shout. "It's very nice to meet you too! This is my first day! I'm still learning to handle everything up here!" Through sheer force of will, Shannon managed to keep a blank stare through the megaphonic greeting delivery. Every word was overly pronounced and accompanied by broad hand gestures. Typical.

Mandy dropped her head onto her arms and banged out a steady rhythm. Mary stood with her hand stretched as though she was going to hold the girl back. "Um, Rebecka, Shannon isn't—" She started to say but Shannon had already reached for her back pocket and pulled out a note book.

Because it was rare for anyone to know sign language, Shannon had always kept a pen and a notebook of paper stashed somewhere on her person. This allowed her to communicate with anyone. Whenever an old book needed to be replaced the first thing that she wrote in the new book was a series of phrases she used on a consistent basis.

Shannon's practiced fingers flipped to the page she wanted and, smile still in place, she held it up for Rebecka to read. When she saw what it said, the girl's face turned a shade that would compete with any tomato. Printed in neat, bold letters, so anyone could understand with ease, were the words, "I am mute, not deaf."

At this point Mary started laughing. She placed her hands on the embarrassed girl's shoulders. "Don't worry too much about it. I did the exact same thing when I first met her too. A lot of us did, actually. I'm afraid she is used to it."

Still red, Rebecka dragged her gaze up to look Shannon in the eye, "Wh...Why can't you talk, o... or do you just choose not to?" she asked, her voice small and carrying a smidge of a stutter of nervousness.

Shannon used her pinky to catch the next page to flip it over. "My vocal cords are nonfunctional. They won't make any sound. I do not know why, they just don't."

"Oh, okay," replied Rebecka to the written answer.

An awkward silence fell over the trio. A situation hastily managed by Mary redirecting the teenager to the spreadsheet opened up on her computer. With her charge parked in front of the screen, the older woman shot Shannon a sympathetic look. Shannon only shrugged. Like Mary had said, she was used to it.

The front desk busy, Shannon faced the front entrance. "How many tours are you doing today?" she asked Mandy

"Only two. But the last one is Ms. Hartworth's class."

Shannon winced, "Good luck with that." The blonde nodded solemnly.

"Dinner at Mellie's?" Shannon suggested. Mandy sagged against the counter,

"If today is anything like last year, absolutely. Chocolate cake can cure anything." The easy laughter was broken by Zeke's voice scratching out of Shannon's walkie.

"Shannon, I need your help with tank C1, please. Bring your wet gear when you come. This one could take some finagling." Shannon pressed the talk button twice making the box sound two piercing pings, letting Zeke know she had heard and was on her way.

Shannon threw a sly grin at Mandy then hunched her spine and looked at her friend across a hiked shoulder. "The master is calling." Mandy snorted and swatted at Shannon's retreating back, pushing her on her way.

"Oh yes!" Dripping with sarcasm she called, the words laced with restrained giggles, "The slave driver will have your hide if you don't hurry along.

$\mathcal{A}$ squeal of worn brakes brought Mandy's attention to her own job. The long, street-dirtied, yellow beast was pulling up to the drop off zone. Swiping the small stack of papers off the counter Mandy put on her camp counselor's smile and marched through the glass entrance to the start of her day.

The doors of the bus were not yet open, but the roar of excited children filtered through to her anyway. Even though she did not need to, Mandy glanced down at her itinerary. Mr. Bennet's 1st grade class was here for a three-hour long tour around the main exhibits, then the brave teacher had opted to take over for the minor activities.

Mr. Bennet was a relatively new teacher, but despite that, the few other times Mandy had interacted with him, and his previous year's class had gone surprisingly well. Still, there was only so much control you can put on a group of seven-year-olds, but he did as well as possible. It should be a decent start to the morning, which boded well for a sleep deprived Mandy, who had spent far too much time the previous night watching sci-fi classics with her insistent younger brother.

"Just get them organized and moving toward the bug rooms. Then you should hit your first wind," Mandy told herself as she went to introduce herself to the chaperones trying, in vain, to corral the munchkins into a more manageable group.

Most looked as though they had never seen a child before in their lives, which was marginally concerning since, in all likelihood, at least one of the bouncing packages of energy belonged to them.

Abandoning her initial idea of talking with the adults, Mandy switched gears and moved to plan B. Letting herself skip a few steps gave her walk an extra spring to her natural gait, allowing her to part bounce, part walk, part land in front of her tour group.

"All righty now!" Her voice nearly sang out over the cacophony, crisp and clear. "You must be Mr. Bennet's class. My name is Mandy, and it is an absolute pleasure to have you all here today."

Thirty pairs of eyes slowly came into semi-focus on her. Progress. Sweeping a pointed finger over the crowd, she continued, "Who here has ever been to the marine center before?" She tapped her chin as if she were pondering each face.

Five hands shot into the air along with calls of, "Me!" and "I have!"

"Wonderful! So you know all the amazing things we have inside. For those of you who haven't been here before, there are a few rules I have to go over before we get to the fun, so can I get all your listening ears?" Mandy grinned and pushed her ears out farther than needed. This earned her the laughter and full attention of the class.

After a quick rundown of the Center's rules, Mandy clapped her hands together and grabbed the door handle to swing it wide. "Let's get started then. All of you, please go on in and stand by the big fish between those two halls." The kids began filing over to the Marine Center's unofficial mascot, a five-foot tall marlin statue the crew had lovingly named Marvin the Marlin. Over the heads of the mini stampede Mandy caught the eye of Mr. Bennet, "Very well handled," he said with a respectful nod. Mandy shrugged in reply.

"You learn what works." She stepped a touch closer to the teacher and lowered her voice slightly so it would not carry over to the children now taking photos and selfies of each other in front of Marvin.

"Are there any troublemakers I need to keep an eye out for?"

"Only Lucas and Jonny," he pointed to two boys elbowing their way trough the crowd to get to the statue ahead of the other kids, "but I'll keep them in my line of site. You shouldn't have any problems with the others and the parents will help if there is an issue."

Mandy nodded at his words but sighed as he walked ahead of her. A nice thought, she mused. Let's hope Mr. Bennet had chosen his chaperones as well as the last time they met. Most often the parents who volunteered for field trips were quite eager to spend the time with their kids. However, there was the occasional instance where the adults were unequipped to handle more than their own child. A situation normally ending with Mandy's wits being stretched to their limit.

No matter, this was her tour, and she would make sure the kids had a great time. If she got through this without any petrified fish, or kids with bitten fingers due to an annoyed turtle and curious hands, Mandy would call the morning a success. Then it would be Ms. Hartworth's turn. "Oh joy".

Mandy shook herself. One thing at a time. "Who wants to see some bugs?" Mandy asked Marvin's paparazzi onslaught. An excited chorus and a forest of raised hands answered. "Well then, let's get started!"

The morning rolled by smoothly. Mr. Bennet, though new to being a teacher, certainly had a talent for the job. Her first tour hardly felt like work. The children were well behaved. Even the two mischief seekers the teacher had pointed out at the beginning only attempted to bang on the shark tank once. That would make the tank cleaning crews who had to dive in the tanks with potentially annoyed sharks happy, Mandy smirked. She had been said diver several times, and it was always a bit of an adventure, but you learned to get used to a lot of things "normal" people would consider strange.

Mandy waved goodbye to the tour as they were herded outside with bag lunches and headed for the break room. With any luck, Shannon would be at a stopping point as well and they would be able to chat over lunch.

Rounding a corner Mandy found her answer. There were not many people around. This could be viewed as a blessing or a curse. Nevertheless, Shannon stood in the middle of the hallway, her passage being blocked by two incredibly tall men.

Height, unless you are looking strictly at the numbers, can be a very subjective thing. A child can look at his father who barely reaches 5'5 and think him a giant. Meanwhile a woman of supermodel height can look at the same man and say he is quite short. It all depends on one's point of view.

However, Mandy doubted her median sized frame was much influence in this particular case. The shortest of the two was 6'4 at the very least. Both were quite lean, as well, angular and lithe. A sense of menace surrounded them, though she did not know what gave her the impression. Mandy just knew somehow, the walking skyscrapers were dangerous, and at the moment they were blocking Shannon from moving anywhere. Not good.

Chapter Three

Shannon hated when things like this happened. She was already in a bit of a foul mood after Miss Molly, the marine centers local sea turtle, had decided that she was not moving fast enough for her liking and attempted to take a bite out of Shannon's backside. Twice.

Zeke had laughingly taken pity on her and sent her to lunch, while he spoke with Mrs. Lennot. Mind focused on the tuna sandwich she had waiting for her, Shannon was a bit startled when she was stopped by the two giants coming down the hall opposite her.

"Hey, we heard you guys had a hammerhead somewhere around here," the big one said, the bigger one at least. Both the men standing over her were beanstalks and seemed to loom over her. Their sudden proximity created a weight of claustrophobia. The one speaking wore a smile that Shannon assumed was meant to be reassuring but had the complete opposite effect.

"All we've seen are boring sand sharks and manta rays. Those are just about everywhere. Where's the interesting stuff?" Shannon tried to back up a step to point down the hall toward the larger tanks where the shark in question had made its home, as well as gain a buffer zone between herself and the two men.

"What's with this?" the other man said waving his arms at the hallway. He stepped closer to Shannon again. "My friend asked where the hammerhead was. You going to tell him?" Gesturing wasn't working. *"Perfect,"* Shannon thought.

This was why she preferred to work behind the scenes with Zeke, less chance to run into situations like this. Shannon tried to look around the giants to see someone who could speak to the men directly. Having no luck, she went for her pen and paper and started to write out directions. Not that it would do much good. Most likely these two were just looking for someone to bother and she was an easy target, but she could at least try to answer their question. Hopefully they would get bored if she did her job and did not engage. It had been a tried-and-true tactic for the majority of her life.

Pasting on a smile, Shannon held out the pad for them to see, and got the paper slapped out of her hand for her trouble.

"Too good to talk to us, huh?" The bigger man laughed at his own joke and again moved closer, forcing Shannon to take another step back to maintain some distance. Her smile was gone now. Her breathing grew heavier in an effort not to lash out. Shannon had always had difficulties when it came to her inability to speak, but it had been a while since she encountered this much blatant hostility.

Shannon bent to pick up her notepad, but the taller one was much faster than his size would suggest. He snatched it before her fingers had a chance to brush the cover. The man held the book before her between two fingers, a self-satisfied grin on his face. A face in which Shannon was rapidly developing the distinct urge to smack.

Shannon straitened and raised an eyebrow at the paper thief. How old are these guys? Ten? The pair continued to make jeers at her but Shannon was not paying attention to what was spilling out of their mouths. *"Ten is too generous,"* She thought; *"maybe seven. No, five, seven-year-olds are much more imaginative when it comes to insults."*

The slightly shorter of the giraffes began edging around her left side penning her in further, but something made him jolt to a halt. He nudged his friend's shoulder and nodded behind Shannon to whatever he had discovered. It must have been just as much a surprise to the partner because he became ridged at the sight.

Exchanging a look, the two sauntered off without another word, leaving a confused Shannon in their wake, and tossing her notepad to the ground as they left. Shannon spun to look at the hallway behind her trying to spot what had spooked her temporary headaches, but nothing seemed to jump out at her that would scare off the bullies.

What she did spot was Mandy walking in her direction. Her face was twisted in a scowl that would give a growling Rottweiler pause. Shannon could practically see steam coming out her ears. She must have seen the short encounter. Mandy always got angrier than Shannon when it came to incidents like the one in the hall.

Shannon held out her hands to forestall her friend's bull-charge.

"It's fine! I'm okay, they left." Shannon caught Mandy by the shoulders. Mandy's eyes ran up and down her friend. Looking for some hidden injury or pain. Waving a hand in front of her face Shannon redirected Mandy's attention. "Hey, I'm okay."

Mandy nodded and took a few deep breaths. Shannon nodded as well, watching the spitfire come out of "berserker mode."

"Who, the heck, were those guys?" Mandy asked.

"Just a couple of morons wanting to cause trouble. They left, and I'm hungry, so can we just go to lunch?" Shannon began pulling Mandy along by the arm.

"You're going to let them get away with treating you like that?" Mandy gritted out, her voice and hands synchronized in her vehemence.

"Whatever spooked them did more than I could have and I don't want them to spoil our break. Please, just drop it." Mandy huffed but relented and let herself be dragged onward to the break room.

There were a few people milling about and chatting in the small room. Shannon made a beeline for the fridge while Mandy snagged the last remaining chairs at the table, slouching in one and propping her feet up onto the one to her left.

"We should at least put a call on the radio. If they made trouble for you, it's possible they'll try and make trouble somewhere else in the building." Shannon glared over her shoulder. The woman had deliberately waited until they were surrounded by the flock of mother hens before making that particular suggestion. Judging from the smug grin plastered across her face, she was quite proud of her little bombshell. The comment had the desired effect.

All heads in the cramped room turned to face Shannon, and more than one set of hands landed on hips.

"What do you mean?"

"Who's causing trouble for our Shannon."

"Somebody need a boot to the backside?"

Mandy leaned back in her chair so that it balanced on two legs, while she recanted what she had apparently witnessed but had been too far away to do anything about. The more she spoke the more agitated the other occupants in the room became. Shannon attempted to assuage some of the tension by throwing out as many calming gestures as she could think of. It was useless. The mother hens had turned into mama bears before her eyes, and one of their cubs had been messed with.

Mary was the first to grab the walkie off her belt and broadcast Mandy's description of the two trouble-makers across the staff channel. What amounted to much of the same reactions as before scratched through the multiple speakers in the room, including a very loud comment from Zeke about the sharks still needing to be fed that afternoon. Shannon smiled. As annoying as the confrontation had been, it was nice to be reminded every now and then how many friends she had here. Even if they did tend to overreact.

Despite a determined effort on the staff's part, the two giants were not spotted anywhere in the complex. Shannon surmised that whatever had scared them away from her had scared them clear out of the building. It was no matter to her. They were gone and she had work, which needed to be done.

Zeke's reaction to the incident, after his initial and thankfully brief dose of bloodlust, was to be extra nice to Shannon for the rest of the day. Looking from the outside it was not obvious. He let Shannon feed the manta rays, took over her chore of cleaning out the otter enclosure. He even let her take over training with the one dolphin, Lilly, in residence at the center. It was a very sweet way to end an otherwise tiring day.

As they were making their way out after wrapping things up for the night, Shannon turned to the big man and signed. "Mandy and I were planning on going to Mellie's for dinner. You want to join?"

Zeke jerked the door closed and slammed the lock into place. Shannon was always amazed he could get the troublesome thing to do what he wanted on the first try. Looking the large man up and down, she determined the lock was simply afraid of him like most everyone else.

Zeke shoved his keys into his front pocket freeing up his hands.

"Haven't been to Mellie's in a while. I'll call Sarah and see if she wants to meet us there." Shannon smiled wide. It had been too long since she had seen Zeke's petite wife. The two were as opposite as humanly possible, so it amused Shannon to watch how they fit like two bizarre puzzle pieces.

"See you there," she signed as she walked backward down the walk. Shannon's stroll was interrupted by Mandy snagging her arm and dropping her into the passenger seat of her car.

"The sun is still up; I can walk to the diner!" Shannon exclaimed.

"It's close enough. I am giving you a ride whether you want one or not." Mandy's tone brooked no argument as she climbed in behind the wheel.

Mellie's Diner was not far from the Center; however, Mandy was always much more cautious than Shannon when it came to wandering around in the dark. It was not that Shannon was not careful; she simply had grown up trusting their sleepy town and those that lived there. Mandy, having been raised by born, bred and rehabilitated city dwellers, was less inclined to such notions.

The bell hanging over the door chimed as they walked into the crowded restaurant. You would never find Mellie's Diner on any tourist map, but ask any local and they would tell you it was the best place to eat anywhere around. Opened by a third-generation lobster fisherman, Joe Milner, hopelessly prone to seasickness in the late 60s when his father wanted him to take over the family business.

What was originally an escape route turned into a focal point of Shelter Bay. Joe, along with his wife, the restaurant's namesake, though silver-haired and a bit more weathered with time, still ran the place the same way as the day it was opened. Joe, in the back, hollering and moving around the counters and stoves as though everything would burn if he left a dish for more than a few minutes; Mellie gliding to and from each table with an easy grin and a pleasant word. Every face and order memorized perfectly. No matter how many times customers tried to trip her up, their meals always came out to perfection.

Over the years, different remodels, while providing more space for the larger crowds, also made it so the building had the appearance of having four floors. The main dining area, and largest section of the space, stepped down from the entrance and hostess stand into a sort of square well. Two higher platforms branched out from two edges of the square allowing more seating with the kitchen tucked off the third edge. A staircase by the entrance gave access to the second-floor bar and deck areas. Whitewashed, wooden tables, simple carved chairs, and broad windows gave the place a homey feel.

One of the younger waitresses greeted Shannon and Mandy, showed them to a four-top in one of the alcoves, and got them their drinks as they waited for Zeke and Sarah to arrive. They did not have to wait long. As soon as they had received their sodas, the couple swung through the door and began scanning the crowd.

Sarah was the first to notice the duo and begin wading trough the press of tables. Somewhat of a challenge due to her swelling abdomen. Shannon smiled and stood to give the small woman a tight hug around the shoulders.

Sarah and Zeke had begun dating a few years after Shannon had met him at the Center. He had talked endlessly about the gorgeous, intelligent woman he had met when he had gone home to Alabama to visit his family for weeks before the famed beauty had ventured north.

Zeke had been nearly as nervous to introduce the woman he had fallen for to Shannon, a girl he had adopted as another sister, as he had to his parents. His fear was unfounded; Sarah spent one evening with the silent girl and she fell just as hard as Zeke. There had been many days where Sarah had "kidnapped" Shannon and Mandy for a shopping excursion or hiking adventure further inland. Dinners at Mellie's were certainly a staple among the odd group.

Shannon started to take her seat again when a table on the opposite side of the restaurant caught her attention. What she saw made her heart sink to the floor. Seated at a table on the edge of the first floor were the two bullies from the afternoon. Her apprehension must have shown on her face, because Sarah's smile faded and a slight crease settled between her brows.

"What's up, Sweetie?" she asked. Shannon's focus shifted back to her friend. Plastering on a smile she hoped didn't look too forced, she waved her off and motioned to the seat across from where Mandy sat. Shannon threw Sarah the sign for tired and over embellished the body language to cover up her distress. Sarah seemed to take her explanation in stride and lowered herself into the offered chair.

Shannon dropped into her own chair a bit harder than she intended. The last thing she wanted that night was to make a scene in the middle of the town's most popular restaurant. Zeke blessedly only had a basic description of the men, but Mandy had been a proper witness to the incident. If she noticed the two in the corner, a scene would be the least of her issues. All Shannon had to do was make sure Mandy stayed occupied and she would hopefully go home with one less headache.

Most of the evening passed by smoothly. Mandy entertained the group with exaggerated tales of Mrs. Hartworth's unruly class. Shannon passed notes to Sarah asking how she and the baby were doing, which launched an entire, in places one-sided, discussion with the new parents to be, about all that was happening in the pregnancy. The food was amazing as was per-usual. With the good food and laughter, the occupants of the table behind them were forgotten.

Forgotten until the men rose to leave.

Shannon was breathing hard from laughing, silent though her giggles were, at Zeke describing an old diving excursion in college, when she happened to look across the room and locked eyes with one of the beanpoles. She saw recognition flash across his face, and then anger. It was the anger that got her attention. Why would he, be angry with her?

She was about to find out as he had changed directions and was heading for her table.

Shannon slouched over her plate as she watched his approach. At this point she was more irritated than anything else. With Zeke sitting at the table, she knew he couldn't hurt her. All the confrontation would do would be to bring back the stress she had forgotten for the last hour.

The tall man caught the attention of the rest at the table just before he leaned his tented fingers on its surface.

"Well if it isn't the rude little imp from earlier." The man's enjoyment of the awkward situation was clear, but the sneer twisting his lips gave him a sadistic streak.

"Don't have that filthy Skinner hovering now, do you?" He growled, the word skinner coming out like a curse. That was as far as he got before Zeke shoved his bulk in between Shannon and the aggressor. Why this man was continuing to target her, Shannon could not fathom. Most of his caliber had their fun teasing the mute and then moved on to more interesting prey. Not him.

It was not the wisest move, as this time she was not alone. Shannon only regretted they were in the middle of Mellie's. "Whatever your issue is, you need to turn it right back around and back out the door. You ain't comin' near her." Zeke said, his southern drawl thickening with each word as he tried to control his temper.

The fool did not seem to take the warning. His smile widened. "I've no issue with the girl. I simply want to have some fun." His head tilted slightly as he smiled down at the black man. Not an easy feat with Ezekiel Timmons. "Now get out of my way before I move you."

"You ain't movin' jack squat!" Zeke shoved the man back a couple paces, but this just made him laugh. They were beginning to attract the attention of some of the other patrons. Shannon's chest tightened and she half rose from her chair, looking for somewhere to take the girls out of the way if a fight was truly about to start.

Looking at the beanstalk's face as he moved back toward Zeke, that was exactly what was going to happen. Zeke saw it too, and he braced himself for the man's first swing, and clenched his fist to deliver his own in return.

The smack of a fist hitting flesh cracked through the room, but it was not Zeke who took the blow. Unseen, and unheard, a man, somehow even taller than the beanstalk, with short cropped, night black hair stood in the middle of the two potential combatants, the beanstalk's fist caught in the man's hand like he was catching a baseball.

All trace of merriment fled the bully's face at the sight of this new man. Every muscle in his body went ridged. Shannon thought if someone had said "boo" too loud next to him he might shatter.

While the lanky man could look down at Zeke, the newcomer loomed over the beanstalk at a height approaching seven feet tall. His shoulders were somewhat broad but his body angled down to narrow hips, giving his torso a triangular shape. He stood like a fencer, or given his position between a potential boxing match, a matador. His height and his structure gave the impression of a living weapon, constantly ready to move with great speed and power. A skill he had just demonstrated in a not completely subtle way.

When he spoke his voice was low and smooth like a cello bowed on the lowest string, beautiful, yet somehow menacing at the same time. The words the musical voice used however, were not ones Shannon could understand. Some of the words sounded almost like Italian but not quite. The pitch would change up and down in a way that said it was part of the language itself and not simply inflection.

Whatever the strange words coming out of the man's mouth were, it seemed to whither the trouble-maker's confidence to nothing. He seemed to wilt, standing in place. Who was this man that he could defuse a situation that quickly with only a few words?

After bending the fist he still clutched back at an odd angle, just long enough to draw a wince from the beanstalk, he released his grip and straitened to his full, impressive height. The beanstalk came to attention, then marched to the front and out the door, leaving the raven haired man and a very confused group of friends.

The newcomer turned from the door to face them, his movements fluid. He met Zeke's gaze first. "He will not trouble you or your friend again, you have my word. I commend you for standing up for them, not many would do so against Ottician." The man inclined his head. His accent was thick and was a cross somewhere between Spanish and Italian, but never fell fully on either side of the spectrum, but it was the closest comparison Shannon's brain could come up with for the shape of his words.

Zeke grunted and said, "Why does he keep comin' after my girl here?"

The man heaved a sigh of long suffering, "Ottician's taste in entertainment is not to my liking, but that is the plain truth of it. He enjoys making mischief. A habit I am attempting to break him of. Unfortunately, I have not quite succeeded.'

"I'll say."

"His behavior tonight will not go unpunished I assure you." he said, and judging from the glint in his eye as he glanced at the door, Shannon believed him. The man moved around Zeke, his movements again smooth as flowing water, to stand in front of Shannon.

"You have my greatest apologies Miss. Ottician was under my watch and I take full responsibility for his actions." he said, sincerity lacing every word.

Shannon glanced at Mandy then started signing to the towering man. "It is forgiven, I am just glad no one was hurt." Mandy's voice cut across the table as she translated for Shannon. This brought the man's attention to focus momentarily on the blonde. Mandy ducked her head slightly and shifted on her feet. Shannon suddenly had to make an effort not to laugh at her friend's pink-tinted cheeks. It was a new look on her.

The man's inspection did not last long and he shifted back to lock eyes with Shannon. "I thank you for your grace, and as I said before, it will not happen again" he promised making a point to look each of her friends in the eye, before turning to Shannon once more. He placed a long fingered hand over his heart, and bowed in her direction. The gesture was so unexpected, Shannon stood in uncomfortable shock, not knowing how to respond.

When he bowed towards her however, something changed in the man's. It was as if a switch was flipped and as he rose, all genteelness had fled his features. His nostrils flared slightly as he breathed in, and his jaw set in a hard line. When he spoke, the words, though still holding that musical tone, no longer held any warmth.

"A pleasant evening to you all." He said, pivoting on his heel and strode out the door, his long legs making quick work of the distance. Had Shannon not known better she would have looked to see if ice had been left behind in his wake. An odd man to be sure.

With the raven haired man's departure the noise of the restaurant, which had petered to nothing in order to watch the drama unfold, rose to its crescendo once more as Zeke and the women retook their seats.

The table sat silent for a while until Mandy heaved a sigh, leaned onto the table and in a voice, too chipper, with a smile too broad announced, "Well, that was fun."

Chapter Four

As the days rolled by, the unpleasant memory of the encounter with the thugs was pushed to the back of Shannon's mind. While not yet forgotten, it had begun to fade. The look the raven haired one gave her was what refused to release its hold on her thoughts. Something had shifted in the last moments before he left. Whatever it was, Shannon had the distinct impression it would not bode well for her.

The majority of the staff had gone home for the night by the time Shannon was putting away the last of her tools. Normally, Zeke and her would do this together, but Sarah had been to see the doctor that morning to see how their baby was doing. The bear of a man had turned into a nervous kitten in his anxiousness to hear what happened.

Shannon had taken pity on him after he managed to trip over the food bucket for the second time in five minutes; everything was nearly set for the night anyway. The father-to-be gladly snatched up the excuse and had hurried for the door, throwing his thanks behind him as he went.

Once all was back in its place and set for the morning, Shannon made her way to the front of the building to gather her things and start for home herself. Approaching the break room, Shannon scanned the lobby in passing, only to have her gaze catch on Mandy perched cross legged atop the front desk. She smiled and shook her head at the blonde who was too distracted with her phone to notice Shannon had emerged from the back.

Collecting her things quickly, Shannon headed back out to the lobby. The closing of the break room door was enough to startle Mandy out of her technological world, and into the real one.

The woman tossed herself from the counter. "About time, I'm starving," Mandy groaned, the sound louder in the large, empty space. "Let's get some burgers before movies. I can call Mellie's and we can pick it up on the way to the house. Sound good?" she asked, looping an arm through Shannon's.

Shannon in turn raised her eyebrows and nodded. In truth, Shannon had forgotten it was Thursday, their set movie night, but after pushing through the extra work tonight, a burger and movie were quite appealing. Mandy would find no objections on her end. With her focus glued to the screen as her rapid fingers tapped Mandy called over her shoulder,

"You want the usual?" Shannon slapped her leg once and Mandy nodded at the affirmative.

Shannon finished locking things down while her friend was busy placing their order. Mandy's car was parked in the middle of the lot, the lone vehicle in sight. She hung up the phone when they were halfway. "Mel said it would be about ten minutes, so we shouldn't have too long once we get..."Mandy never had a chance to finish the thought, as an arm wrapped around her torso and lifted her off her feet. Shannon heard her friend scream and turned to face her. Yet in doing so she failed to see her own assailant coming from behind.

A band of iron muscle wove its way around her throat and cinched tight. Panic shot through Shannon and she began raking her nails against the flesh trapping her, drawing a curse from the man attached to the arm. Even as scared as she was, a sense of satisfaction settled in Shannon's gut at her attacker's frustration. The satisfaction was short lived as the immovable arm somehow tightened further in warning, then eased to allow breath back in her lungs, labored, but any air was appreciated. Shannon got the message, she did not like it, but she understood.

Across from her Mandy was kicking and writhing, throwing her weight in any direction to try a get free. Shannon began to try the same but the hold her captor possessed made it impossible for her to do anything without cutting off her air further.

Strained, the man attempting to control Mandy said something in a language Shannon found vaguely familiar. Given her mind's desire to focus on the arm around her neck, she could not place it. Shannon's captor spewed something back in the same tongue, anger lacing every syllable of the foreign words..

Whatever they were saying, the tiny conversation was enough to take the focus off Mandy and the blond used it to get a hand inside her purse. Finding what she was after Mandy tore her hand out of her bag and raised it above her head. There was a hiss, then Mandy's attacker was howling in pain, and the girl wriggled free.

At his partner's scream, for just an instant Shannon's assailant loosened his grip. Not letting the opportunity slip by, Shannon let her knees buckle so that all her weight was suddenly unsupported and she dropped to the asphalt, out of the noose hold. Pain shot up her back as her tailbone collided with the pavement. Her palms stung, most likely scraped by the hard landing.

Shannon ignored it all. She tried to scramble away, but was caught by her upper arm. Breathing now ragged with fear, Shannon's hands floundered for something, anything she could use. Her fingers brushed cloth, her lanyard. Clutching tight, she whipped her wrist around letting the band of fabric bring the cluster of jagged metal keys toward her assailants head. The makeshift weapon made contact, but he was taller than expected, so instead of hitting him in the temple, or ear, the hunk of keys slammed off the edge of his jaw, jangling like tiny bells as they fell to her side.

The blow seemed to only piss the man off. He roared what she assumed was a curse, and cocked back his fist for a punch Shannon knew would be aimed at her head. There was no doubt that blow would knock her cold. She should brace herself, or try to dodge, but for some reason Shannon could only watch as the fist swung toward her face.

There was a sickening thud, and a distinct cracking of bones as a foot slammed into the chest of the man who held Shannon. His grip was torn from her arm as the man was thrown yards away from her, deeper into the parking lot. Focus still trained on the man that had gone airborne, Shannon was oblivious to the sounds of fighting behind her until a sharp crack, shocked her back toward the mayhem.

Mandy sat curled on the pavement, hair in a tangled mess, with the contents of her purse scattered all around. Ignoring the pain of being tossed around like a rag doll Shannon used her borrowed energy from the situation to get to her hands and knees, and crawl over to her friend.

The blonde girl jumped when Shannon touched her arm, then seeing it was her, tears welled up and she flung her arms about the her neck. They clung to each other for a few moments, both too relived to speak now that, at least for the moment, the fighting was stopped. Heavy footfalls crunching the asphalt drew their attention instantly, adrenaline still pumping, doing its job of keeping them alert.

A young man with light brown hair crouched down in front of the two women. He wore jeans and a simple blue t-shirt, heavy boots, and a thick leather jacket. Not the kind a biker would wear though. This was sleek, rich brown leather, which just begged to be touched. From his crouched position, the coat draped around him slightly, but when standing, Shannon would guess it would reach a just passed his hips. The collar was cut in sharp, clean edges, but the stitching was slightly worn. The same for the pockets, which were simple splits in the leather. The strangest part about the garment was the hood which was attached to the collar itself. While an odd choice, Shannon came to the conclusion the coat would look incomplete without it.

Normally, Shannon would not pay so much attention to what a person was wearing, yet on this man, the coat was worn in a way which made it seem a part of him. The two could simply not be separated.

"Are you lasses alright?" His words were low, soft, and carried a smooth brogue. At the sound, Shannon's body melted. A sense of safety washed over her at the familiar tone, which only confused her more. She had never seen this man before, so why was there a wash of nostalgia running over her? The attack must have rattled her more than she thought.

The man looked behind the girls, then behind himself, at the thugs sprawled on the ground. There was a third man Shannon had not previously seen laying next to the one who had grabbed Mandy. It was dark, yet Shannon could still make out a sheen of liquid starting to pool around him. Shannon shivered at the thought of what it most likely was. Common sense tried to drag up fear, or at the very least apprehension, as she moved her gaze from the growing pool to the man before them, but the feeling simply would not rise to the occasion.

The stranger frowned slightly then held out his hands to help them rise. "You need to get home. There may be more of them coming and you two shouldn't be here if they do."

"Seriously?" Her bedraggled friend scraped herself off the asphalt, and managed to gain a vertical, if a touch shaky, balance. "Three guys wasn't enough; you think there'll be more? Who are these psychos anyway?" Mandy's voice cracked under strain. She attempted to run a hand through her hair, but it got stuck among the many knots tangled on her head.

"This could be all of them, but on the off chance it's not, you two need to leave. Get somewhere safe." The man gathered Mandy's things together, shoved them in her purse and handed the bag over, pressing the keys into her hand. His tone brooked no argument. Still, Shannon turned to Mandy

"We need to call the police. These guys attacked us! They need to get locked up." she signed.

Mandy was about to answer when the stranger cut in. "You can call the police when you are safely away from here." He turned their shoulders and started gently, but firmly pushing them toward the waiting car.

Not given much of a choice, the two shaken girls got in, and started down the road. Shannon watched out the window at the man in the leather jacket as they left. He watched them too. *"I know you,"* Shannon thought, *"How do I know you?"*

Mandy turned the corner and their rescuer was lost from view, the question unanswered.

Waves lapped against the hulls of the various boats moored along the docks. Somewhere further down, a ship's bell continuously chimed as the boat, which housed it rocked in the calm water.

Tyrus hung back from the rest of his unit gathered around their centurion at the end of the dock. While they were focused out to sea, Tyrus watched in the opposite direction, toward the city. The soft lights in the distance gave the illusion of warmth and peace. A comical thought. As if the dirt stompers were capable of such a thing. However, Tyrus had to concede this tiny town on the edge of their main society was less vulgar than the rest. Tyrus leaned his lithe form against one of the rain-pocked concrete pillars of the dock. "Less vulgar, yes, but that's a long way from being actually civilized," he thought chuckling to himself.

"Still nothing?" Centurion Atticus's voice was hard, cold, matter of fact. Not much different from every other day. Tyrus answered him without turning away from the path into town.

"Not since they said they had spotted her."

A grunt was the only acknowledgement his answer had been heard. Seconds passed until the centurion spoke again. "It shouldn't take this long to grab, one girl." Annoyance tinged his last two words.

"Magnus, go with Tyrus and see what is taking those three idiots so long."One of the five men at the end of the dock separated from the group and marched down the narrow planking, toward Tyrus, toward town.

Tyrus pushed himself off the pillar and matched his stride. Once on the main stretch of land, they picked up their pace and settled into an easy jog, their long legs eating up the distance. Not ten minutes later their feet were hitting the faded pavement of the Marine Center's parking lot.

They had slowed when the building came into view, but at the sight of three long shapes laying on the ground Tyrus cursed and broke into a full sprint.

He reached Ottician first. The man's still eyes and grey skin told him all he needed to know. Grabbing a shoulder Tyrus turned the dead man over slightly to get a better look at him. He winced at the large dent in the man's chest, it was like his sternum and ribs had caved in on him. One of the bones must have pierced his heart or lung, he would not have lasted long after the impact. There was comfort in that thought at least.

"Ottician is dead." He called to Magnus who was crouching over the others.

"Damien and Leon as well." Tyrus turned at the words. Given how the men had been laying out in the open he had expected the answer, yet hearing it said aloud, he found himself still surprised.

Tyrus moved to join Magnus where he stood between their two former squadron members. Thinking aloud he said, "Ottician and Leon, maybe I can see them getting bested... maybe. But Damien?" Tyrus stared at the blood circling his comrade. "He was nearly as skilled as you and me." Magnus nodded and looked between the three bodies.

"This feels chaotic to me. I don't think any of them saw what killed them in time to react, or were too preoccupied. Leon has scratches all over his arms, and something is wrong with his eyes."

"Ottician had scratches too, but nothing compared to the chest wound." Tyrus rubbed a hand across his brow, breathing slow in an attempt to hold in his temper. Three of their men were dead, and there was no sign of who killed them.

"You need to tell him." Magnus said still staring at Damien. Tyrus groaned but knew he was right.

Closing his eyes Tyrus found the link in his mind, which wound back to his commander. At such a short distance, the task was not difficult. Grasping the thread, Tyrus was able to speak directly to Atticus. It never failed to amuse him when Atticus jumped at the connection of minds. His talent unnerved many, even those in the military, which looked for people like him to help with long distance communication. It was a rare gift, but not unheard of. Other Waders tended to take offense at the fear or disgust associated with the gift, but all Tyrus thought of people's attitude, was an opportunity for free entertainment.

He summarized to his commanding officer what he and Magnus had found, and through the link Tyrus could feel his commander's fury at the loss of his men.

"How can one tiny girl take out three of my men!" Volume was a tricky thing when speaking mind to mind, but Tyrus still cringed slightly at Atticus' 'shouted' thoughts.

"Quite frankly, sir, I do not think this was the woman."

"Why not?"

"The girl I saw in that diner was a Skinner; of that I am certain. But this attack would have required much more strength than I think someone her size could manage. Even if she is one of those beasts."

"Then what, by the tides, killed my men?" Tyrus surveyed the damage once more. No possible way it could have been done by the girl he saw. There was too much skill, too much power and precision. He glanced at Magnus and knew he was thinking the same thing.

"We're looking for a Bacainn."

Chapter Five

Concealed from those in the parking lot, Tristan watched with growing frustration and concern. There were now seven men gathered in the empty space. Their irritation at what was before them was clear even from a distance. *"Good. Let em' pitch a fit all they like. Serves them right trespassing into our territory."* The men made short work of collecting their comrades, and were gone nearly as fast as they had come.

Waiting a few minutes more to be sure they were gone, Tristan turned, and let his feet carry him down the well known path while his mind mulled over the ramifications of what had happened.

"Seven to come collect, plus the three I killed makes ten. A complete squad. The overgrown eels sent a full squad!" he said to himself swiping at a low hanging branch, not caring about the whiplash catching him in the shoulder as he continued to walk.

Tristan forced his temper down and picked up his speed. Nothing more to think on. They were exposed now and a decision had to be made. They were not going to like it, but it was his call, and it was time.

*T*he car jerked to a stop in front of Mellie's. Blessedly, the report they submitted at the police station did not take as much time as expected. The officers had not been thrilled they had left the scene of the crime, but since they were fleeing what amounted to a mugging even though nothing was taken, they understood the girls' need to get away as fast as possible. A description of the event and those involved was taken, then Shannon and Mandy were sent on their way. Mandy's stomach had caught up with her so instead of going straight home, the car ended up depositing them outside the diner. Neither girl seemed to be capable of getting out of the car.

Mandy's finger had not stopped tapping on the wheel since they had reentered the vehicle. Shannon had yet to break her vigil of staring out the side window. Not the most pleasant view, as the only thing currently in her line of sight was the large dumpster sitting around the side of the building. "Our food is probably cold by now." Shannon had never heard her friend's voice so small. The vulnerability pulled Shannon out of her stupor, making her refocus on

Mandy. She in turn wouldn't, or perhaps couldn't, meet her gaze.

The neon of Mellie's sign reflected off Mandy's eyes. Shannon turned so her back was against the door and pulled her feet into the seat to curl around her. Shannon would have liked to pull her friend into a hug; it could have helped the both of them but in this particular situation she was faced with a dilemma. Mandy despised tears. Hated them even more when they were her own. If Shannon were to touch Mandy right now, all it would accomplish would be to shatter what was left of the rattled blonde's self control. So, Shannon rested her hands in her lap and waited.

Silence was something both of them were quite comfortable with, a happy accident of Shannon's condition. While most people grew awkward with its extended presence and attempted to fill it, Shannon lived in a world of silence. It was an old companion, and when Mandy had come into her life, the energizer bunny had found a kind of beauty in her friend's stillness, had learned to love it. It was in the quiet both women gradually settled their nerves and settled back into themselves.

Dragging her hands over her face in order to not so subtlety clear away any rebellious tears, Mandy nodded and said. "I'm starved, let's eat." then promptly shoved herself out of the car. "*That's the Mandy I know.*" Shannon thought watching her friend dive into the restaurant.

What was originally going to be a movie night turned into take out eaten over a center console. The girls ate and talked about what happened, then talked about anything but what had happened. While both were still jittery from the attack, surrounding themselves with normalcy allowed them to relax. By the time Mandy dropped Shannon off at her house, refusing to let Shannon walk, a point Shannon did not argue with, she was ready to be done. It had been a trying end of day and Shannon was eager to be rid of her work stained, fight scuffed clothing, and dive into the cloud of blankets and pillows towered onto her bed.

The front door of the shoreside home Shannon and her mother shared had a habit of complaining quite loudly every time it was moved in any direction more than three inches. Over the years they had tried to silence the poor block of wood with any and every trick they could think of, but to no avail. At some point it was just an accepted part of the house. Anita in surrender would simply say, "At the very least, any burglar coming through would find it impossible to surprise us."

Late as it was, Shannon did try her best to ease the door open just enough for her to squeeze through so as not to wake her mother, the early riser. To her delight the door only gave a slight moan and Shannon slipped inside.

The colliding scents of smooth vanilla from scattered candles, the sharp salt from the sea not a hundred yards off their back porch, and mixed with a tiny hint of drying paint drifting down from Anita's studio on the upper floor, blended into a messy harmony to create the smell of home. Hooking her knees on the armrest of the couch, Shannon flopped back onto her back and threw her hands over her face. Breathing in the familiar scent, listening to the soft creaks and clanks as the house settled in for the night. It was like the house itself had said it was okay for her to let go. She was safe. She was home.

Tension bled from her body as she melted further into the couch.

How much time passed was unclear while Shannon lay sprawled over the couch; upstairs, a door banging against the wall as it opened and brought her focus back to a razor's edge. Nerves still frayed from earlier in the evening, she got to her feet without truly making the conscious decision to do so.

Voices, loud but dampened by having to work their way through walls and floors, trickled down to her strained ears. She recognized her mother's voice, but was that a man's voice?

Shannon picked her way to the stairs, though she still could not make out any of the words, it was clearer. It was definitely a man up there. Fear wrapped itself around her chest making it hard to breath. If one of the men had woken up and followed her home.

Shannon forced herself to take a deep breath. *"You don't know that is what happened. Maybe it is Mr. Gregory come to fix the drip we've been having in the bathroom."* Shannon put her foot on the first step and stopped. *"At eleven-thirty at night? Sure, that made all kinds of sense."* Shannon shook her head, when even her thoughts turned sarcastic, she was in trouble.

A soft hiss slipped between her teeth. Eyes darted around the room and snagged on the long, folded umbrella by the door. Not the best weapon but Shannon would take what she could get.

Impromptu bludgeon in hand, Shannon creeped up the wooden stairs, careful to avoid the ones that would scream her approach to anyone above. Although as she got closer and the conversation transitioned from incoherent babbling to actual speech, Shannon doubted the squabbling pair would have noticed her either way.

"...out of...blue...can't just drop...especially this important!"

"It...your choice... keep in the dark...she is certainly old enough to handle it now."

"But- "

"And whether she can cope well or not is now out of the equation completely."

Her mother sounded stressed, but not scared or in pain. Shannon's shoulders relaxed slightly. The man's voice was more familiar than expected, especially the accent. After hearing a couple of full sentences, it hit her. The man from the parking lot who had helped Mandy and her! He had only spoken a few words to them, but Shannon was certain it was him. His next words held a tinge of anger, and it made her clutch the umbrella tighter.

"Having one or two guppies come ashore for a laugh is one thing. Scare the daylights out of them and throw em' back over the border. But this was not kids testing the lines. They sent a full squad of legionaries to capture her, Mrs. Rowle. We were lucky they used three for the actual grab." He chuckled "I don't think they expected the girls to put up such a fight either. Shannon wailed on the one grabbin' at her. Banged him right up and Mandy pepper sprayed one of the urchins of all things. I didn't even know that worked on them! Gave me time to get to them."

Shannon crouched low on the stairs out of their immediate line of sight, but she could see them. Her mother, still in a paint splattered t-shirt and jeans, perched on the edge of a barstool with her fingers tightly laced in front of her mouth. The man from the parking lot braced his palms against the island of the tiny kitchenette tucked in the corner of the upper floor.

Dropping to lean on his elbows, the man ran a hand over his face and blew out a heavy breath. His shoulders slumped slightly, he suddenly looked as tired as Shannon felt.

"I almost didn't make it. When I heard Mandy scream..." removing his hands he leveled his gaze at Shannon's mother and his voice became hard.

"There is no more time for us wait, Mrs. Rowle. They know what she is, where she is, and I cannot protect her on my own up here any longer. I have to take her back to the Grotto and the sooner the better." He straightened up again as he said these last words. "Now where have you stashed her coat?"

Shannon's mother sniffed and wiped at her face. Shannon almost slipped on the step when she saw the motion. Her mom never cried. Never.

Anita's voice was quiet, but was set with resolve as she said "My parents have it. They live further inland, maybe a three-hour drive. I thought it would be safer away from the coast." The man nodded his agreement.

"Well then," he said coming around the island, "As soon as Shannon gets home we can leave. Why don't you gather a few things for the bo-" his words cut off. The pair had started moving further away and it had become harder to hear what was being said, but when Shannon tried to lean forward, she lost her balance slightly. The sound of their eavesdropper preventing herself from doing a face plant startled the occupants into an about face.

With as much dignity as she could muster, Shannon took the last step up the stairs, stood to her full height, umbrella still in hand and asked with one hand, "Who exactly are you? Who were those men who attacked me, and what the heck is going on?

Chapter Six

Over the next thirty minutes Shannon never truly got an answer to her, in Tristan's opinion, quite reasonable questions. Did this make him stop from herding the two women into packing up their essentials and stuffing a thoroughly annoyed and exasperated Shannon into the car? No, absolutely not. They would have plenty of time for talk while they drove.

Mrs. Rowle took the wheel as she would have a better handle on the fastest route to her parents' house. Anita set her phone down in the cup holder after calling the half-asleep couple to give them at least a little warning the trio was on their way. Not the best of situations, but under the current circumstances, Tristan was willing to forgo his manners if it meant keeping his charge safe. A charge who was currently stewing in the front seat curled against the window. *"Well, this is going to be fun,"* Tristan thought as he checked the rear window once more. To his memory, he could not recall ever seeing a Nereid drive a car, but better to be overly cautious now, than be caught off guard later.

"How long do you think it will take to get to your parents' house, Mrs. Rowle?" Tristan said turning back around and leaning toward the front seats.

"About three, three and a half hours, but there is hardly anyone on the road this late so maybe less." Anita kept her eyes forward as she spoke; focused on the few hundred feet of road the high beams illuminated.

Taking a deep breath to brace himself, Tristan turned to the surly woman in the passenger seat. "Alright Shannon; let's have it. I know you have questions, we have time now, so ask away before you explode." At first, Tristan thought Shannon was going to ignore him, a thought proved false moments later. The shadow of her head turning to face him in the back was the only warning he had before she lunged for the gap between the driver and passenger seats. Her sudden movement caused her seatbelt to lock, halting her forward progress, but not her hands.

Tristan could make out rapid movement and could hear the slap of hands colliding for various signs but could not distinguish more than that. He held up his hands to try and push back the onslaught of motion. "Woah! Hold on a sec." He grazed along the car's felt ceiling, swiping in random directions until his fingers found what he was looking for. Pressing a small button, the cab was flooded with muted yellow light. After blinking a few times to allow his eyes to adjust, Tristan turned back to Shannon, her own lashes fluttering at the assault on her vision.

"There, that's better, now I can see you. Why don't we try this again shall we?" he said. It was true, with the light on Tristan would be able to see and understand her signing, but he would also have the pleasure of witnessing the full range of her annoyance and anger at the situation. *"Oh yes this will be a barrel of fun. Why did the Rowles have to put off this conversation for so long? Now I have to be the one to explain this whole mess. This was not part of my job description!"* Out loud he said. "To start out, in the rush I don't believe we were ever properly introduced. My name is Tristan McKenny. I was sent here by your father to help keep you safe since he can't be here himself."

Shannon sat up straighter in her seat, her gaze flipping back and forth between her mother and him before her hands lifted and she asked. *"How do you know my dad? Why would he need to send someone to protect me?"*

Not wanting to exclude Anita from the conversation, who had to keep her eyes on the road, Tristan spoke aloud. "Your father is one of the leaders of my clan...our clan really," he said tilting his head in acquiescence. "As for why I was sent, I think the events earlier this evening are as good an explanation as any. We knew the Nereids would come after you two sooner or later. It was better that someone with training was here to make sure things stayed under control. You have always had a guardian. I'm simply the most recent."

"And the longest posted. Most of the others only stayed a year or so. Tristan has been with us for about six years now, " Anita chimed in.

Shannon's head whipped to her mom. "So you know what is going on too! Why am I the only one in the dark? What clan? What the heck is a Nereid?" In her fury, Shannon's signs had begun to arc in wider, sharper sweeps. Understandable, Tristan would be angry too if the roles were reversed.

Tristan found the direct approach worked best in most situations. He only hoped when he dove over this cliff he'd find water at the bottom instead of hard concrete.

"A Nereid is a being that lives in the sea. They have been called many names over the years, but the most common name now is, mermaids." The blank look overtaking Shannon's face was not exactly encouraging, but he pressed on.

"I'm not talking about pretty, little cartoon characters on a movie screen for kids. Nereids are more monster than man really. They are *brutal*, relentless, and an incredibly powerful military force. We have been fighting them for generations now, defending our territory."

Shannon held a handout to stall him, "Who is we?"

"Me, you, your father, our clan, Selkies in general have been fighting the Nereids for as long as I can remember. The arrogant leaches have been trying to take over our waters." Seeing the confusion on her face, as well as more than a little disbelief, Tristan anticipated her next question and answered it before she could pose it.

"In the most basic terms, a Selkie is someone who has the ability to transform into a seal, or in our clan's case a sea lion, when we enter the water. We look human on land, so do the Nereids for that matter, although they have the obscene height thing to make them stand out. But other than that, on land, both species look completely normal. It is only when we get to the water it's obvious what we are."

Shannon clicked her tongue in disgust. "You have got to be kidding me! I am not stupid! If you don't want to tell me what is going on fine, but stop trying to pass off children's stories as an acceptable explanation."

Anita was not able to catch all of what her daughter signed as she was focused on the road, but she caught enough and jumped in between Tristan and her daughter. The poor man did not deserve to have the brunt of Shannon's anger thrown at him.

"We are not making up stories, Shannon. All of what he is saying is the complete truth. Your dad is a

Selkie." Anita shook her head as Shannon, with doubtful eyes, pointed at her. "No, I'm completely human. That's why you were able to stay with me here on land while he had to return to the sea. "

"Had to?"

Tristan took that question. "Being a Selkie has many advantages. Superior strength, agility, more finely tuned senses, we even live longer than regular humans. There is nothing like being able to shift and move in the ocean like you're a part of it. But all that does come with a price. There's an old saying that sums it up quite well I think, "What is taken, must be given." It's a timecard of sorts. However long a Selk steps on land, he has to spend the same amount of time in the ocean; Doesn't matter how much time it is, it must be given back. The longer you hold it off, the more time you are locked in your seal skin."

Tristan leaned back against the car seat. "For most, this is just a normal part of our lives, and it doesn't bother us. For others..." Tristan's eyes darted to the front of the car "it becomes an anchor that drags them down. I've seen a few people try to push the limits of the balance, but the coat always takes what it is owed. The longest I have ever heard of someone lasting on land was seven years. At that point the coat will force the Selkie back to the water."

"It's what happened to Eoin," Anita said, her voice carefully measured. "It's why your dad left

Shannon. He tried *so* hard to stay for us but couldn't manage it any longer. He had to give his time back."

Shannon leaned her side against the seat; and looked between the two other occupants of the car. Without really deciding to do so, her fingers found the worn, braided necklace she always wore. There were many more knots on either side of the pearl than when she had first received it, but the pearl itself was exactly the same. Smooth, cool, and a touchstone to help her stay calm. The day he had given this necklace to her was the last she had ever seen of her father. Sitting there, she did the math in her head and sat up. "Say I believe this nonsense. If seven years is the max a...Selkie can spend on land, and the price is equal to the time taken, then Dad should have come back to us years ago. Why didn't he?"

Tristan looked a bit uncomfortable. Anita glared back at Tristan in the rearview mirror. "*That* is a question I would like answered as well."

Tristan leaned against the door opposite Shannon so he could still see her, and keep an eye on their tail, propping his arm on an upturned knee.

"You both must understand, Eoin Rowle is not just some random Selkie in our clan. He is The Lann, the greatest warrior we have. A genius when it comes to battle tactics and our top general. The only one who outranks him among us is our Clan Chief, Nolan, who also happens to be his brother."

"There have been Selks who have married humans before with no issue. As much as I admire the man, Eoin did not handle your situation well at all. Spending that much time away from the lines was bad enough, but then he got himself locked in the skin for seven years. It was devastating for our clan. We are still trying to recover the ground we lost during that time. When the coat released the Lann, he did try to go straight back to you two, but the chief thought history would just repeat itself, and he couldn't allow that. He forbid Eoin from leaving his post again. Said it is what was best for the clan. In some ways he is probably right, in others..." Tristan let the sentence hang in the air.

Movement brought his attention back up to Shannon, "Sorry, I missed the first part of that."

"I asked why he never tried coming anyway?"

Tristan laughed flat out. It startled the women, but he could not help it. "You're assuming he never did. I assure you that is not the case."

"Wait, he defied Nolan?" this from Anita.

"He tried, and nearly succeeded many times. But the chief holds his position for a reason. Eoin, for the past few years, has had a permanent escort to make sure he doesn't run off. It has become a normal thing to bet on in the clan. How long the Lann can go without making a break for it. Once a month he allows Eoin to come topside to at least see you both, but his guards have strict orders not to let him interact with you. The chief is too concerned with losing his best general again. Without going so far as to kill his own men, there is not much the Lann can do."

Shannon ran her hands over her face, blowing out a huff of frustration. *"So— Dad is a shapeshifting seal-person who left because the sea forced him to. Even though the sea let him go, he is now being held hostage by the local overlord because he is too good at his job. Yet he is still allowed to see us once a month at a distance, with supervision like some sanctioned stalker. I am being attacked by a nightmare version of a childhood fairy tale, which is why I am currently stuffed into a car with a guy I met a couple hours ago, going to my grandparents' house for some unknown reason. Did I leave anything out?"*

"No, I think you covered the basics," Tristan said, swiping a palm across his mouth in an attempt to refrain from laughing. By contrast, Shannon's expression was twisted in a fascinating combination of weariness, confusion, and annoyance. It was the annoyance Tristan saw most clearly, making him proceed with caution.

"Do you have any idea how crazy all this sounds?"

"I am fully aware, yes."

"This is still the story you're going with?"

Tristan forgot his mirth. He leaned closer to her in the dim car so she could see his face and know how serious he was. "I am not making up stories, Shannon.

Everything I have said is the truth. You can believe me or not, that is your choice, but it will not change simply because you're having trouble wrapping your brain around it."

Shannon's gaze darted across every inch of his face, looking for any sign that he was lying. She could see nothing but pure sincerity. This almost scared her more.

Tristan leaned back against the car door once again and looked back out the rear window. "Why don't we save the rest for later? Some of this might make more sense once your grandparents give you back what we need."

"Give me back what? What do I need?"

He did not answer, his attention back on the road behind them. Whether he did not see her signing or more likely simply declined to respond, Shannon was not sure, but it was clear this particular conversation was over. She faced forward and made herself be content to watch the trees zing by as the car sped past.

"That part will be easier to understand if you see it for yourself," Anita said, angling the car to follow the curve of the highway.

Whether good or bad, the next few hours will be interesting at the very least. With this thought Tristan slowly let his body relax into the seat but never stopped scanning their surroundings.

"Who knows. Could be fun."

Chapter Seven

Shannon had not been to visit her grandparents in quite some time, but as they pulled up the gravel drive the impression of the small ranch style house being frozen in time would not leave her mind. Same flowers in the beds around the front, tended with a loving hand. The shutter on one of the side windows still hung a bit crooked. Even the frayed rope swing she played on as a kid still hung from the massive oak across the yard.

Normally, the street, though quiet, would always have some type of activity brewing. Children playing in any one of the many yards, or two neighbors having a shouted conversation from their respective porches. Things looked different so late at night or early in the morning as it were. Still, it jarred Shannon at how a place she had loved and played around most of her life could look unsettling in the stillness. She shrugged. *"Shadows can shift anything to creepy mode, I suppose."*

Taking care not to slam her door and disturb the neighbors, Shannon trotted to catch up to her mom who was already stepping up to the front door to knock. Tristan trailed behind.

Shannon could not get a read on the man. The story he tried to push on her in the car was completely absurd, and almost insulting that he would think her gullible enough to fall for something so insane. What troubled her was her mother's support. For an artist, Anita was not a person Shannon would have ever called flighty, and certainly not stupid. For her to throw her weight behind an explanation firmly belonging in the fantasy section of the library was confusing.

Then there was the fact both had nearly thrown her in the car and driven her three hours to her grandparent's house at o'dark-thirty in the morning. Shannon glanced at the man behind her. Weird as he may be, he did put himself in harm's way in order to save her. Maybe...she could give him the benefit of the doubt. They said it would make sense when they got here. Shannon did not know how, but out of respect for her mother and, begrudgingly, Tristan as well, she would listen. Semi-kidnapping aside, she could give them that much.

The front porch light turned on above them. The curtain covering the glass top of the door inched aside and Shannon could make out the side of her grandmother's face. A moment later the door flew open, and she stood before the trio in her entirety. Anita had inherited her willowy frame from her mother. Though well into her seventies, Rosemary

Henesey exuded a kind of soft strength Shannon had always admired. Long and straight, her once blonde hair pulled back into a simple silver braid, small wisps loosened to gently frame her face. Even though she knew her grandmother had been a teacher, as a girl Shannon had liked to picture the elegant woman as a ballerina. The grace in which she did everything seemed to fit a dancer more than a schoolmarm. Wrapped tight in a soft, cream robe, Rosemary ushered them all through the door.

Once inside, she pulled her daughter into a tight hug. Her husband stood behind her in the living room. Leaning around the embracing women, he caught his granddaughter's eye and signed, "Hey Beautiful." Shannon smiled. Ralph was not the best signer in the world, but he tried his best for her sake. Beautiful was one of the first signs he had learned, and his favorite. It had quickly become his sign name for her.

"Hey Granddad," she signed, stepping into a bear hug of her own. Unlike his wife, Ralph was rough and a galumphing boar of a man. Being around mechanics and army grunts all his life only made him more gruff. Those who did not know him would be afraid of the big man. Those who did know him, thought this a wise instinct. Reasonably tall and broad in the shoulders, the man was like a boulder of muscle despite having a bit of a pot belly. According to him, that was just extra padding if he was ever in a fight. Over the years his hair had thinned out on top of his head, but this was balanced by an impressively thick beard with eyebrows to match. Both made it hard to read his expression, raising his already high intimidation level. Yet on the rare occasions he did smile, mostly around his family, it would transform him from a biker gang leader, to a grizzled version of Santa Clause.

"What is going on Anita?" Rosemary asked, finally releasing her daughter. "Not that we don't love seeing you, but your phone call didn't exactly promote calm."

Looking between both her parents, Anita said, "I came because, I need you to give me the coat." Whether he was aware of doing so or not, Ralph tightened his hold on Shannon. Over her head he stared down Tristan, still standing by the door. To his credit, Tristan met the older man's gaze without flinching, not something everyone could do. In the end, it was Ralph who broke contact first in order to address his daughter.

"It was my understanding that you gave that thing to us so no one," he released Shannon and took a step closer to Anita, "including you would have any idea where it was."

Anita nodded in acknowledgment. "Initially, yes, it was safer that way. But now it is more of a danger for Shannon if she doesn't have it with her." Anita brushed Shannon's thick curls behind her ear. "Honestly, I should have told Shannon about this years ago so she could make up her own mind. But with Eoin not here-" Ralph scoffed at the mention of Shannon's dad. He had never been his biggest fan. A fact that had caused some tension between him and his daughter. His outgas now was rewarded with a scowl aimed in his direction.

"I am not having this argument with you again, Dad. Not right now." Her expression softened slightly as she looked between her parents. "Where did you hide it?"

"It's safe," Rosemary answered.

Anita rubbed her hands over face. "Can you get it for us...Please?" Ralph crossed his arms, unmoving; Rosemary seemed torn between her two family members. Seeing the stalemate, Tristan entered the conversation. "We only have a limited amount of time. The decision has been taken out of all our hands. Shannon needs her coat, and quickly." He stepped closer to Ralph, within striking range. Looking at the roughened man, Tristan was not sure this was the wisest move, but he did so anyway. "I understand you are trying to protect your granddaughter. But this action is putting her at greater risk. I only have a small window where I can get her somewhere safe without a couple of squadrons on our tail. The longer we stand here debating, the smaller that window gets. So please, get the blasted coat."

Ralph's expression remained cold, and hard as granite. Tristan could not tell if his words had any effect. Two sharp stomps on hard wood swung everyone's attention to the subject of conversation. Shannon, still confused and annoyed from the conversation in the car, stared down the group of people who all seemed to have more information than her. This angered her more than anything else. Obviously, she was the focal point of whatever they were discussing, so why was she the only one still in the dark?

"Why is a coat so important?" she drilled Tristan with her eyes. "You said you would explain more when we got here."

"Yes, I did, but I also said it was easier to show you than tell you." He focused back on the Heneseys as he said, "Kinda hard to do that when I don't have what I need."

Shannon huffed, "Whatever is happening, I need answers. Please give them what they are asking for so I can understand what the heck is going on." Shannon leaned against the door, the weariness of a long day hitting her all at once. She took a few steadying breaths so she would not start crying in the middle of her grandparents' foyer, not the simplest of tasks with the emotional rollercoaster she had been on in the last twenty-four hours.

Shannon's input seemed to tip the scale in Rosemary and Ralph's mind toward their visitors. Ralph pressed a hand to his wife's shoulder as he left the group and headed toward the garage. Rosemary herded her impromptu guests into the living room.

A fire had already been set to a happy dance in the hearth, its warmth calming Shannon's frayed nerves. She sunk down next to her mother on the plush couch and leaned against her shoulder. Anita shifted and tucked her daughter closer to her side, pressing a kiss to top of her head and squeezing tight. Rosemary sat across from them in her favorite wingback chair, the navy fabric neat, but well loved. Her focus drifted between the two women and the sturdy man they had come with, who had chosen to peruse the bookshelves on either side of the mantle rather than taking a seat. She knew he was one of them; one of those creatures like her son-in-law. When she had first met Eoin, she had liked the man. He adored Anita and their little girl, but she had never fully understood why her daughter had gotten involved with him when she knew he would have to leave at one point. She never liked it when her girl was hurt and her marrying Eoin was taunting heartbreak. Rosemary did not want to think what having a Selk back in their lives would entail.

Before that train of thought could run any further, Ralph returned with a crowbar in hand. He pointed at Tristan with the metal rod. "You're sure she can't be safe without it?"

Tristan squared up to Shannon's grandfather. "Not in the time I've been given, no."

Ralph nodded, the action feeling like a final seal on the situation. This was happening no matter the opinion of anyone in the room. He motioned for the women to stand from the couch, then waved at Tristan to grab the other end. Together the men hefted the bulky piece of furniture to the far side of the wall.

With a grunt, Ralph kneeled down and flipped the edge of the thick rug over on itself, exposing the wood flooring beneath it. Using a fist he began systematically pounding on each of the wide floor boards. Shannon had an idea of what he was doing, and it was confirmed when his fist landed on one of the boards towards the center of the room. The dull beat of solid wood transitioned to a hollow "thock." Shannon shook her head. Of course her grandparents had a secret compartment underneath their floor! Didn't everyone?

Ralph flipped the crowbar in his hand and then jammed the flat edge into the crack between the hollow plank and its neighboring plank. After a bit of jostling, he managed to wedge the iron bar under the wood. Slight cracking made Rosemary cringe at the damage being done to her beautiful floors,

A sharp jerk and the plank popped free into Ralph's hands. Three more boards quickly followed, revealing a hole in the floor a little over two feet wide on each side. From where she stood, Shannon could not see in the hole, but this was not a problem for long as Ralph was leaning down and, with a muttered complaint, dragged out a medium- sized metal box with a heavy lock on the front. The box landed on the main floor with a bang.

Pressing a hand on the lid for leverage, Ralph shifted so he was sitting on the floor facing the lock. "Rosie, grab the key for me would ya."

Lips tight, Rosemary nodded and stepped over the hole to get to the far left bookshelf. There she brought down a clay figurine of an elephant that had sat on the shelf for as long as Shannon could remember. When she was a child her grandmother had always said not to touch it; it was too fragile to be played with.

Rosemary felt along the edge of the blanket painted onto the animal's back until she found the small latch hidden there, then popped open the back. *"The darned thing is hollow!"* Shannon thought as Rosemary reached in and retrieved a single key on a ring, handing it to her husband. *"I'm in a mystery movie where hidden keys and secret passages were a normal thing. That s what's happening here. The only question is, when did I wander onto the set?"* The lock clicked, the lid was thrown back and puzzlement appeared on all her family members' faces.

Suddenly nervous, Shannon backed up till her knees hit the couch and she was forced to sit down. She wanted desperately to see what was inside the box, what had caused all this mess. She wanted answers, but at the same time she was completely terrified of those answers. She knew instinctively they would change her life in ways she could not possibly predict.

Rosemary was the first to move. Her delicate hands disappeared into the metal container and came free with a long span of fabric. No, not fabric, the smell of the disturbed material filled the small space. Leather.

Draped across her grandmother's arm was a large span of treated leather. It looked as if it had been worked into some kind of garment, but with it bunched up the way it was, Shannon could not figure out what the garment was supposed to be. Whatever it was, it snagged Shannon's attention and held it with an iron grip. Someone could have screamed right in her ear, and she would not have noticed. Not at that moment.

She was no longer nervous, quite the opposite in fact. A strange sense of calm rushed over her like it was the first time in a while she was allowed to take a deep breath. Without making the choice to do so, Shannon found herself rising from the couch and slowly walking toward Rosemary and the object in her hands. Tristan was the only witness to her trance-like movements from his relaxed stance by the bookshelves. Everyone else was focused on the bundle that had been tucked away under the floor.

"I don't get it," Rosemary said her hands running over the treasure they held, "This is much larger than the one we put in here. Ralph did you switch it out or something?"

Ralph shook his head, just as confused as his wife. "I haven't touched the thing since we buried it 'neath the floor."

"Well then where is the real one?" Anita cried out in dismay, snatching the garment from her mother. Shannon's throat tightened in a sudden panic, breaking the bit of fog she had fallen into. Why was she so concerned for a scrap of leather? But even this thought ground against the grain. It was hers. Shannon knew this to the marrow of her bones. It was hers and she did not like the fact her mom was the one holding it and not her. Shannon moved once more toward it. She wouldn't let it be snatched around left and right like a dog toy. Tristan watched, encouraged.

Anita was speaking again. "She needs the real one. If it's not here, then where is it?"

"That is the real one." Tristan's Irish brogue cut through the debate. All eyes save Shannon's swung to him. "I'm assuming you were expecting something a bit smaller. A coat fit for a child?" Anita clenched the material, her voice tense. "I could almost fit the whole thing in both my hands when I gave it to them."

Tristan's accent became thicker as he explained, taking on the air of a storyteller, "No matter when you took it from her, that coat is just as connected to who she is as her hair color, or the way she walks, or the way she smiles. Our coats grow and change right alongside us. You could have put it on the moon and it wouldn't have made a difference."

Tristan's gaze had yet to leave Shannon. An easy smile spread his lips as she gently rescued the leather held hostage by her mom. "Her coat will always fit her perfectly. It's a part of her, it can't not."

The second she touched the coat Shannon felt better. It was heavier than she first thought it might be, but then with the amount of material in her hand she could not say she was especially surprised. The leather was so soft against her skin Shannon was having trouble believing it was leather and not silk or velvet. What her hands doubted, her nose had no such qualms. The heavy sent of treated leather surrounded her yet still managed to not become overpowering.

Running over the length of it, Shannon found the top of the shoulders where she grasped tightly and held the jacket in front of her letting the base fall loose so she could examine what had been unearthed from her grandparents' floor.

It was heavy, making it an effort to keep suspended in front of her. The shoulders were tapered and fed down into the sleeves until about where the elbow would be. There the sleeves widened into a bell with thick embroidery threading the edge. The front lapels of the bodice overlapped each other completely so the coat was fastened on the left, as opposed to down the center, with large wood-like buttons carved with an intricate, interlocked knot Shannon didn't recognize, but they matched the sleeves and bottom hem perfectly.

The crossed top of the coat allowed for the bodice to be form fitting up till Shannon's eye found the tails of the coat. Flaring at the hips, the base of the coat fell in folds of deep, walnut-toned material down to a length which would hit Shannon just passed her shins. This made it seem more dress-like than jacket. Old-fashioned for certain, but it was without question the most beautiful thing Shannon had ever seen.

Boots connecting with wood pulled Shannon's attention from the coat to Tristan coming closer. Stopping to her right he reached for the coat in her hands, her coat. Why was he reaching for her coat? Shannon flinched away, but his smooth voice stalled the action. "Easy Lass. I'm not goin' to take it." His tone was one you would more often use to calm a spooked horse. Despite her lack of four hooves and a mane, it did the trick on Shannon.

She watched as his hands found the buttons and one by one, he released all four. This done, he stepped in front of her again and placed his hands over her own which were still clutching at the shoulders of the coat. His eyebrows raised, silently asking permission; he waited.

Shannon hesitated only for a moment before loosening her death grip. Tristan took the weight, then gently shaking out the collar he fanned the coat open and held it out for her. An eagerness stole into Shannon as she realized what he was doing. She spun so fast her head became a touch dizzy, needing to adjust to the sharp movement. She could hear Tristan chuckle behind her as she, with his help, fed her arms into the sleeves.

The second the leather settled onto her shoulders, Shannon felt something shift inside her. A snapping of puzzle pieces she didn't know were lost, locking together. It was like being sucker punched, or coming up for air after being trapped underwater for too long, or the difference between watching a movie and living it yourself. It was all of these and more. She truly couldn't put words to the feeling, except it simply felt...right. Undefinably right.

Her cheeks all of a sudden felt cool and damp, and Shannon realized with a start she was crying. Wiping at her face, she looked up to see her family. Rosemary and Anita were crying right along with her, Ralph's face was screwed into a scowl, so Shannon knew he felt just the same.

Anita stepped forward, only just remembering to avoid the large hole in the floor before tumbling in. "Are you okay? It doesn't hurt does it?" She asked not daring to touch her yet.

Shannon nodded, "I'm fine, Mom. Better than fine. I feel amazing!" She turned to face Tristan. His broad smile matching her own. Glancing down at the leather hanging off her shoulders Shannon took a moment to bask in the feeling of contentment, before making herself get back to the business at hand.

Tristan had answers, answers she needed. *"Is this what you were wanting to show me? If so, I still don't understand. What is this thing exactly?"*

A look of confusion, or perhaps worry, flashed across the man's face but it was gone so fast Shannon was not entirely sure she had seen it.

"A selkie's ability to transform is tied into our coats." he said, lifting the right edge of her lapel to look at a series of small loops attached to the end. These corresponded to smaller flat buttons which Shannon found running along the inside lining of the left lapel. Shannon began fastening these, closing the coat around her as Tristan continued to speak.

"We receive them at birth. One of our parents takes a piece of their coat and gifts it to us as soon as we are born. A connection is made, and that strip of leather becomes the newborn's Selkie coat. We are not sure if the coat imprints on the infant or the other way around, but it doesn't make too much of a difference. At this point the child is truly a Selkie."

Shannon finished buttoning the four outer buttons of the coat and ran her hands down the soft leather. Her fingers touched each button, the sleeves, the collar. It was when she reached the collar Shannon realized she had missed seeing a span of material attached to the collar itself and falling to the back. A hood? She would have to ask later.

"The coat is what allows us to transform. It is also what maintains the balance we were talking about in the car. It's an odd relationship, but one selkies need. Without it, we are never fully ourselves." He stepped forward and tugged on the collar. "This is your coat, Shannon. Always was, always will be. You just got separated for a little while."

"Why?"

Tristan looked over her head at this question.

"When you were born," Shannon turned at her mother's voice, "your dad and I made the decision to remove your coat so you could grow up like a normal kid." Anita ran a hand along her forehead. "Or as close to normal as possible." She smiled or maybe grimaced, Shannon wasn't sure which. "We thought it best if you were able to grow up with at least one parent who could be around. We knew he couldn't stay, and not being able to shift back for so long would have been disastrous with you being so young. So...we made you land locked."

"That's a nice way of putting what you did to her." The heat in his voice made Shannon focus on Tristan again. His face mirrored his tone, anger pulling his features into a scowl.

Rosemary stepped in front of her daughter. "They made the best out of a bad situation. Took care of their child the only way they could figure to."

Ralph grumbled from the back of the room. "She was better off with us on land anyway."

"Better off? You call having half your being stripped from you better off?" Tristan shouted, advancing on the older man. Shannon pushed against Tristan's chest trying to slow his forward momentum. This did slow his movement, but it didn't stop him from continuing to rant. He had spent too many years watching over her. Watching her struggle and fight for her place in the world with only half the cards she had initially been dealt. It was the one thing he had ever pushed back against Eoin on in the six years he had served the Rowle family. Shannon could not defend herself, because she did not know anything was wrong. Even the idea of having one's coat taken was repugnant to a Selkie, and these people were acting like having a chunk of yourself stolen from you was a blessing! It infuriated him.

"Taking her coat doesn't just stop her from shifting, though that would be bad enough by itself. Stealing a Selk's coat dulls everything, senses, strength, endurance. You took away her damn voice for the love of all that breaths!"

Shannon went rigid. Tristan halted himself, his eyes falling shut realizing what he just said. He'd let his anger get the best of him for half a minute and blurted out what should have been told to Shannon gently. Tristan peered down at the woman in question, her face void of any emotion. This, in a way, was more disturbing than had she broken down screaming.

Shannon kept her palm pressed to Tristan's chest as she shifted to face her mother. She needed something solid to hold onto, otherwise she would buckle, so the man would just have to stand there and be a wall for a minute. Served him right if he was going to drop bombshells.

Anita raised her hands up in placation, "Sweetheart, it was the only thing we could do at the ti"

"You knew why my voice was gone this whole time?"

Chapter Eight

Shannon tried to pay attention to what her mom was saying. It was an explanation as to why she had spent her whole life with her lips zipped shut. Why she had to fight to be taken seriously, because most people assumed she was stupid because she couldn't talk. The taunts, the whispers behind her back, or insults directly to her face, debatable which was worse; all explained, granted bizarrely, by the coat she was wearing. A problem her mom could have fixed this entire time instead of dragging her to countless doctors only to be told the same thing every single time, no she was fine, no there was no explanation as to why she was not able to speak. They had no cure.

Shannon knew she should listen, knew it was the mature thing to do, but at the moment she was tired, bone tired, and could not seem to find the patience in order to listen to an excuse she was far too emotional to consider rationally.

"Maybe it's best if we call it a night," Anita said, her hand going to brush back Shannon's hair but pulled away when she flinched.

"I should really get her back. I don't want them to think of coming further inland after her and finding you all here."

"We have all been up half the night. A couple hours of sleep is not going to kill anyone. It may even give you an edge when you get back into town. I would imagine facing those brutes while struggling to keep your eyes open would be a bit of a detriment." Anita raised a knowing eyebrow at the Selkie. Much as he hated to admit it, she was probably right. Shannon did look about to fall over, and getting back to the coast was only half of their journey. Once they hit the waves they would have miles of ocean to cross to get back to the Grotto.

Tristan nodded in acquiescence. "A couple hours, then I truly need to bring her home." This time it was Anita's turn to flinch, the word home digging into her harder than she expected. She hid it well by shedding her thick sweater. "Sleep first, talk later."

Ralph grunted. "Your rooms are all set." He turned to glare at Tristan and growled. "You get the couch."

"You do spoil your guests, Sir." Tristan quipped, a crooked smile finding its way to his lips. The jest only seemed to make Mr. Henesey grouchier, much to the Selkie's somewhat guilty amusement. Tristan did not blame the man for his temper. In his shoes, he very well might have been the same. He chuckled to himself as he splayed out onto the gaudy flower-printed couch. Who was he kidding, he would be worse. He must have been more tired than he thought, because it was not long after he first laid down that Tristan slipped into the quiet black of sleep.

After a few hours of sleep and a light breakfast, Rosemary insisted on everyone eating, Tristan and Shannon were back in the car and making their way back to the beach, aiming a bit further south than Shelter Bay. If they could avoid the Nereid squadron all together, it would be one less thing for Tristan to worry about. He was still a little surprised he had managed to convince Anita to stay behind at her parents' house rather than joining them on their return trek. Even more surprising was Ralph Henesey being an ally to the idea.

The highway was more or less a straight shot through trees, and rocks, and more trees. He knew in the autumn the massive oaks, maples, birches, and pines would transform the hillside into flaming bands of vibrant color, however now, in the late spring, everything was varying shades of green. Granted the land did have its own kind of beauty unique from the submerged sights Tristan was used to. Stubborn patches of wildflowers brought in a bit of color, but after a couple hours of, for the most part, the same monotonous surroundings, the sightseeing got old. Turning the radio on had helped for a while, but now even that was grating on his nerves. His only other option was to speak to the stoic woman riding shotgun. Not the best choice for his health if her expression was anything to go by.

A singer came on through the speakers whose voice was not so much singing as wailing, and Tristan had finally had enough. He slapped the large power button, and the car was dropped back into silence. His ears seemed to sigh along with him.

Movement caught his periphery, and he glanced to the seat beside him. "I'm sorry, what was that?" Shannon began to sign again, and Tristan managed to read the words *where* and *go* his attention pulled back to the road as it began to wind around through some denser woods and he missed the rest. Luckily, he got the gist of what she was asking. "Where are we going?" He asked to clarify. She nodded.

"We are going to the Grotto. It's a bit hard to describe, but I suppose the best description is a half sunken island part way out into the Atlantic." Shannon did not respond so Tristan went on. "It has never been breached, and not for lack of trying on the Nereid's part either. You will be safe there." Tristan hesitated before saying. "Your father is there."

Shannon stared at him for a few heartbeats, her hand moving to the pearl on her necklace. *"How do you know my Dad?"* she asked.

Tristan's brow furrowed, "With your coat back, your voice would have been returned as well. You should be able to talk if you want to," he said; her stunned face distracting him from the road. He did not think that had occurred to her yet.

Shannon leaned forward in her seat, crossed her legs and then made an incredibly exaggerated attempt at what Tristan thought was meant to be, "hello.", At least it would have been, had any sound came out. She tried again; same result. She tried a few more words and still nothing. Seeing her riling herself up, Tristan placed a gentle hand on her forearm in an effort to settle her.

"It's alright Lass. Talking is a skill. You have to learn it like any other." His gaze shifted back and forth from the road to her face. "Take a breath and try again." Nodding, she sucked in air through her nose, forcing herself to be calm. Her mouth moved in the general shape of words, but silence was the only result for her efforts. Frustrated, Shannon leaned back in her seat and watched the passing trees.

He did not let it show, but disappointment weighed down Tristan's shoulders as well. He had not realized how much he had been looking forward to hearing her voice. It had been a curiosity of his for years as he had watched over her. He shook himself. It was her voice, he was just her guardian, and he did not have the right to be disappointed. Still the thought persisted, what would she sound like?

"In answer to your question," he said changing the subject, "Your father is one of my superior officers. The man who trained me, raised me really, is good friends with the Lann." Shannon turned confused eyes on him at the unfamiliar term. "Lann means Blade." He explained, "It's a title of sorts for the best warrior in the clan. Eoin Rowle has been the Lann for as long as I can remember. Thats why it was such a problem when he got skin-locked. Our best fighter was stuck with half of his abilities useless, to him, and to us. Made a lot of people nervous."

"That's why he never came back?"

"That's why he was never allowed to come back."

The rest of the car ride was devoid of conversation. The only break in the awkward silence being the various radio stations which never completely lost their static. Needless to say Tristan was relieved to see the outline of the coast come into view at last.

The sun glinted off the grey-green waves in the midmorning light and Tristan could not help the grin that split his face at the sight. Salt tinted the breeze that whipped his hair into his face, an inconvenience easily ignored. It felt like this was the first deep breath he'd had the whole day. Despite her anger at the situation, Shannon seemed to relax as well as they left the car and headed for a secluded stretch of sand hidden from the rest of the beach, away from potential, curious eyes. Not that there were any people around to see them anyway, but it never hurt to be a bit cautious.

Grabbing Shannon's hand, Tristan pulled her toward the water and stopped just shy of the incoming tide, the thin edge of waves lapping at their shoes every now and then. He faced her. "This next part will probably be a bit scary and feel more than a little weird since you have never changed before. Once you are in the water, instinct should kick in and guide you without any issue, but just to be on the safe side, we are going to go in at the same time so you can see me change as well. Hopefully seeing what it's supposed be like will help remind your body what it's meant to do. Okay?" Fear flashed in her eyes but was gone so fast if Tristan had not been watching for it, he would have thought he had imagined it.

He squeezed her hand. "You're going to do fine. I'll be right next to you the entire time." Releasing her clutching fingers, he reached toward her collar and pulled the deep hood up over her head. Tugging it far enough forward so the wind would not rip it off as soon as he let go, he placed his broad hand atop her leather shielded curls. "Ready?" His gentle, lilting voice and small, soft smile helped to calm her nerves.

Breath shaking, Shannon nodded, a tiny grin fighting its way onto her face. Tristan took her hand again, threw his own hood up, and towed her off the beach and into the waves.

$\bullet$

$\mathcal{F}$rigid water seeped through her shoes and climbed up her legs making her jeans cling to her claves. Shannon had always had a higher tolerance for cold than most, but the icy bite of the waves and ripping wind should have had even her shivering to the point of vibrating bone. Instead, Shannon found herself thrusting farther into the water, reveling in the cold. Something in her bones ringing through her that this was right. She looked at Tristan's back as he pulled her deeper into the waves. They were standing in water well above waist high, approaching the dangerous territory of being swept up by a riptide. He did not seem to care.

Shannon shook off the thought. If what he claimed they were about to do was true, she would not have to worry about the temperamental, watery hands of exhaustion and possible death ever again.

Their feet still technically touched the bottom, though Shannon was only managing the feat by balancing herself on her tip toes, the rolling waves easily lifting her off the sand to have her float weightless for a few seconds, then depositing her back down to continue her bouncing march into the ocean.

Meanwhile Tristan seemed to have no problem standing in the now shoulder deep water, his larger frame anchoring him more solidly to the earth.

"Alright." He said stepping closer so his voice did not have to fight with the wind. "You work with the seals at the marine center, right?" Shannon nodded. Tristan continued, "Since you don't know what you look like in your sea lion form, I want you to picture them and think 'change'. You should already be feeling a bit of an itch to shift with how deep we are." As soon as he had pointed it out, the pricking along Shannon's skin intensified to the edge of pain. Grimacing she looked back at her impromptu magic shifter guide. Whatever her face looked like, apparently it was quite amusing because Tristan laughed and grabbed her shoulders.

"Don't worry. I know it feels odd. It's not normal to hold this long in the water before changing so you don't have to get used to the feeling. Once we submerge completely the shift should go into full swing. I just wanted you to have some idea of what to do. I'm afraid it won't be much help. Most of this is instinct. Just watch me and try not to fight too hard." He griped her shoulders tighter, "Ready?" Shannon rattled in a breath and nodded. Tugging her with him, Tristan sunk beneath the surface of the ocean.

Shannon's eyes burned slightly as she forced her eyes to stay open underwater. Following his advise, she watched Tristan who had moved a bit away from her in order to have room to accommodate the larger body of his sea lion form. In the span of a few eternally long seconds, the man she had been practically tied to for the last twenty-four hours vanished into sleek, dark skin, a thick barrel chest, double what the already broad man had been, wide black eyes constantly shifting around evaluating their environment and long thick flippers. The man had just turned into a sea lion, a no kidding, real life, right in front of her, sea lion.

Her mind reeled at what she had just seen, but did not have time to dwell on the matter. A pulse shot through Shannon like a massive heatwave starting at the center of her chest and spreading out through her limbs. The coat wove itself around her, wrapping tight, until there was not an inch of her not covered by the thick leather. Where the extra material had come from Shannon did not know, but she suddenly did not care as the previously benign hood had begun to meld itself to her face.

Panic surged through Shannon; her hands clawed at her face through the material but had no effect. The coat had covered every sliver of her, and now it was getting heavy, unbearably heavy. She was sinking further into the water under the weight of the coat. Shannon writhed, and tossed, churning the water around her into a frothy mess. The coat was going to drown her!

Shannon heard a series of intermittent clicks before something large and smooth brushed against her side. Instantly Shannon felt calmer. Flashes of color and emotion, ease and a solid wave of safety swept over her, but it did not belong to her. Shannon was unsure how, but somehow, she knew this influence was from Tristan. The bump from earlier was most likely him as well, trying to calm her down. It worked. Shannon's mind hushed and focused on what her body was doing.

Whatever Tristan had done, it allowed Shannon to push past the panic brought on by the strangeness of the change to realize, it did not hurt. Quite the opposite in fact. Her body elongated, morphing into a creature foreign to her senses, yet comfortable and natural, like holding a blanket from her childhood she had forgotten about but still knew.

Fingers and arms melted into long flippers, legs fused together, chest expanding into a more compact, streamlined shape. In concept the idea of shifting into a completely different form would be a painful one. In reality, every bone that rearranged, every muscle pulling to a different position felt like finally stretching after being still for hours on end; Sore, but a wonderful relief at the same time.

It was hard to judge how long it had taken to fully shift into her new form, but eventually Shannon felt her new skin settle down and lock into place. From head-to-toe Shannon could sense the reach of her new body just as well as her human one. Her mind reeled.

Shannon was not human. She never had been, and the truth of that knowledge hit her all over again.

Tristan apparently was not inclined to let her tarry on the concept. He glided past, bumping into her again. The touch prodded her into opening her eyes for the first time since the change had begun. Normally, when underwater, Shannon's vision was a jumble of blurry shapes and shadows. Now everything around her came into focus with as much clarity as she was privy to on land, perhaps more so. The water itself acted as a magnifier. Everything seemed more vibrant, details popping out at her which normally would have gone unnoticed in the plants, the sand, the water itself. It was overwhelming but exciting to think of exploring this new world.

An image of two sea lions floated into her mind. The smaller of the two, mottled shades of light brown, swam toward the larger darker male. Shannon stared at Tristan's sea lion, identical to the one in the vision. He waited patiently, his flippers moving back and forth in a lazy effort to keep himself in the same place. Shannon had yet to move and was sinking, moving with the rhythmic waves.

Tristan tilted his head at her and let out an amused bark. The same vision flashed in her mind, a feeling of encouragement, or was it goading, and a hint of the humor she just heard in the bark threading the image. Shannon finally got the picture. How he was doing that she would bug him about later, but obviously he was wanting her to swim towards him.

Her head bent down to look at herself then sprang back straight. She had just folded nearly in half trying to see what she looked like. Since when had she been that flexible?

Ignoring Tristan's barely contained laughter, Shannon attempted to move the way she'd seen in Tristan's mental demonstration. Pulling her flippers up high, then tilting her head toward Tristan, Shannon pulled her flippers down hard against the water and...threw herself into a summersault.

When she stopped spinning, Shannon looked around in confusion. Tristan had disappeared. Where on earth would he have gone? He wouldn't leave her stranded, would he? But looking around she was unable to see him.

A bark drew her attention behind her, and she swirled her head to look over her shoulder. Oh. Tristan had not moved. She had spun herself to face the opposite direction. Using smaller movements, Shannon turned herself around. Tristan's battle not to laugh, while watching her sorry attempt at swimming in her new form, was almost worse than had he openly guffawed. Picturing her wild turning, like a broken bath toy, was funny even to her. His restraint was impressive, and she did appreciate the effort not to embarrass her.

Shannon's lungs began to sting a bit, she glanced up at the shimmering surface. How long had she been underwater? Having made it work before, Shannon kept her movements as small as possible and moved toward air. A mass of dark fur circled around her twice, popping up right next to her when she emerged, blinking away the saltwater from her eyes.

In the open air now, Shannon was surprised to find she was not as desperate as she had assumed she would be for having been submerged for so long. Her breaths were even, measured, pulling easily in and out of her nose. Strange. Shannon could have sworn she had been down for at least five minutes if not more. Deciding to test out a theory Shannon pushed her confusion in Tristan's direction. If he could send his thoughts, or what she assumed were his thoughts, to her, why not send her thoughts to him.

Tristan opened his mouth wide in a toothy grin, and flashes of joy and pride flooded back toward her. Shannon felt her own grin split her face at her apparent success. Tristan sent an image of himself going under the water and staying there swimming back and forth not coming to the surface. Shannon got a sense of time passing, hours flying by even though the picture was only at the front of her mind for a few seconds. She thought she understood.

Selkies could stay underwater for an obscene amount of time. But how? Shannon focused on the word 'how' and pushed it toward her companion.

Tristan had yet to use any solid words, but she hoped the meaning she wanted would get through. All she got back was a feeling of certainty. She thought about what that could mean. Tristan pushed the previous image at the same time as a brief flash of curiosity then the certainty again, solid and unchanging. Shannon nodded at him. *"He doesn't know why. Just that we can. It's just how it is."* she thought.

Tristan dove below again, his back flippers splashing her in the face just before they followed the rest of him down. Shannon huffed in amusement and without thinking, dove down herself, the action much smoother than her earlier attempts.

Instead of staying in one place Tristan wove in and out and around boulders, up into open water, then swooping down to the sea floor stirring the sand into clouds. You would think a creature with such a large, bulky form would be comically awkward to watch, but he glided through the water as though he were born to it, which Shannon mused, he had. There was no wasted movement. Every action blended seamlessly into the next to make it look more like he was flying through the water rather than swimming.

His flippers, both front and back, were used like rudders to cut whichever direction he wanted. The tilt of his body added and controlled his momentum almost if not more than his flippers did, which he only used occasionally to give a burst of speed.

Watching him, seeing how swimming was supposed to be done in this form, made it easier for Shannon to mimic, rather than the singular visions Tristan had sent before.

Locating which muscles did what was a bit tricky, but after some trial and error, Shannon managed to smooth out her strokes and finally she was moving in a straight line.

A yip sounded on her left as Tristan swept in to swim next to her. His wide, dark brown eyes shone with delight, and a thrill of pride shot through Shannon at his silent praise. She could do this. She could really do this!

Thrusting in a broad sweep, Shannon quickly propelled herself toward a jutted outcropping of boulders. Tristan kept pace, glancing back and forth from her to the rocks. With a flick of his flippers he edged ahead. Without previous agreement, Shannon and Tristan found themselves in a race.

Chapter Nine

They played for a few more hours letting Shannon get the hang of moving in her sea lion form. Races, chasing after fish, and throwing themselves above the surface only to dive back down again was a much more fun way to learn than simply swimming laps. It also let her get out of her head a bit and let her natural instincts tell her how to move rather than her brain freaking out about how different it felt to swimming like a human.

Still, Tristan was surprised at how quickly Shannon was learning how to navigate in her new form. For someone who had not even heard the word Selkie before yesterday, it was nothing short of remarkable.

Not only that, as soon as she had figured out the basic mechanics of how to move, a kind of effortless grace had gradually seeped into her strokes, until Tristan found himself watching, fascinated. It was beautiful. Granted there were times where she over-corrected or would push a bit too hard on one flipper or the other and go tumbling like any new pup. Entertaining and adorable, it was a challenge not to laugh with joy every time it happened. What was fun to see, was after such a spill, she would pause, and Tristan could almost see the gears in her mind running back the last few seconds, finding where she went wrong, and adjust. Then she would fall back into her watery dance.

Tristan had lived around Selkies his entire life. There were very few who could compete with her level of finesse, and they had spent their entire lives in their coats. Shannon had found her's only this morning. It was a marvel.

Shaking himself out of his musings, Tristan glided in a smooth arch above, then below Shannon. The muscles needed to perform the spiral stretched and pulled wonderfully, he ended the curve next to her, his left flipper catching hers on a downstroke.

Sending the image of them heading east out of the bay, he watched her expression. Shannon had a wide grin, showing off her pointed, black teeth, from their various games. At the projection, her mouth closed and while her glee from the "lessons" did not completely disappear, it was dimmed. A flash of a much younger version of the Lann walking away down a stretch of beach whipped across his mind and was gone. Pain and grief rose and fell with the image. He was suddenly more nervous than he was before. No, that wasn't right, the nervousness was coming from her, not him.

It had been a long time, since someone else's emotions had effected his own to that degree. He would have to pay closer attention in the future to what was his, and what bled off of her when she communicated. Pushing the feeling of anxiety down, he made a mental note to teach her how to not send stuff like that if she did not want to. It was a skill taught to pups early on, and so had not occurred to him as being an issue he would be faced with. Tristan took the lead and headed in the direction of home.

Normally the journey from the mainland to the Grotto only took about three hours, less if you found a good current to coast on. Unfortunately, Shannon, being new to the coat, was making things a bit more complicated than usual. At first, she was fine, but the "play/training" they had done earlier, plus a long-distance trek had started to wear her down. In the end it seemed wisest to stop and rest about every hour or so, breaking the journey down into more manageable legs. A bit frustrating for someone, like Tristan, who was accustomed to making the trip in one straight shot, but understandable.

What held Tristan's concern was the final stretch of the journey, for two reasons. First, surrounding the mount which housed the Selkie clan's home, was completely open water. To a certain extent this was part of the natural landscape but was exaggerated and maintained by the Selkies as a defensive measure. By putting the Grotto in such a place, it was incredibly difficult to achieve any large-scale attacks without being spotted far in advance. Most small incursions were shot down quickly as well for the same reason. They simply could see any Nereid strike force coming. However, this also made it so there was nowhere to hide when escorting an untrained, shiny new Selkie to safety, while an entire squadron of Nereids were searching for the Selk who had killed three of their men.

Second, while their approach was landside and well within Selk controlled waters, it was not unheard of for scouts or advance teams to be sent out by the enemy to test their defenses. If one of those units met up with the remains of the one he had encountered in Shelter Bay, he would have one heck of a fight on his hands.

Tristan's eyes took in Shannon's elegant frame as they prepared to dive. *"The only way through, is through,"* he thought. Six years he had been this woman's guardian, at this point it was no longer just his duty, but a need. He would see her home safe to her father, no matter what.

As it turned out his worries were unfounded. They did not encounter so much as a stray look out. Still Tristan breathed a bit easier when at last his home came into view. When seen from above, the Selkie stronghold looked like a speck of an island. Its high, irregular cliffs made it uninhabitable despite the scattering of trees at the top of the rocks. However, like a stone iceberg, the landmass expanded far beyond what peaked out into the sun. A solid, immovable mountain face stood proud in the open ocean.

Grinning at Shannon, Tristan took the lead and dove further down. About midway down the hillside, dozens of feet below the surface, and tucked away between a cluster of boulders, a hidden opening for a tunnel that burrowed into the stone; its end not visible from where they floated.

Looking over his shoulder at his companion, Tristan sent the image of her staying close to his side, pushing a mild urgency to it. She bobbed her head up and down as she continued to swim forward, and he plowed on through the fissure.

Once past the narrow entrance, the tunnel widened slightly so they could swim side by side, but even then, it was a bit cramped. It was dark, almost too dark to see, and Tristan found himself navigating more from memory rather than actual sight. The temperature had dropped as well. This far north, even though they were still technically in the Atlantic Ocean, the water here never truly warmed up, no matter the season. Sheltered away from the sun, the tunnels felt more like swimming through melted ice. To Tristan though, protected by the thick blubber of his Selkie form, it felt wonderful, refreshing, like walking into an air-conditioned house in the middle of summer. He just hoped Shannon wasn't too uncomfortable. If you were not used to it, the cold could be jarring.

The tunnels were specifically made to be befuddling. It was one more measure to protect against invaders. Would be attackers would find themselves hopelessly lost in an endless series of dead ends and looping turns before coming close to the main compound. Allowing the defenders to pick intruders off one by one, popping in and out through the dizzying maze of hollowed out stone.

To someone who had spent their childhood playing and training within the tangled labyrinth, it was like walking the halls of your own home. Soon the walls of the tunnel widened and opened into a large cavern, the edges curving up like a giant had blown a bubble in the stone long ago and here it remained.

The water only rose to about the midpoint of the space. Tristan broke the surface first, Shannon not far behind, and skimmed toward a wide slab of rock forming an edge to the underground pool.

Tristan with one strong push, flung his body out of the water and onto the stone. Using his front flippers, he walked, or rather waddled away from the pool in order to give his companion room to get out herself.

A massive splash whipped his attention back toward the water. Shannon was gone. He scanned the dim interior, his concern rising when he could not spot her. He trotted back to the edge and looked down into the pool. Nothing. Blast it, it was too dark down here.

He was readying to dive back in when her head slowly poked above the surface again right under his nose. For some reason she kept staring at the rock, at his flippers, anything instead of his face. He had never seen a sea lion look so sheepish before. It hit him an instant later, and he began shouting at himself. Don't laugh. Don't laugh. Don't laugh!

Sliding back into the water Tristan sent her the image of how to get out of the water. He made it as slow as possible so she could see every detail. Unfortunately, he had not managed to contain all of his amusement and it leaked out into the projection. He got a slap of flat annoyance back at him. Only a small portion of it was directed at herself for flubbing the exit.

It took a few tries, dragging a body almost double the weight of your human one out of the helping, buoyant hand of the water could be trickier than one first assumed. Hence Shannon's glorious, repeated tumbling return to the pool. But practice makes perfect, or at the very least possible, and eventually both slumped comfortable on the flat stone. One more gracefully than the other, but at least they were on dry land again.

A scrape from the other end of the cavern had Tristan rising and moving to put himself between Shannon and the unknown sound. On a rock outcropping a bit higher off the water than the wide ledge Shannon and he occupied, Tristan spotted the shape of another sea lion. Male from the size, but he could not tell who it was in the dim light.

The male launched himself off the boulder and arched beautifully into the water below. Seconds later, he emerged onto the ledge in front of Tristan. When he saw who it was Tristan relaxed his mouth opening wide in a toothy seal grin. It had been far too long since he had seen Kent.

In hindsight Tristan should not have been surprised to see him stationed here. The eastern cavern was one of the three main entrances to the Grotto itself. There was always a Reidh stationed at the choke points. He had seen a few on his way in, but Shannon's dramatic exit of the pool was apparently enough to distract him from the fact. He was sure Shannon would not be happy to have any witnesses to her debacle, but Tristan knew without a doubt Kent Harrok would not say a word.

Kent bopped Tristan's shoulder with his head, a flipper coming in from the side to push at his head. Tristan did much the same. The two Selkie males barked, and shoved at each other in mild play. When Tristan had been chosen to be Shannon's guard it had made it so Tristan was not able to come back to the Grotto nearly as often as he would like. As it stood, Tristan had not been home in quite a few months.

Settling down, Tristan looked behind him in order to introduce Kent to his charge. But when he did, his eyes found Shannon tucked against a cut of rough boulders. He would not call it cowering per se, he did not smell any significant rise in fear, but it was certainly a high level of caution at the arrival of the new male. Tristan tilted his head at her. If he was honest, in her shoes, he was not certain if he would not have given them a wide berth as well.

Tristan projected as much calm as possible in Shannon's direction. He flashed pictures of Kent and him as boys growing up; Them going through training together. Kent being chosen to join the Reidh, the best and most committed warriors they had. He knew the words would not travel but he hoped the intent would. *"You are safe with him. With us."* He touched the tip of her nose with his own. *"I promise."*

Stumbling awkwardly tying to walk in a straight line on her flippers, Shannon approached Kent. Kent in turn held still as a statue as she came closer. Tristan could have laughed at how ridged Kent held himself, doing his best not to scare the cautious woman.

Kent was a terror in battle. Moving art when it came to combat, no matter which form he chose to use. Tristan was skilled, more so than most, but when compared with his friend he looked almost klutzy. Put Kent in any social situation however, and the roles were reversed. He could not seem to get a handle on how to interact with people when not fighting them, especially women. Shannon though bumbling slightly in her unfamiliar form, was quite pretty and Tristan knew that would make Kent all the more nervous.

Finally, having made it to stand next to the two Selkie men, Shannon looked up at Kent. He was not as tall as Tristan but was almost twice as broad and jet black. Kent looked down at Shannon scrutinizing and unmoving. Shannon shrank toward Tristan. When Kent was nervous he tended to lean on the utter silence side of things as opposed to babbling. This combined with his coloring, his size, and the less-than-cheery interior of the cave made for quite the intimidating presence.

Tristan slapped Kent in the back of the head, jarring him from his impression of a breathing statue. He barked in surprise. Not many were willing to do that to him so it did not happen often. Tristan pushed his irritation at him. "You're scaring her, idiot!"

Kent lowered his head and shifted on his flippers, making yips at Shannon. She tilted her head at him. Tristan caught the hint of amusement and kindness slip from her, and even a bit of empathy. It made sense. Shannon had had to deal with mis-communication issues her entire life. Tristan did not know why, but it made him happier than he would have expected that she was not put off by Kent. A train of thought for another time.

Tristan turned his focus inward and tested the hold of his coat. As he pushed against, what could only be described as seams, the coat resisted with just as much force. He tried another angle, same result. With the force the coat was fighting him with, Tristan probably had a few more hours before he was released again. He sighed. He had hoped with the time spent teaching Shannon and the journey itself would have equalized. Apparently not.

Knowing Shannon would not be able to understand a more complex thought stream quite yet, Tristan directed his thoughts toward Kent instead. As smoothly as water sliding off glass, Kent's form morphed and reshaped to reveal the human face behind the coat.

Kent was a man of average height, but sported shoulders as broad and solid as a professional wrestler. Stocky build, barrel chest, he was the type of man who would make it seem a tossup as to who would win in a man verses semi-truck collision. Kent Harrok was the definition of sturdy. His coat was thick, tough and had the look of something expected to be seen amongst a motorcycle club, with the exception of the deep hood, he threw back to showcase a square jaw and dark brown eyes.

Being around Zeke for so many years had made Shannon very accustomed to men who dwarfed her, both in height and breadth. It did not scare her as it would most others, so when he crouched down so they were eye to eye Shannon swore it was not because of his size she had to force herself not to shrink away.

Three, tiny, nearly imperceptible scars textured his jaw and brow, but it was his eyes, hard as forged steel; the way he held his body even in the crouch, as though he could spring at her with barely a thought, that made her wary. When Shannon watched Tristan move, she could tell he knew how to fight, every movement was smooth, measured, balanced. But this man was violence contained and controlled to a wire taught tension. His smile was an easy expression, one he was used to making. It lessened the instinctual fear running through Shannon— slightly— but not near enough for her to be comfortable.

"You must be the lovely Shannon I have heard so much about over the years," Kent said, shooting Tristan a glance. His words held the same brogue as Tristan's, but the voice was much lower, vibrating like a drum from the stockier man. "He wanted me to let you know that he'll be stuck in his skin for a while yet. You can either stay here with him and wait it out, or I can escort you up to the main hall and he will catch up later." He waved his hand like he was physically putting the choice at her feet. "Up to you love."

Shannon blinked at him a few times, looking him over, but ultimately she shifted closer to Tristan. He, in turn, exchanged a nod with his friend and settled in a more comfortable position on the stone. It took a moment for her to figure out how to situate herself, but eventually she calmed down, and was soon drifting off to sleep.

Kent dove into the pool, transforming midair with ease, and swam across to retake his post in the upper corner of the room. Within the gates of his home, and his friend watching over them, Tristan let himself slip into slumber as well.

Chapter Ten

$\mathcal{A}$ nudge to her shoulder woke Shannon hours later. Cracking her eyes revealed Tristan crouching over her, once again in his human form. A smile spread over his face as she slowly worked her way back to full consciousness. At first, it had been odd being on land in this new form, but Shannon had been surprised with how natural it had felt to fall asleep like this. Strange, how something could be completely new and entirely familiar at the same time. She had a feeling there would be many things about this new aspect of her life that would feel the same way.

Rising up onto her fore flippers, Shannon looked Tristan up and down, tilting her head in question. His grin widened and he chuckled, understanding the meaning behind her gaze.

"The easiest way I have found to shift back, is to picture my human hand removing my hood. If you feel a tightening around yourself, it means not enough time has passed to equal out what you spent on land. You haven't had your coat for long, so that should not be a problem this instant." He waved an encouraging hand at her. "Give it a shot," he said as he rose to his full hight and crossed his arms comfortably.

Closing her eyes, Shannon tried to do as he instructed. Given this was the first time she had ever been a sea lion, it was not terribly difficult to picture her own hands doing any kind of task. As soon as her mental fingers touched stiff leather Shannon could feel a release of pressure along her entire body. The feeling was similar to rising slowly from a pool of water. The surface tension clinging to your skin, as though it is reluctant to let you leave, but helpless to stop you anyway. Just as simple as walking out of that pool of water, her body shrunk and slimmed into smooth curves, flippers turned to hands and feet, and coffee toned fur faded to pale skin.

Completing the motion she did mentally, Shannon let her hood fall back, allowing her chestnut curls to fall about her shoulders. Tristan grinned with pride. "Well done. That didn't take you long t'all." Shannon grinned back, strangely thrilled at his praise.

"Come on. I'm starvin' and I suspect you are too," he said, waving her on as he walked toward a tunnel she had not seen when first entering the chamber.

Shannon did her best to keep track of the route, but after the fifth turn she had to admit she was hopelessly lost. Tristan smirked over his shoulder when she huffed a breath after climbing up the second incline of their jolly jaunt. "The tunnels are a maze on purpose. Safer that way. You'll get used to it. Promise."

They walked for a good ten minutes before the sound of running water drifted to her ears. It was here Tristan paused and swung an arm ahead in an elegant sweep, inviting her to pass. A heartbeat later, when her eyes allowed her to stop squinting at the sudden flood of light, in contrast to the shadows of the enclosed stone at their backs, Shannon gaped at the reason for the theatrics.

The opening for the tunnel sat midway up the bowl of a deep canyon valley. Switchback trails curved their way down the sides of the cliff-face, pockmarked with other entrances both above and below. At various levels, small waterfalls cascaded into one another like dominos to merge once again at a large stream running the length of the canyon and disappearing out of sight. This must have been the source of the running water sound that echoed to them, even when they were still underground. It was no wonder, there were at least a dozen of the rushing manifestations of a postcard photographer's best dream.

One of the smaller falls ran off to the right of the platform where they were standing. Shannon shuffled over, conscious of the edge, her shoes crunching the thin layer of grit over the stone, then reached out her hand to break the stream. The water was biting, and unless her nose had decided to play tricks on her today, fresh. She cupped her hand and tentatively brought it to her lips. Cool, fresh water washed over her tongue. The contrast was interesting as she could still pick up the salt on the breeze from the ocean beyond this bizarre oasis.

Shannon tilted her chin up. The walls themselves rose high above where they stood, curving over their heads, to form an elongated dome-like structure. The dome was incomplete, however. Three massive gaps in the rock above, like the crater of a volcano, allowed beams of yellow, orange, and pink light from the dying sun to peak through the stone onto the valley below.

Small, old-fashioned houses made of stone and thatch dotted the deceptively large space in no particular order. These quaint homes gave acclaim to their builders and those who lovingly maintained them over the years. While spread out enough to not crowd their neighbors, they all circled what could only be described as a castle.

Large stone walls, turrets, towers, and an incredible keep at its heart. Three of the waterfalls draped behind the southernmost wall and fed into a wide moat that surrounded the entirety of the castle, providing both protection and water to those who would take shelter behind her battlements.

Shannon stood mesmerized by the dazzling, fertile valley. It was as if someone had taken a masterpiece painting of a child's fairytale land, plucked it out, then lovingly placed it in this tucked away corner of the world where it could not be smudged. There was only one word for it, beautiful.

From behind, Tristan's smooth brogue, thicker now as he breathed the air of his home, said with pride, "Welcome to the Grotto."

Shannon stood stunned. Her hands twitched at her sides but were unable to form words. It boggled the mind how such a scruff of dirt, rock and spindly trees as the island appeared from the outside, could hold a breathtaking sanctuary within. The fact there was an inside to begin with was enough to make a person's thoughts turn summersaults.

Eventually, Shannon got control of her appendages to an extent where a simple, *"How?"* was manageable.

Tristan beamed in muted satisfaction at her floored expression. Tugging at her elbow they began working their way down the stone trail to the bottom. His hands moved at the same time as he talked, "We think at one point this island was a volcano." Shannon's eyes saucered at this insight. The walls certainly gave the impression of a volcano, but she had not considered the place to actually be one. He waved her off her concern.

"No. No, long time ago. Our clan has lived here for generations, and the volcano went dormant centuries before that. This is one of the safest places for our kind to be. The tunnels we walked through," he jabbed a thumb over his shoulder, pointing at the opening they had emerged from. "We believe at one point were lava channels, and this," he gestured to the valley below them, "was the main magma chamber. Over the years we have expanded and shaped what nature carved out. But you can still see what it used to be."

Reassured they were not going to be blown to kingdom come, Shannon let herself admire the breathtaking scenery. *"It's beautiful."* She signed.

Tristan sighed in contentment and nodded thoughtfully. "The Maker blessed us with a remarkable home." Shannon looked down at the path upon hearing this. Focusing on putting one foot in front of the other, so as not to trip. At least that was what she said to herself in her head. A nudge to her shoulder made Shannon look back up at her companion. His smile was warm and a little too knowing for her comfort. "This can be your home too." He jumped down to a lower ledge and held a hand out to help her down. "If you let it be that is." Shannon took his hand, but did not respond to his statement.

"I am going to need to work on my poker face. He read me way too easily." she thought.

Being welcomed, even if it was by just one person, did not mean she could flip a switch and suddenly sink roots into this place. Her home was Shelter Bay, where her mom was, where Mandy, Zeke, Sarah, the Marine Center and its staff were. Those buildings, roads, and smiling faces within that small town were entangled with every minute of her life. Every pivotal moment, which shaped the person she was today, had been witnessed by Shelter Bay and her people. Until today. If Tristan was to be believed, she could not go back there at all.

The abrupt change was more terrifying than Shannon would ever admit to anyone.

The walk down the canyon walls took a bit over fifteen minutes, but within the hour Shannon and Tristan were stepping up to the gate of the castle. Shannon craned her neck up to see the top of the stone walls. *They have a darned castle in the middle of a stone island!* she thought, still flabbergasted by the idea. Tristan shouted up to the men standing guard in the gatehouse, and after seeing who it was, they waved them through.

"Why are the gates not closed?" Shannon asked.

"They are closed at night and anytime there is even the chance of an attack from the outside, but many people who live outside the castle come in and out throughout the day to work, or visit those who do live here. So the gates remain open. It is a weak point, but one we can compensate for quickly if the situation calls for it."

As Shannon watched his explanation it struck her once again how proficient he was at ASL. In fact, he had never batted an eye when she was talking to him, even though, through the chaos of the last couple days, Shannon had not slowed her sign rate down at all like

Darbie Hamilton

she normally would with an English speaker. The only time he had asked her to repeat herself was when they were in the car the first night, and that was because the lights were out.

She must have been staring more than intended, for Tristan shot her a sidelong look and asked bluntly, "What?"

"Where did you learn to sign? When did you learn to sign?" Shannon asked. She tried to be nonchalant about it, but Tristan still chuckled at the question or rather, the delivery of the question. Could he truly blame her for being taken aback? The man had shown himself to be not only competent with her language, but proficient, and for the most part that skill had flown over her head.

Tristan chose to answer fully in sign, letting his voice go quiet. "Started learning about three days into my taking the job as your guardian." Shannon raised her eyebrows, he nodded and continued. "When I saw it was your primary language, I thought it would be wise to know what you were saying. Plus..." He looked uncomfortable, and for a minute Shannon thought he was not going to finish the sentence, but after a beat Tristan shook his head and pressed on awkwardly. "I thought it would be a good way to get to know you. To... know who I was protecting." The sentiment made Shannon smile. Tristan was still essentially a stranger, but it was clear he had put a lot of effort into learning sign. Few people in her life had gone to the trouble of trying, let alone becoming as skilled as he clearly was. If even a bit of that was for her, rather than just him doing his job, well, she was flattered.

Tristan held open a large oak door across the bailey and up the stairs of the main keep. *"Me being able to insult Kent, without his knowledge is just icing on the cake."* This made Shannon hiss in a laugh. How many times had her coworkers asked her to show them the insults and curse words in sign just so they could use them on each other! She had lost count.

The Great Hall, despite its name, was a simple room. Incredibly large, both in width and height, but the smooth stone, and long, polished wood tables made the grand space utilitarian rather than extravagant. Iron chandeliers and sconces provided a bright, lively atmosphere, echoed by the laughing, chattering people filling the room.

The tables were arranged length wise on either side of the door. Two to the left, two to the right, leaving an aisle down the middle for easy movement. At the back of the hall on a raised dais was a smaller table of the same make, running perpendicular to the ones on the ground. Only four people sat at this table, though there were seats for seven available.

The way they were sitting, in the center of the head table, had the subtle feeling of a king's family watching over their court. The man at the head of the table seemed to be the source of this perception. Broad shouldered, heavily muscled, and while relaxed and smiling with the others, he sat in a way so he could move to attack or defend at any time. It was a body language Shannon had seen many times in the men who had come back after serving in combat overseas. But rather than making him appear nervous or on edge, it gave an aura of readiness and protection.

Tristan, noticing her interest, leaned in and whispered, "That's Nolan Rowle. He's the chief of our clan... and your uncle." Shannon whipped her head around eyes wide. Tristan nodded.

"May be wise to make introductions when there is less of an audience." he teased. Come on, looks like the section on the end just had a fresh tray put down." He led her to sit midway down the far table on the right.

People seemed to rarely stay in one spot for very long, even while eating. Every now and then someone would rise and take their food to visit with a friend they saw on the other side of the room, only for the space to be taken up by another doing the exact same thing. Shannon was reminded of the massive block parties or fairs Shelter Bay would host every few months. No one stayed put for long there either. The comparison in her mind allowed her to breathe a bit easier in the new environment.

They slid into a newly vacated spot and Tristan began filling plates for them from one of the large trays set up every five seats or so along the massive table.

The smell of some kind of savory stew flirted with Shannon from where she sat as Tristan ladled a portion into two bowls. Steaming bread and fresh fruit with vibrant enough colors for a magazine display quickly followed and Shannon's stomach flipped in excitement.

When the plate was placed in front of her, Shannon quickly blessed the meal and started with the stew, careful not to make the bell sleeves of her coat a casualty of supper. One bite and she was in heaven. Every flavor blended together perfectly with the next. Savory and smokey, rich and light, and a bright sweetness to tie off the bow. If pressed Shannon was not sure she could say which part she liked best. "Whoever cooked this is a magician!" Shannon said, popping another berry into her mouth.

Tristan grinned as he tucked into his own food. "Duncan will be thrilled to hear you say so." The motion of their hands must have caught the attention of those around them for a young couple across the table suddenly called over the voices closest.

"Tristan?"

The man in question looked up at hearing his name called and gave a friendly wave. The pair got up from their seats and scooted the two who were sitting directly parallel to Tristan and Shannon over a few spots so they could take their place.

"Thought that was you. Found someone else who knows that hand thing of yours, eh?" This from the man as he sunk into his newly acquired spot. His accent was thicker than any Shannon had heard so far. Still understandable, but she had to concentrate in order to decipher it. The woman elbowed the man in the ribs. The man just grinned and gave shrug. The woman rolled her eyes at his antics then leaned into the table. "Wasn't expecting you to be back so soon after your last visit." she said, a question lacing her tone.

"All the time with the sandies must be getting to him." The man piped in. Tristan glared at the comment. "Can it Bruce. You know I don't like you callin' them that." He said at the same time the woman smacked his arm. The man waved them both off.

"So, you finally giving up your post and coming back? You know Callum will take you back in a heartbeat."

The woman laughed, "No truer words. He still compares the rest of us to you."

Tristan took another bite of stew letting the silence hang for a beat. "I'd need to talk to the Lann about something like that. Have you seen him about?"

Both shook their heads at the same time. "It's the last week of the month," the man said distractedly, while snagging a stray hunk of bread off the serving platter.

Tristan groaned, running a hand over his face, "I forgot about that."

"What's important about the last week of the month?" Shannon asked.

Glancing at Bruce and his as yet to be named counterpart, he switched to sign, "It's the one time of month the Chief lets your dad go and see you and your mom."

"Dad has never come to see us. Not in seventeen years!" Shannon replied with gritted teeth, her hands cutting sharp lines through the air, and cracking when the signs required them to connect.

Tristan took a deep breath, "Yes, he has. He's forbidden from interacting with you two, but he goes to see you every chance he can," he rebutted.

The conversation was cut short by Bruce who was quickly getting on Shannon's nerves. "Who's your friend, Tristan?" he asked, now making a pointed effort to look her over. A chill went up her spine at his gaze and Shannon moved a bit closer to her guardian. Sensing her discomfort, Tristan put a protective hand on the back of her chair. This calmed Shannon significantly, a topic for later pondering. But for now, the thought could be set aside for the current conversation. "This is Shannon," he introduced after a small debate with himself, "Shannon, this is Bruce and Emma. We used to work together. They are both part of the Bacainn." In sign he added. "I'll explain Bacainn later." Shannon nodded and waved at the pair. Emma was now studying her too, but more like Shannon was a puzzle piece she could not quite figure out where to put. "Why do I know that na... "

The main door to the hall swung wide and in strode a man in his mid-forties, frustration pouring off him in waves. His footsteps pounded into the stone as though he meant to break them. He did not care he had gained the attention of the entire room. Murmurs instead of shouts and laughter chased each other around the space.

He moved straight to the front table, and dropped down into the seat on the end, farthest from the family in the middle and started putting together his own plate of supper. It was only two chairs, but the message was clear, "don't talk to me now". He didn't slam his plate, or slosh his bowl, but every movement was a bit too sharp, a bit too hard. Running clawed fingers through his hair, he took a deep breath and visibly forced himself to calm down. Only when his emotions were back under control did he allow himself to take his first bite.

Bruce grumbled underneath his breath. "They must not have been at home." He cursed. "That does not spell good things for the next few days training." He cursed again as the room slowly settled back into its normal volume, ignoring the stewing man at the front.

Shannon, in contrast, could not take her eyes off the figure. His hair was longer and had wings of grey at the temples now. His beard was thicker and also heavily peppered. Somehow, he was more solidly built than she recalled, but there was absolutely no chance she would ever forget that face. A face she had last seen on a beach as a child. Her father, Eoin Rowle, sat like a gargoyle at the end of the table, every muscle in his body warning others to stay away.

The hard man before her did not match the laughing eyes and playful smile which danced through Shannon's memory. The contrast scared Shannon, striking a nerve she did not know was exposed. Before she had made the conscious decision to do so, she was rising from her seat and tugging at Tristan. "*I need to go,*" she signed, pulling harder.

Tristan rose as well, his gaze taking in her panicked expression. "*Okay, let me find Patty and she can get you settled in one of the guest rooms.*"

Before he had finished the sentence, she was already shaking her head. "*No. I want you to take me home. Take me home now!*"

"*I can't do that. You know it's not safe.*" Tristan tried to take her arm, calm her down, but she ripped her arm from his grip.

"*I want to go home!*" She was starting to hyperventilate. Tristan had to calm her down. He tried again, "*Shannon I cannot do that. Let's just get you settled and maybe—* "

"No!" The word ripped from Shannon's throat and echoed off the stone walls. Shannon threw her hands over her ears and pressed as hard as she could while the sound built louder and louder, ricocheting all around her. Where was it coming from? The awful noise played havoc in her head, first shrill and high, then swooping low and wailing only to pitch up again, bouncing along the inside of her scull until she was afraid the bone would crack. "*Someone, make it stop!*" she begged in her mind, "*It hurts. Too loud. Too loud!*" In the back of her consciousness Shannon could hear Tristan's voice attempting to say something, but it just added to the vicious noise.

After an eternity of ceaseless clamor, a callused hand clamped firmly over her mouth, beating the sound into reluctant submission. It was enough for Tristan's smooth baritone to come to the foreground, a moment more for his words to register. "You're screaming Shannon!" Shannon locked eyes with his. Seeing he had at last grabbed her attention, Tristan put an arm around her shoulders and tucked her into his chest. Shannon's tears poured down her cheeks. The horrid sound still came in bursts, rattling around her head, but at least it was not constant anymore. "Deep breaths. It'll stop, but you have to calm down."

Her fist clutched his shirt as she pulled in a stuttering breath. Then another. Tristan continued to murmur softly as he stroked her hair. Bit by bit the noise ebbed and gave way to the familiar sound of steady breathing. Not once did Tristan pull away or suggest they get up and move. Shannon frowned. When had they sat down on the floor?

She pulled back slightly. Tristan's arms held at first, resisting, then let her sit up. The instant Shannon looked around she wanted to curl up in a ball all over again. Every eye in the great hall was on her. Every eye, including her father's.

"Come on," Tristan coaxed as he pulled her to her feet, and gave Shannon someone else to look at. Draping his arm back around her shoulders like a protective cloak, he began moving them down a hallway Shannon had not seen before. Where he was taking them, she did not know. At the moment however, as long as it was away from here, neither did she care.

Chapter Eleven

Tristan had never been in the position of having to calm someone down out of complete hysterics before. It was a far more unsettling experience than he would have thought possible. Nevertheless, as he sat on the stone with Shannon folded into him, it was both for her benefit and to get his own heartbeat back into a somewhat normal rhythm.

Through the wall of people surrounding them, the stupefied face of the Lann could be seen. The raised dais allowed him to rise above many of the heads. He had obviously discerned who exactly had been shrieking like a banshee. Tristan's ears were still ringing from being so close to the shaken woman.

For that to be the first time in her life to hear her own voice, mentally Tristian shook his head as he tried to put himself in Shannon's shoes, traumatizing to say the least. But to watch your daughter go through that and be helpless to stop it. Tristan dreaded to even contemplate the matter. Still, sympathetic as he may be, when Tristan saw Eoin had at last propelled himself into motion, pushing through the crowd toward his daughter, he could not allow it.

Pulling Shannon closer, Tristan glared at the older man and held up a hand to forestall his charge. To his shock, the Lann did slow, and at Tristan's small but sharp shake of the head, came to a full stop.

Tristan knew how much Eoin loved his daughter. Knew keeping him from her would rip him to pieces. Yet this entire mess had started because of him. Tristan would have had to have been blind to miss the coincidental timing of Eoin's grand entrance to the hall, and the beginnings of Shannon's panic. Clearly the woman was not ready to confront her father yet. And after the previous episode, there was no way in hell Tristan was going to force her to today.

Shannon was his charge. Her safety, both mentally and physically, came before anything else. Including, his boss.

Shannon had calmed down to a degree, her breathing slightly more at an even keel. So, before the best warrior of their clan lost his patience and decided to test the resolve of the man he set over his daughter's protection, Tristan as gently and quickly as possible, got her to her feet and wove through the crowd toward the eastern wing.

Blessedly, Patty was standing at the entrance to the corridor. The woman had an uncanny read on anything needing to be done in the castle. Not that this particular situation required a mind reader, but the steady presence and honey smile of the middle-aged housekeeper loosened the knot on the last of Tristan's nerves. The melting of Shannon underneath his arm told him she had found the woman's presence soothing as well.

Waving a hand to them both she swept them down the corridor and into the main living section of the castle. "Come on Deary, let's get you settled." She nodded back toward the great hall and the now abandoned crowd. "If that was a sampling of your day, I'd imagine you're plum worn to the bone." Shannon sniffed and nodded to Patty, giving her the tiniest smile Tristan had ever seen. However, when she did, a small hum slipped out of her at the same time, making her flinch back against Tristan, her smile forgotten altogether.

Patty and Tristan exchanged a concerned glance. It was like watching a duckling fear water. Something which should have come naturally, was utterly terrifying to Shannon.

Determination settled onto Patty's face, warm as the summer sun for its intent, but no softer than steel. Despite the tension of the situation, Tristan found himself fighting a laugh. Shannon had no clue she had just been adopted by the castle housekeeper. Time would tell if it was a good or bad thing.

Patty was not one to waste time. Before long, she was turning the key in the lock of one of the many guest rooms in the eastern wing. The matronly woman scooped Shannon out from under Tristan's arm before either of them could think to protest and swept her into the room. With Shannon inside, Patty turned to bar the door. "I've got her, lad. The girl needs rest more than anything, and you know she will be safe enough in my care," she said, raising an eyebrow, daring him to contradict her statement.

For half a heartbeat Tristan was inclined to do just that, but they were in the heart of the Grotto castle, and should it come down to it, Tristan pitied the man who tried to go against Patty. Both the Chief and the Lann would be wanting an explanation. Sighing in resignation Tristan nodded. Before he left, he caught Shannon's eye and signed, "You can trust Patty." He gave her a lopsided grin, "She could probably put those mother hens of yours at the center to shame." That earned him a chuckle from the distraught woman, and a wince at the unfamiliar sound. Tristan's grin vanished. He hated leaving her here in this state, but Patty was right, she needed rest. "I won't be far if you need me." Whether he was reassuring Shannon or himself Tristan wasn't certain, but the sentiment managed to put the tiniest smile on Shannon's face. It would have to do. Heaving a sigh, he nodded, turned an about face and marched back to the Great Hall.

As expected, Nolan, his wife Fiona, and of course Eoin were still in the hall. What he did not expect was the rest of the hall had been emptied of any other occupants. His entrance had not gone unnoticed by the trio. The chief was the first to speak, "You're not normally one to make an entrance, Tristan, but that was certainly an impressive one."

"Would not have been my choice, m'Lord."

"Care to tell us why the incident occurred then?" The words were phrased as a suggestion; the tone implied otherwise. Yet it was Eoin Rowle who gained Tristan's complete attention. He rose from leaning on the lip of one of the tables and stalked toward the younger man.

"Yes. I would very much like to know why my daughter was screaming in the middle of the hall!" Eoin's voice gradually rose until he was yelling himself. With effort, Tristan managed to not flinch from the enraged father.

"Shannon and I were having an argument. I don't think she meant to, but she said one of the words aloud. To my understanding she has never done that before." Tristan shrugged helplessly, "I believe... it scared her. That's when she started screaming. My guess is she didn't know how to make it stop."

Pain flashed through his eyes as Eoin sagged down onto one of the chairs, and dug his fingers through his hair. "No, she wouldn't know how to stop. She s never had to be taught before." Fiona walked over and rested a hand on troubled man's shoulder. It was as much support as he would likely accept right now. The chief brought Tristan's attention back to him, leaving his brother to his own thoughts... for now.

"You still have not answered my question, Tristan." He leveled his gaze on the young warrior, and Tristan unconsciously stood straighter under his chief's scrutiny. "Why are you here? Why did you bring the girl?"

"Shannon!" Eoin rose to his feet once more and glared at his brother. "Her name is Shannon you pig headed brute. Your niece, my daughter! The least you could do is use her proper name." Nolan measured Eoin's words and stance before tilting his head in acquiescence.

"Why did you bring, *Shannon*, to the Grotto?" Nolan had asked the question but it was Eoin, once again, Tristan faced when he answered,

"Nereids attacked Shannon and Mandy last night." The older trio stiffened at his words, anger rolling off them. "Three of them. They were waiting for her, Sir. It was a miracle I was nearby. As it was, I barely made it in time."

"What did you do with the urchins?" Eoin growled.

"They're dead," Tristan said matter-of-factly. A savage grin spread over Eoin's face.

Nolan nodded in acknowledgment of the situation but otherwise not reacting. Tristan continued, "Only three attacked her, but an entire squad was on the mainland. I watched them come to claim the bodies." He ran fingers through his hair and leaned against the table. "They were targeting her. Went strait for Shannon, Mandy only got caught in the crosshairs. Half the reason I made it in time was because they were not expecting the girls to put up such a fight." Tristan chuckled, "Mandy hit one of them with pepper spray of all things."

Eoin laughed, "I always liked that girl." He sobered and asked, "So with a direct attack you chose to bring her here then?"

Tristan nodded. "The best security she had was that the Nereids did not know who or what she was. With her anonymity gone, I could not guarantee her safety. Not on my own at least. I chose the next best option." He leveled his gaze at the Lann, "You should know, Sir, Shannon was not fond of the realization she had been, as she put it, lied to her entire life." Eoin flinched. "The threat to her life is the only way I could convince her to come here."

Eoin dug at his eyes. "It's not completely unexpected," he cursed, "We waited too long to tell her."

"Per usual," Nolan muttered. The comment coming offhand as his gaze became distant, evaluating the situation. Eoin growled and began to rise from his seat, but Lady Fiona put a staying hand on his shoulder. "That was a might harsh Nolan," she said

At his wife's chastising words the chief shook himself out of his thoughts and took stock of the small group in front of him, but especially his brother. "I will apologize for the tone, but not the words Brother. Procrastination is what put us in this mess in the first place."

"My wanting to stay with my wife and child? How horrible of me!"

"Staying with your human wife and child so long the Debt was called in!" Now the chief was getting angry. Tristan saw the makings of a brawl if things kept to the current course. It would not be the first he had seen between the brothers due to this very subject. Fortunately, the Lady of the house was not one to suffer wrestling matches in the middle of her Great Hall. Her smooth, melodic voice carried over the men's shouting with the ease of practice. "This argument never goes anywhere, and I don't have the patience to listen to it again tonight. Perhaps our energies would be better suited to deducing how the Nereids may have found the poor lass?"

Tristan watched fascinated as both men reigned in their tempers. He thought it wise not to weigh in on this conversation until he was asked something directly. Easier to keep all his limbs where they currently were that way.

"Do you know how they found out what Shannon was?" Fiona asked, letting the brothers collect themselves. Tristan crossed his arms as he thought back. "Earlier in the week Shannon ran into a couple of hot heads on shore leave. They came to the marine center and were causing trouble, were picking on her. They started to get aggressive, so I let them see me. I was hoping they would think I was just defending claimed territory."

"You think they realized you were protecting her?" Eoin asked, his focus now completely on the bacainn.

Tristan shook his head. "No, they were more rankled by the fact I was there spoiling their fun. It wasn't until that night I think they figured it out."

"What happened that night?" This time the question came from Nolan.

"Shannon and her crew went to supper, and the same Squids were there. Started picking a fight right there in the restaurant. I thought Zeke was gonna knock their teeth in." Tristan snorted, "Honestly would have liked to have seen it, but an older one came over to put a stop to it before I could interfere again. He moved different than the other two. And the way they reacted makes me think he was some kind of officer. He certainly moved like a fighter. He made the loud-mouths heel like pups." Tristan narrowed his eyes at the memory and crossed his arms, "Made a whole production of apologizing for the scene. He was standing close to Shannon. Maybe he caught her scent?" Tristan met Eoin's gaze. "Three days later she was attacked. Two of the Fish I killed were the ones harassing Shannon, and the older 'officer' or whatever he was, was one of the ones to come collect the bodies.

So, at the very least the incident was related. Whether it was their first contact, or confirming a suspicion, I can't know. Either way she was too exposed."

Eoin heaved a sigh. "Sounds like you made the right call. I just wish she didn't have to go through something like this. Her first taste of being a Selkie was violence. I didn't want that for her."

"Nothing for it now." Nolan walked over and gripped the back of his brother's neck, "At least she's safe. She's safe, and now you have the opportunity to get to know her again." Nolan gripped a bit harder, pulling the man's eyes to his, "And this way she can get to know her father. Both who and what he is. No more hiding."

As much as his brother's interference had angered Eoin over the years, he knew Nolan only did what he thought was best for everyone involved. And despite heated words, he knew his daughter's well-being was not excluded from his thoughts. It was in their nature to take care of their own.

Relaxing, Eoin turned back to Tristan and asked the question he asked every time he saw the man, "How is she?"

"Shaken, confused, angry, tired. She's been through, and learned, a lot in an incredibly short time. I think tonight we saw a release of that pressure. Despite everything though...She is handling it all better than I hoped she would." Tristan straightened in an unconscious defensive stance, but his voice remained calm. "She needs time to adjust. Give her a day, maybe two, before you try to approach her." His words came out harsher than intended, verging on the edge of an order, but Tristan did not apologize for his tone. Not on this.

Eoin nodded seeing the wisdom of the suggestion and graciously ignored the note of command. If anything, it comforted Eoin. Tristan had, and would, protect his daughter...even from him if needs be.

Walking over to the young man he slapped his arm, "You've done well Tristan. Thank you." Eoin caught the minute, satisfied tip of the soldier's lips at his praise. "Now go get some sleep. You look like you've been fighting a rip current."

Tristan gave a slight bow to the three figures in the room. "Good night, M'Lord, M'Lady, Sir." Then strode from the hall.

In the silence his departure had brought, Fiona spoke up, "I wondered if that would happen."

The brothers looked at her simultaneously. Fiona glanced between their identical confused expressions. "You didn't see it, did you?" When they continued to look befuddled, she out right laughed. "Seriously! The man has protected her for years, gotten to know her *for years*. It was bound to happen eventually." She patted Eoin's shoulder and kissed her husband before heading to her own bed. Before she was out of sight she called back. "Mark me. Before this mess is squared away, you're going to regret not putting Angus on her protection detail."

Now the two men were utterly lost. Why in the world had she brought up the old battle instructor?

🝱

$\mathcal{M}$andy had never been more grateful for an early shift in her life. Sleep had been an elusive friend the night before. The mugging refused to stop replaying itself over and over again. For once, the blare of her alarm clock was a welcome sound. At least by going to work she would be productive instead of staring at the ceiling for hours on end.

Swinging through the door, Mandy flipped on her chipper voice and called over to the desk, "Morning Mary!"

Mary gave a smile and a wave, busy with something on her computer. Snatching her earpiece and walkie from the staff room, Mandy did her best to set aside the night before, despite a sore shoulder from "sleeping" funny, and focus on the ready distraction only thirty plus kids could provide.

She was halfway through her first tour of the day when Mandy realized she had yet to see Shannon the entire morning. When her tour group entered the sea lion enclosure, Dr. T was the only one working with the playful animals.

Mandy shot a confused look at the marine biologist. Reading her meaning in an instant he kept a smile on his face for the kids but shook his head. With the kids distracted by the barking chorus, Mandy snuck out her phone and shot Shannon a quick text asking where she was. When they were leaving the sea lion enclosure, and she had still not gotten a response, she texted again. Still no answer. She tried Mrs. Rowle but got sent straight to voicemail.

Mandy got the kids through the manta ray exhibit and settled down in the cafeteria with their teachers as quickly as feasibly possible, then hurried back. Dr. T was examining one of the males' flippers when she barged through the doors. "I can't get a hold of her. Can you?"

Releasing the sea lion to go play with his friends he rose and walked over to Mandy. "Not a peep. I've tried since this morning when she missed morning prep. It's not like her to just not show up."

"Or not to answer. She never takes this long to reply. Especially with both of us trying." Mandy tapped her phone against her palm. "Zeke, we got jumped last night."

"What!" Somehow his already bass voice dropped even lower. "Who? Did they hurt you?" His eyes started scanning her for the slightest injury.

"Couple of the guys who gave us trouble at Mellie's a few days ago. They tried to grab us. I pepper sprayed one of them, Shannon gave the one after her a good whack, then this random guy came and beat the crap out of the creeps."

"Who was he?"

"I don't know. I've never seen him before, but he saved our backsides and got us out of there. I never got his name. Zeke...What if those guys came back? We have no idea why they went after us. What if they tried again? You know and I both know Shannon would never skip out like this. What if..."

Zeke grabbed her shoulders before Mandy could hyperventilate. "Shannon lives with her mama, right? Have you tried her?"

"Yes! Same thing, no answer." His hands tightened trying to ground her.

"Alright, let's see if anyone else here has heard from her and if not..." Mandy whimpered, but Zeke pressed on trying to keep his own emotions in check to think clearly, "If not, we can swing by her house. If she is still not there we'll go to the station. You already told the police about last night, right?" Mandy nodded. "Maybe they found the guys and we can at least rule them out from what is going on." Zeke bent to look her directly in the eye. Mandy forced herself to take slow breaths and nodded again. With a plan, she felt less like she was going to cry.

"Come on." Zeke put an arm across her shoulders, and they walked toward the front. "Please God," Mandy prayed under her breath, "Please let her be okay. Or show us how to help her if she is not."

*N*ormally Atticus was the perfect picture of an officer. Strait laced, unflappable, some would even go so far as to say his personality was about as colorful as his blunt, blue-grey scales. However, it was at times like this when the pressure gauge of his temper malfunctioned, and Tyrus would wonder how his brother had ever obtained a reputation for being level-headed, or even sane.

A poor ship which had wrecked several years before had the unfortunate fate of being on their path back to Nereid territory, was currently bearing the brunt of Atticus's fury. All the windows were now completely gone from the light cruiser. Half of the railing was ripped out of the gunwale, the water-warped planks of the deck were scarred by several spike slashes, and to round everything off, the hull now sported several large dents from the heavy impact of his tail. The entire spectacle uncomfortably reminded Tyrus of a youngling pitching a fit when his toy was taken away from him.

Not that any of the unit said anything to imply such a thing. Large guppy or not, the man could likely kill most of them without too much effort if he wanted to. If destroying a speed boat helped redirect his temper away from them, then they were content to let him batter the poor ship until he came back to himself.

To some degree, Tyrus did understand his frustration. They were his men too, his comrades, although, he would not go so far as to call them friends. Magnus was the only one of the squad who had earned that right. But at the very least they had lost three good fighters. It was a loss no one took lightly. Tyrus almost pitied the Bacainn who accomplished the deed. Mercy would be the last thing on Atticus's mind when they found him. If they ever found him.

His brother was finally winding down. His fins flexing into smoother strokes to keep him in place. His breathing evened out and his shoulders relaxed into their normal square line. The officer was back in residence. The rest of the men saw this too and began moving closer, feeling it was, somewhat, safe to be within range again. Tyrus stayed where he was. If his brother needed him, he would say so. As if to prove his thought correct, Atticus barked his name and waved him forward.

Tyrus pushed off the boulder he was leaning against and approached his commander, covering the distance in a few easy strokes. "You're staying here to keep watch." Atticus ground out.

Tyrus forced himself to not immediately bite his brother's head off. Like it or not Atticus was his superior officer. "Sir? Forgive me, but watch for what?"

Atticus pointed up at the surface toward land. "That should have been an easy task. A lone skinner on land. No clan, no training, not even her coat to protect her. It should have been simple, but instead I lost three men in the deal." Atticus's spikes flared and his voice took on more of a growl. "That girl, whoever she was, was important enough to place a Bacainn with enough skill to take out three of our own…by… himself. They had her on land for a reason. I want to know what that reason is. I want to know what makes her special from the rest of the skinners that she warrants a personal guard when she's on shore."

Tyrus did not move as his brother got so close to his face their noses were inches from touching. "If she is important enough for a bodyguard, I want to know why. And when she comes back to shore, seeing as how he was so successful the first time, it stands to reason they will send the same slug as before. I want you here when he does." His voice began to rise. "I don't care if you have to wait through the next moon cycle. The second his foot touches dirt, your spikes are at his throat. Am I clear!"

The iron in Atticus's eyes did not leave any room to argue. Not in his current state of mind. Tyrus swallowed his protest and even managed to speak without gritting his teeth. "Yes, Sir." It seemed Tyrus was going to be spending a lot more time on land than he ever cared to.

There were times when he really would not mind smacking his brother. Hard.

Chapter Twelve

Whether it was the sunlight spilling in through the window or force of routine, but Shannon found herself wide awake at the crack of dawn. The bed was surprisingly comfortable. The severe lines of the solid wood bed frame were softened by the soft simple pattern of the heavy quilt and linen sheets. The mattress almost looked stuffed rather than the spring mattresses she had grown up with. Still, it was one of the most delightful collections of fluff she had ever curled up in.

Shannon sank deeper into the pillows, letting her mind float between sleep and awareness. If she stayed in her cloth fortress, maybe she could ignore the chaos of the last couple of days. It would not be hard. Most of what had occurred was so outlandish it was not too far of a stretch to allow herself to think it was all a delusion. A stress response from the attack, and she would open her eyes, walk to the kitchen, and her mom would be there making eggs and singing completely off key.

But then pesky logic intruded, and she had to face reality. Bizarre as that reality was, it did not change. Her father was a creature of bedtime stories, and therefore, so was she. She had been saved by a fairytale from a group of other mythical creatures. Yep. Her life made sense.

"Well, since when has your life ever made a whole lot of sense." she thought. Throwing the covers off, Shannon swung her feet over the edge and forced herself to stand. *"Whining won't change anything. This is your life now. Adapt and press on."*

First things first, she needed to find her father. Shannon was in no state of mind to talk with the man last night, but she needed answers to a whole slew of questions she had had bouncing around in her head since she was six years old.

The room she had been ushered to the night before did not have much in it. A bed, a nightstand, and a narrow wardrobe made up the bulk of the decoration. Shannon had slung her coat over the foot of the bed before she had crashed into the pillows. It was still odd to have the thing, to feel that pull of self toward what her eye told her was an inanimate object, but every instinct in her body said it was a part of her. She may not have wanted to sleep in it, but she also did not want it out of her sight.

Her clothes on the other hand were an entirely different story. Having left in the middle of the night, last night? Or was it the day before? Either way, there had hardly been time to change into more comfortable clothes. So not only was she wearing the same thing she had for the last two days, but it was her work uniform "fresh" off a shift.

"Maybe Tristan knows where my bag went," she thought, humming to herself. The noise startled Shannon, her hand clutching at her throat as if she could catch the sound in her fingers. She pressed her eyes closed against the tears welling up. Shannon had lost count of how many times as a child she had prayed to hear her own voice. How many days she had to fight not to be jealous of the other people who could laugh when they were happy, cry when they were sad, shout when they were angry or hurt. Shannon loved who she was, and a big part of that was her being a mute. It made her think, act, and respond to the world around her differently than most. It made her observant, thoughtful and as ironic as it might seem, an incredible communicator. She would not be who she was if she had not grown up the way she had. But that acceptance had taken time and had cost more than a little pain. Now, without warning, she had the one thing she wanted more than anything. It was unnerving.

Pulling in a deep breath, Shannon snagged her coat and threw it around her shoulders. Once again, the feeling of a puzzle piece snapping into place washed over her. If nothing else, this felt right.

Shannon had not exactly been paying attention to where the sweet woman who smelled like bread had marched her the night before. As a result, it was more guesswork rather than any sense of direction that made her hang a left outside of her door. If she was wrong, there were plenty of people in the dining hall last night. Perhaps one of them was wandering around the corridors as well and could show her the way to food.

Shannon should never play roulette. Random selection was evidently not where her luck lied. After at least five minutes of walking, the direction she had chosen proved to be not only completely devoid of people, but also managed to get her more turned around than she already was. Shannon remembered Tristan saying something about the tunnels being designed specifically to be confusing for the purpose of befuddling intruders. She made a mental note to ask him if the castle was made to do the same thing.

Shannon was just about to give up and do an about face when she heard the flutter of women chattering just ahead of her along the corridor. Finally, someone who knew where they were going. Speeding to a light jog, Shannon moved towards the voices and possible directions to food.

Swinging around the corner, Shannon found three women talking, laughing and not really paying attention to what was around them. All three were very beautiful, but the one at the center of the group was the most striking. Medium height and build but perfectly proportioned as if she had been carved from marble by a master craftsman. Her skin was smooth, and pale as milk except for the smattering of freckles along her nose and cheeks. Rather than looking like blemishes, they instead drew the attention to her vibrant green eyes. Tight curls of blazing red fell past her shoulders. She looked more like a painting than a person.

The woman turned to face Shannon more fully, noticing her presence at last. The look in her eye made Shannon wary. Intelligent, yes, but cunning seemed a more fit description to the glint she found in the emeralds staring her down.

Taking a deep breath to steady herself, Shannon smiled and stepped toward the clutch of women, the other two coming alert as she came closer.

Shannon waved at the women in greeting. Putting her fingers together she motioned to her mouth in the sign for eat, then pointed down either hallway and shot them a confused, questioning look. With people who did not know sign language, Shannon had learned broad obvious motions worked best. She may look like she was playing charades, which to an extent she was, but communication happened, which was the goal. She had lost her ability to be bashful about situations like this years ago.

The redhead scrunched her face in feigned puzzlement. "I'm sorry. I don't know what you're saying. You're going to have to speak up." The other two tittered at their ring-leader's comment. Her brogue while strong, trilled like an old folk singer. The delicacy of her voice, in a way made her words all the more biting. It was like your ears lured you into letting your guard down. How could something that sounded so pretty hurt you? Then the mind would catch up, letting you comprehend what the lovely sound was actually saying, and the blow would land where you were not expecting it.

Shannon saw in the minuscule smile tipping the woman's lips, she knew Shannon could not talk. Wonderful. These women would be no help to her. But them being here at least meant there were people in this section of the castle. So rather than turning around, Shannon shot the three "ladies" a smile, a nod of thanks, and tried to slip past them down the hall. The redhead stepped into her path, forcing her to stop where she was. *"Really?"* Shannon thought and swung her palm forward trying to ask permission to pass. The peacock wasn't having it.

"You know, I always wondered what kind of pitiful creature you would turn out to be to need Tristan's constant supervision," she said, sounding exasperated. "I mean really. How helpless are you to need our best warrior's presence to make sure you don't hurt yourself? I don't see what's so special. You're just as pathetic as I imagined you would be." The women laughed again.

Part of this performance was for the peanut gallery Shannon was sure. But there was something in this woman's stare that made her believe a portion of her rant was indeed personal, which made no sense whatsoever. Shannon did not even know this woman's name, and yet the venom in her eyes, and tone was palpable.

"If you're so useless as to need a babysitter, why don't you scamper off where you won't be a bother to anyone else? Look at you! You can't even say one word in your defense."

Shannon raised an eyebrow, then signed, *"One word in my defense."* For a glorious moment all three women were struck silent. Naturally, Miss Redhead Ringleader, was the first to recover. "What was that?" she took a step forward, but Shannon held her ground, "What did you just say, you freak?" she demanded.

"Oh, lay off Lyra!" A voice called down the hall. Footsteps steadily made there way to the motley group. From behind Shannon, a young woman about a hand shorter nudged her aside and stepped in front, effectively placing herself as a barrier between Shannon and her would be tormentor. "Everyone in this place knows you can't go two hours without hearing the sound of your own voice. Shannon here has managed just fine her entire life without any of the advantages that comes with being one of us." This woman seemed to be the opposite of the redhead.

Lyra. Shannon made a mental note of the name. This new woman, while pretty, was not the heart-stopper Lyra was. However, her bearing and presence exuded confidence and authority. This one knew her place in the pecking order and used it to her advantage. The fact she seemed to not care one bit about Lyra's opinion instantly raised the young woman higher in Shannon's eyes.

"Shannon has finally rejoined the Clan, rightfully so," she emphasized. "I'm sure you can understand our family's joy in having her home at last, and will do everything in your power to make her feel welcome." The last was said in a tone which made it an order rather than a suggestion. Lyra bristled, but did not contradict her. Giving a shallow bow, and throwing a glare at Shannon, she, along with her two friends, turned and disappeared down the hall.

The woman sighed and shook her head at the retreating women. "I swear those three get sourer every year. Especially that harpy," she said pointing at the redhead's back. Spinning on her heel, the edge of her coat flaring behind her, the woman faced Shannon. They each studied the other for a heartbeat or two.

She had dark, curly brown hair that was only partially tamed into a twist at the back of her head. Her face was round, but not plump; sported wide, doe brown eyes lit with laughter, and paired well with her contagious grin. She released a contented sigh, "You have no idea how long I have waited to meet you," she said, her accent thicker with restrained emotion.

Shannon tilted her head in question. The woman shook her head and waved her hands as if to clear away wayward dust. If Shannon did not know better, she would have sworn there were tears in her eyes, but they were gone the second she took a closer look. "I'm sorry. Where are my manners?" She stuck her hand straight out like a she was thrusting a spear. "My name is Miriam. I'm Chief Nolan's daughter," her grin turned playful, "your cousin."

Shannon's brows did their best to climb completely off her face. Tristan had explained that her father was the chief's brother, but somehow her mind had not made the leap to it meaning she would have a cousin. Shannon checked herself. She may have more than one cousin. Her mother had two siblings, and they all had children, though she didn't see them much. Why not on her father's side as well.

"Nice to meet you, Miriam," she signed, even though she knew the petite woman would not understand. Though she seemed to understand the context and smiled sweetly.

Linking their arms, Miriam started tugging them further down the hall they were on at a leisurely pace. "If you don't mind, would you like to have breakfast in my rooms? I would love to get to know you a bit better before I have to share you with everyone else." She asked nonchalantly, but from the forced ease of her movements Shannon could tell it meant a lot to her. Her heart softened; it had been a while since someone new made an effort to get to know her. Shannon smiled and nodded at her cousin.

You would have thought Shannon agreed to teach her how to fly the way she lit up. A squeal of delight transitioned to a fit of giggles. "This way! This way!" she squealed, now towing Shannon's arm behind her as they wove through several different tunnels, all the while she chattered about the food she had set. "I am biased, I know. But Elenor is the best cook in the world. I don't know how she comes up with these recipes, but everything that comes out of that woman's kitchen is fit for angels. Her strawberry tarts are my favorite." She spun the knob on a solid oak door and ushered Shannon inside. "I had her send up some so you can try them."

The suite before her was a lot brighter than Shannon expected for being in castle. Crested windows and a set of French doors allowed a great amount of light into the room. The furniture was all soft birch wood and covered with fine textiles of white and various shades of blue and lavender. The suite was broken into three distinct sections. In the center was a seating area with a love seat and two chairs, with an oval table between them. Wildflowers sat in a low vase in the center, adding a pop of color, as well as sending a wonderful scent of sweet freshness into the air.

To the right, the color scheme flowed into the bedroom. A simple blue comforter with white embroidered pillows to match, posed like the cover of a Better Homes and Gardens catalogue. A delicate bedside table with a lamp and book perched next to it.

On the other end of the suite, Shannon could see the opening to a pristine bathroom. While there were some blues decorating it, pinks and yellows could be seen as well.

It was one of the most feminine rooms Shannon had even seen. Yet instead of being stifling, the room had the opposite effect. Walking into this suite Shannon felt herself breath deep and relax fully for the first time since she had arrived at the Grotto. She turned to Miriam who stood in the doorway letting her take the room in, and she realized the room was an extension of the woman herself, calming without being smothering. It was like she exuded brightness, comfort, and ease with little to no effort at all.

Miriam beamed. It was nice to see her cousin let herself be still, let her tension go. She had been present the night before when Shannon had arrived. Never did she want to see anyone, let alone her family, be that scared in her home ever again. It went against every bit of her training as a lady of the house, against the very grain of her being. But Miriam also was keenly aware her cousin would need time to see where she fit into life in the Grotto. She berated herself for not getting to the woman before Lyra flashed her claws at her. In her defense, Shannon had not been in her room that morning and Miriam was forced to go on a manhunt for the wayward woman.

She was here now and that is what mattered. Miriam was hungry and was sure Shannon would be as well. Poor thing still looked worn out. So, dawning the familiar role of hostess, Miriam stepped fully into the room and to the small trolley pushed out of the way. Removing the protective covers over the platters released the heavenly aroma of baked goods, fresh fruit, and the fluffiest eggs ever to grace a plate. "I will have to fight with Ma for Elenor whenever I leave. There is no way for food to get better than this," she thought as she picked up the two empty plates and handed one to Shannon.

"Take however much you want. There is plenty, and it's all delicious," Miriam said grinning and stepping back to give Shannon access to the cart.

Shannon nodded her thanks again and began loading her plate up with a bit of everything. If the smell of was anything to go by, not to mention Miriam's praise, this was bound to be one of the better meals she'd had in a while. After both women had stacked all they could onto their plates, Miriam lead the way out the French doors onto a balcony. A small round, wrought-iron table with four chairs of the same metal stood in the center. More flowers and ivy draped over the railing giving it the feel of a tiny private garden. From here the two women could see the whole Eastern side of the grounds with a gorgeous view of two of the many waterfalls in the distance.

"Wow." Shannon signed. A look of awe coming across her face as she took it all in. Miriam grinned, "This has always been one of my favorite spots." She set her plate down on the table across from where Shannon had chosen to sit and was about to be seated herself when she stood back up with a start.

Waving her hand at Shannon she said, "Wait right there for just a sec." Then darted back into the room. There was some bumping and shuffling, but before long Miriam came back out to the table, her query clutched in her hands.

She placed the objects down beside Shannon's plate then plopped down into her own seat. "Good gracious this looks amazing." she half moaned, picked up her fork, snagged a bit of eggs and hummed in pleasure. Shannon on the other hand, found herself staring at a notepad and pen.

Noticing her guest wasn't eating, Miriam paused and, thinking she had already managed to offend the woman, tried to apologize. "Tristan says you use sign language to communicate. I know a few words from pestering him and Uncle Eoin over the years, but am nowhere near as fluent as I would need to be in order to have any kind of conversation with you." She grimaced and put her fork down. "I thought with the paper, while it might not be the fastest way of talking, I could at least understand... I'm sorry. Stupid?"

Shannon's eyes widened with each word coming out of her mouth, she shook her head vehemently and snatched up the pen. "Most people don't think of paper and pen. They just let me either sit there, or watch me flap around like a chicken. I normally keep my own with me, but it got left behind in all the commotion. This will make things much easier. Thank you." She wrote, flipping the pad over so Miriam could see.

Her cousin slouched in her seat. "Don't scare me like that!" she said, then started laughing. "While a chicken dance may be entertaining to watch, why don't you just keep the pad. Sounds like you have more need of it than I do." Shannon pointed to the last line she wrote again. Miriam smiled, content she might have been able to help in this small way, "You're welcome."

The two ate in a comfortable silence for a while, but eventually Shannon's curiosity won out. Taking the pen she wrote, "Who is Lyra?" Miriam rolled her eyes and groaned.

"A witch, that's who she is, a bonafide witch. Her mother, Ailis, is our Weaver. Because of it, she thinks she is the best thing in the world and everyone else should think so too. Tricky part is she knows her attitude can put people on edge, so she has figured out how to flip a switch and become this perfect angel. Especially around people she thinks of as important, like my Da. Boy, she turns on the charm when she is around him. Annoys me to bits." She stabbed a blueberry and thrust it into her mouth in indignation.

Shannon's pen scratched, "If you are the chief's daughter why doesn't she play act with you. She seemed quite hostile this morning."

Miriam chuckled, "We grew up together. Most people our age did. I knew her before she got smart enough to hide her colors. Plus, I am not on her "important" people list. My brother, absolutely. But me...meh." She tilted her hand in a so-so gesture. "I annoy her cause even though she doesn't give me much respect, I still have authority over her." Miriam's chuckle turned devious. "I can knock her down a peg or three and she knows it. Ticks her off to no end. Keeps her humble and is marvelous entertainment for me."

Shannon huffed a laugh. She was liking her cousin more by the minute. Mandy would get a kick out of meeting her. At the thought of her friend's name Shannon was washed with a wave of homesickness. Having Mandy here would make things a lot easier. She would find a way to make the whole thing funny or seem like a sitcom movie.

A realization made Shannon sit up straighter. There had been no time to let Mandy know where she was going. She had no idea what had happened, only that Shannon was not in town. And right after both of them had been jumped. Good Lord! She'll be worried sick! Zeke and Sarah too probably.

A warm hand grasped her own on the table, drawing her eyes to it's owner. Miriam's brows drew together in concern. Her hand came up to tap her chin in Y shape. "What's wrong?"

Shannon's eyes brimmed with tears as she wrote down what she was thinking. Miriam read the words carefully, closing her eyes when she was done reading. "I'm sorry Love, but from what Tristan reported last night, we can't risk contacting them right now. The Nereids, now that they know who you are, will be watching your old home and keeping an eye on your friends. I know it is not ideal, but right now, them not knowing where you are is the safest for them." She squeezed Shannon's hand trying to reassure her, "and for you."

Shannon took her hand back and drove her fingers through her hair in frustration. "Give it time," Miriam placated. "Maybe in a couple of weeks when things have died down a bit, we can try and get word to them you are safe." Not looking at her, Shannon nodded.

Miriam sat uncertain how to fix the situation. Contacting anyone on the outside would be disastrous right now, but she also understood. If one of her friends had gone missing, she would do anything and everything to get them back and she knew they would do the same for her. This was the kind of stress that could weigh a person down. With nothing to do for the time being but wait for things to die down, the best Miriam could do was distract. So, she gathered their remaining dishes and piled them on the cart.

"Come on," she said gently grabbing Shannon's arm and pulling her to stand. "I bet you are dying to get out of those clothes. You can borrow some of mine until we can get some for you. I'll take you down to the baths."

Resolving to talk to Tristan as soon as she saw him about possibly getting word to Mandy that she was safe, Shannon wiped her eyes, put on as much of a smile as she could manage, and motioned for Miriam to lead the way.

The baths were heavenly. The design was a cross between a Roman bath house and a hot spring. Not so large as to be cavernous, but there was plenty of space for a group of people to enjoy the luxury they had carved out for themselves. Screens along the walls allowed for privacy to those cleaning, while the rest wrapped in either towels or cloth could bask in the warm water and chat with their friends or family.

It reminded Shannon of a spa resort she and her mother had been to once. The hot water did wonders for all her muscles wound tight as a bowstring, but finally being clean, was the best part of the experience. Scrubbing away the dirt felt like scraping away the strain of the last few days. It did not get rid of her turmoil completely, but it did allow her to refocus. To start feeling a bit more like herself. To feel human. Even if she wasn't exactly that anymore.

Shannon was a bit taller than her cousin so what was a maxi dress on her, hit just above the shins on

Darbie Hamilton

Shannon. Still, it was soft, comfortable, and not her uniform. All good things in her book. Miriam grinned as they made their way back to the main section of the castle.

Unlike Shannon's coat, Miriam's only came down to just below her hips where it flared in a cute, gentle ruffle that continued around the edge of the entire coat. The sleeves were more tailored, and the front was secured with only one button in the front. Altogether, her coat reflected what Shannon had observed of her cousin to a tee, clean, put together, but elegant, and maybe even a bit of whimsy. When Shannon had gotten her own coat, Tristan mentioned they were an extension of the person as a whole. Maybe this was another aspect of this concept. The coat fitting not just the person's body, but them as a whole person: mind, body and character. It was something she would pay more attention to as she met more of the selkies...met more people like her.

"Good idea?" Miriam said, bringing Shannon back to the moment. "Do you feel better now." Shannon nodded, giving her cousin a contented smile. "So much better." she signed, making her movements broad and obvious.

Miriam grinned. "Wonderful. Now," her tone took on a more serious and inquisitive note, "do you want to want to go talk to Uncle Eoin or track down where Tristan ran off to?" Shannon held up two fingers and tapped the second one repeatedly.

Miriam giggled. "Tristan it is. Let's go."

Chapter Thirteen

The training room was filled with the erratic rhythm of strikes and blocks, punctuated by the occasional impact of someone hitting their back on the sparring floor. Kent and Tristan had been steadily sparing for over an hour, neither showing any sign of stopping in the near future.

The display of two of the Grotto's most skilled warriors was mesmerizing. Many had paused in their training to watch and possibly learn something from the young titans. Kent was sturdier on his feet and perhaps even a bit stronger than his friend, but Tristan had a few inches of reach on him. Combined with his finely honed instincts and fast reactions, they were almost a perfect match in ability. It made for very drawn out training sessions. Each taking turns having the upper hand but neither really gaining a true advantage over the other.

It forced the men to get clever in their attacks. Their fighting prowess could be sharpened with any sparring partner with a decent punch. However, being on level playing field allowed both combatants to hone not only their physical abilities, but mental sharpness as well. Tactics, leverage, awareness of environment and how it could be used to your advantage, these were the things that were brought to the forefront when Kent and Tristan fought. It was an incredible sight to behold.

Eventually, they wound down calling a truce, and the spectators went back to work, seeing that the show was over. Kent threw a towel at Tristan's head and grinned. "At least you haven't gone soft hanging around the humans everyday."

"It's not as if I was on holiday. My job was to protect her. I can't very well do that if my fighting skills are rusty."

"You are rusty. I had you three times in there."

"And I walloped you twice. I'm not bad, just didn't have as many decent sparring partners on the mainland." Kent shrugged, conceding the point. "Well, at least now you're back for good this time you'll be able to join the fight again."

Tristan wiped his face and neck of sweat, tilting his head to stretch the taught muscles as they cooled. "I don't know yet if I am. Neither the Lann, nor the Chief has reassigned me, so as far as I know my orders stand as is." This brought Kent's head around in surprise. "Why wouldn't they put you back on the front line? It's not like Shannon needs to be watched round the clock anymore. That's why you brought her back in the first place, right? So she would have more protection than you could provide on your own?"

"Yes, and in theory that would be the end of it. But I think the two of them might be reeling a bit from her being here. They haven't quite figured out where she fits in. Neither has she, for that matter. Speaking of which," Tristan bent and collected his things together, "I should go check on her. She doesn't know her way around the place yet and besides her father, I'm the only face she knows here."

"She knows me," Kent said, indignant.

Tristan laughed, "She met you last night!"

"Maybe, but I'm hard to forget. I have one of those faces that makes people feel all kinds of comfortable." Tristan laughed harder. Kent was one of the most effortlessly scary people he knew. His resting face made it look like he wanted to eat you up and spit you out again. Add his size into the equation, and very few took the chance of messing with him. Ironically, it made Tristan more intimidating to others because he was brave enough to be friends with the Selk.

The only person who may be more threatening was the chief himself. Perhaps it was his air of authority, which gave him the extra edge. Controlled, calculating and the ability to make others follow his lead. A powerful impression to be sure.

Living most of his life around their clan's most deadly and influential people had made Tristan largely unaffected by their presence. He respected them, but he did not fear them. This in turn earned him a great deal of respect himself. It was one of the reasons Eoin had chosen Tristan to be Shannon's guard. The man was simply hard to rattle, plain and simple.

Tristan shoved his friend's shoulder as he left to go clean up and search for his charge. "Whatever you have to tell yourself."

As it turned out, Shannon was the one to find him, with none other than Miriam Rowle in tow. Tristan had always liked the chief's daughter. She was kind, funny, calm in a crisis, and did not seem to play a lot of the mind games some of the other woman favored. What you saw was what you got with Miriam. It was a credit to Shannon's judgement that Miriam was the person she had chosen to spend her time with. The two seemed to be getting along well.

He changed his direction to join them, but was intercepted, "Tristan! I heard you were home, but until I saw you with my own eyes, I couldn't believe it," Lyra said as she came up and tried to hug him. Tristan's forward momentum being jerked to a halt made the attempt a bit awkward. He managed to recover and give her a semblance of a hug in return, one arm going partially around her to pat her shoulder. From her smile an onlooker would have thought he had given her the best gift in the world.

"Hi Lyra. How are things?" he said, still edging toward where the girls were talking. Miriam spotted him and stalled their progress. For some reason, she was making a concerted effort to hold Shannon's attention away from Tristan and his new tag-a-long. Odd.

Lyra was rattling on about something ever so important, but in all honesty, Tristan was not paying mind to any of it. "I'm sorry Lyra, but I have to check in with Shannon." He pointed to the women across the bailey. "Catch up later, yeah?" Without giving her time to respond he scooted out of her reach and on to his charge and her cousin.

Had Tristan not been in such a rush to get to Shannon, he might have seen the flash of anger twist Lyra's face. There and gone in a blink. Of course, had he seen it, he may have thought her frustration was with the way he had shirked his conversation with her. To an extent it was. The issue lay with where her glare was aimed, not at Tristan's retreating back, but at Shannon.

"*Hey. I see you've made a friend,*" Tristan signed after Shannon had turned and spotted him. Her smile at seeing him, at seeing a familiar face, made Tristan relax...a bit. Sleep had done her well. She was much less frazzled today, steadier on her feet. The fact she was able to smile eased his worry for her.

"*Yes, Miriam and I have been chatting all morning,*" she said. Tristan noticed she had already given her cousin a sign name, tapping her shoulder with a curved hand, then popping into an M. "*Boss? An interesting choice. Wonder what brought that on?"* he thought.

"Couldn't wait to kidnap my charge, eh Miriam?"

"Somebody had to rescue her from aimlessly wondering the halls," Miriam giggled. "I've been giving her a tour while we looked for you. Should have known to look in the barracks wing first. Good session?"

"Yes, actually. It's always fun to throw Kent around the training floor."

Miriam raised an eyebrow. "Uh-huh. And how many times did he toss you across the room?"

Tristan shrugged, "Unimportant."

Miriam guffawed at the abrupt reply. "Well, I have to report to Mother before she sends out a search party."

Shannon quickly scribbled down, "I hope I didn't get you in trouble. Did you stay with me too long?"

"Oh goodness no! When Mother hears I got to meet you before she did, she'll have a fit and probably track you down herself. Honestly, she would be more upset if I had left you to yourself. Would not make me a very good hostess, now, would it?" Miriam winked, and pulled Shannon into a warm hug, the shorter woman having to rise on tiptoes to reach. "I'm so happy to have met you, Shannon. So happy you're home with us now." She leaned back to look her in the eye. "I know things are a bit strange now, but you'll get used to it. And if you need anything, you let me know." Miriam squeezed her hand and started to turn but Shannon stopped her with a tug.

"Thank you, Miriam. It was wonderful to meet you," she signed, smiling while holding back tears. Tristan saw he did not need to interpret. Miriam smiled, nodded and walked down the hall in search of the lady of the house.

When her cousin was out of sight, Shannon turned to face Tristan. He gave her a small smile. "How are you doing?" he signed stepping a bit closer.

Shannon smiled back, her lips tight. "Fine."

Tristan raised an eyebrow, "How are you really?" Shannon broke his gaze to stare at the floor, her breathing was even, but a bit jagged. When she looked at him again, he could see tears, fighting to stay right where they were. "It's overwhelming." Tristan nodded and let her go on. "Some people are nice. I really like Miriam. But others..." Her hands paused. "Others come at me like I'm the one attacking them, invading them."

Tristan frowned. "Who is giving you a hard time?"

Shannon waved him off like it was not important. An opinion he vehemently disagreed with. "It doesn't matter," she said, "I am used to people picking on me. I just was not expecting it so quickly. It's not like I chose to come here! But they act like it's my fault."

Tristan tried not to flinch at her words. A task made harder by the fact she was right. The decision to come back to the Grotto had not been hers to make at the time. He wished it were possible for her to have more of a say in the matter but, as vulnerable as she was, how close she had come to being taken, or worse, not even he truly had any better options. Did not make things better in the short term. Not for Shannon.

"I want to talk to Mandy. I miss Mandy." It was with this statement, the first tear lost the battle and trailed down her face. Without hesitation, Tristan snagged her hand and pulled her into a deserted hallway and tugged her into his arms. Protected by someone she knew, and despite the short time, trusted, Shannon let herself bury her face in his coat, and shook with restrained sobs. Her small whimpers tore at Tristan's heart, and he held her tighter, murmuring softly in her ear.

He did not know how long they stayed that way, but eventually Shannon took a final heavy breath, and leaned back. Tristan brushed a thumb across her cheek, wiping away the few straggling tears. It was only after he had done it, he found himself surprised by his action, and even more surprised she had let him.

A bit uncomfortable with how easy it had been, Tristan put his hands on her shoulders to gain some distance. Scrambling for a change in subject, Tristan blurted the first thing to pop into his mind. "Why don't we go for a swim?" The suggestion may have been hasty, but the more he thought about it, the more he liked the idea. "We could get away from the main castle for a bit, burn off some steam, maybe get you used to shifting back and forth." He tilted his head and gave a cheeky grin, "It can be fun, Shannon." He squeezed her shoulders, "Will you let me take you swimming?"

Blowing out a breath in a huff, shaking off the last of her tears, Shannon squared her shoulders, and nodded. She even managed a genuine smile, if a small one. Tristan smiled in return and guided her out of the castle.

As they made their way through the small town outside the castle, Tristan spotted something out of the corner of the eye, which made him pause. Shannon stopped when she realized she had overtaken Tristan and came back to his side. "What's wrong?" she asked.

Tristan nodded to a group of men in pale grey coats, speckled in black, frowning a bit in confusion, "Those Selkies are from the Arctic Clan." He scanned the crowd and his uncertainty grew, though he made an effort not to let it show on his face. He nodded again to another group down the street, "Those are from one of the Southern California clans, and..." Tristan cursed and ran a hand down his jaw as his eyes found another set of foreign coats, "Blazes; They're from the Emerald Isle clan." Shannon took a step closer resting a hand on his arm. Tristan settled. "Come on, let's go," he said, heading towards one of the tunnel entrances.

Shannon gripped his arm to stop him. "If something is wrong, if you need to go, I can wait. Do you need to leave?" Tristan's shoulder relaxed at her words and he shook his head.

"No," he said. "If Eoin or Nolan needed me, they would have sent for me. And we won't be hard to locate if they find they do."

They continued walking. "Why did seeing those men upset you?" Shannon asked. Tristan tilted his head in thought. "It's not the men themselves, but what their presence might mean." Putting a hand on her back he guided her down one of the tunnels. "The clans are spread out all over the world. With us being actively at war with the Nereids, an attack can come at any time. It makes it hard for other clans to visit each other. We typically only do so on massive holidays, clan gatherings, or..."

"Or?" Shannon prodded.

Tristan blew out of breath. If he was going to keep her safe, she would need to be armed with as much information as he could give. "Or when a major military assault is in the works." Shannon hummed noncommittally at this news, but she didn't look nervous which was a good sign. The woman was tough. Tristan could respect someone who adapted quickly.

"Either of the California clans would be one thing. They are close. We work with them quite regularly, both in trade, and allying in battle. But neither the Arctic nor Emerald Isle clans have any reason to be here that I would consider normal. I'm concerned it means something big has been put on the stove to brew."

They reached one of the pools the clan used to get to the outer ocean. Tristan raised his hood over his head, Shannon followed his lead. "If I'm right, things could get interesting in the next few weeks," he said, resting his hands on his hips, meeting her eyes with a steady, unwavering gaze. "Like it or not, Shannon, you are the daughter of the Lann, our best warrior. You may be thrown into the middle of things faster than you may be comfortable with. Are you ready for that?"

"No," Shannon gave a wan smile, *"but I will be."* Tristan adjusted her hood. "I'm here if you need me. Remember that, okay?"

To his surprise, when she replied, Shannon did not raise her hands. Instead, her lips parted, and she said, "Oh...heh" Tristan couldn't help the beaming smile spreading across her face. The word was rough, and simple. More of a mimic of sounds than an actual word, but she was trying. Shannon was trying to talk.

Tristan laughed in delight. "Okay," Still beaming he headed for the water. "Come on. I'm itchin' for a swim."

Smiling herself, and for the first time looking excited at the idea, Shannon ran to catch up to him. The skirts of her coat flared around her legs as they both dove under the water and let their forms wash over them, reveling in the power and freedom of their Selkie form.

Chapter Fourteen

*I*t had been a long time since Tristan had enjoyed his time "in skin" so much. While he could tell she still had her reservations about her life as a Selk, Shannon was like an excited child with each new experience in her unfamiliar form. In turn, it made Tristan pay more attention to the little things he had taken for granted over the years because they had fallen into the category of "normal".

Minute things, like being able to see the massive array of fish that lived in their waters, the feel of moving with ease through the currents, or the joy of successfully hunting down lunch. Shannon was still new to the concept, but her instincts were fantastic. She was quick, graceful, and at least to passing sardines, deadly.

Miriam and her brother, Eoghan, joined them a few hours later. They spent the rest of the afternoon diving and basking in the autumn sun. Bit by bit Tristan watched Shannon grow more comfortable in her skin.

In a word, it was beautiful to watch and gave him an odd sense of pride to watch the woman he had protected for so many years discover his world. Their world, for the first time.

Eventually the time came for them to all head back. They all shifted back as they hit the shore. Shannon was still a bit slow but getting the hang of it. Miriam dropped back with Tristan, behind Eoghan and Shannon who were getting to know each other when they could physically talk instead of interpreting the images. It was somewhat slow going with Shannon having to write down her responses, but like his sister, Eoghan was patient and attentive to his cousin. As they strode through the gates Miriam broke the silence, "Da and Uncle Eoin would like a word. They're in the library." Tristan nodded then looked up at Shannon.

Miriam slapped his shoulder, "I got her. You head on."

Tristan nodded again and moved for the west corridor calling to the pair ahead. "I'll see you in a while, Shannon. Got to take care of something real quick." At the same time, he signed. "I trust Miriam. Stick to her and you'll be fine."

Shannon smiled reassuringly, "I'm a big girl. Go do what you need to do."

Grinning, Tristan shuffled back and headed off to find his commander.

The library was tucked off in a corner of the castle. High vaulted ceilings and shaped windows juxtaposed with the dark woods, and rich tapestries, creating an open, but cozy space. Many in the Grotto loved to come and enjoy the quiet sanctuary of collected knowledge. On the upper floor, there was a more private collection belonging to the Chief and his family. It functioned as a secondary office for the Chief, when he could not be bothered to go back to the opposite side of the castle to his courters and "official" study.

Tristan entered after a call answered his knock on the solid oak door. "Laird. Miriam said you wished to speak to me?"

"Yes, come on in Tristan." Tristan closed the door behind him. The Chief gestured to the last empty chair in front of the wide table. Maps and reports were strewn all over its surface in no particular order. Eoin, of course, occupied one of the chairs, lounging as if this were a regular Tuesday. Tristan paused in his thoughts. Was it Tuesday? Mentally shaking himself, he was losing track of his days, too much had happened in a short amount of time.

The other taken seat was a bit more of a surprise. Angus Harrok, the primary instructor for all the Grotto's young warriors, and Tristan's mentor, sat as comfortably as a ridged back would allow, his hands folded across his chest. "It's good to see you Angus," Tristan said, taking the seat he was pointed to.

"Thought I would come torment my old student since he could not be bothered to pop in to greet this old collection of lard." Tristan smiled at the familiar dig. Long in the tooth he may be, but Angus Harrok remained one of the most dangerous people among their clan. He was the one who took Tristan's natural instincts for battle and turned them into a useable and effective weapon.

"I did not think it wise to scar my charge for life with your ugly face so early in her stay." Tristan jabbed back. A row of white teeth flashed in the middle of the mass of grey scraggly beard around Angus's face.

Nolan grinned at the banter from the two of them but quickly brought everyone back to the subject at hand. "Tristan, you said it was a full unit that went after Shannon on land?"

Tristan squinted in thought at the question. "Well, yes and no," he said. "Only three were present for the attack itself. They probably thought kidnapping one girl would not be a problem. Seven came to collect the bodies. In all, it made up a full squad." He sat back in his chair. "Why?"

Eoin was the one to answer. "Some of the other clans have been having trouble with individual squads wandering further into their territory. Even more than usual."

"Is that why there are contingents from other clans in the castle."

Angus barked a laugh, "I told you he would notice." Eoin grinned at the old man, then focused back on the younger. "Yes, members from many of the affected areas have come to see how widespread it is." The Lann frowned, "Until you showed up, we thought we were unaffected. Obviously, we were wrong."

"Or just early." Tristan mused. "The Squids only showed up in Shelter Bay at the start of the week. The clans I saw in town were from pretty spread out sections of the world. Maybe, we were just next on the list."

Nolan tapped a pen on the surface of the table, leaning into the wood. "Was there anything about the men you fought that stood out to you? Any skill set, or ability you were surprised by?"

Tristan took a moment to think back on his fight, but in the end shook his head. "Honestly, it wasn't much of a match. They were not very good fighters. They didn't pay attention to their surroundings at all, were uncoordinated, and did not adapt well when what they thought would happen didn't turn out. If anything, the only odd thing about them was how easy it was to defeat them. I would not be surprised if they had sent the new recruits to do the grunt work." His eyebrows rose, "That, and the fact they were willing to fight me on land," he said, his eyes locking with his chief, "Never had a scale brain take me on in the dirt before. They know we have the advantage there."

Angus's gruff voice cut in, "Could be they did not expect to fight you. Chief said you thought they were on shore leave."

Tristan shrugged noncommittally, "It was just my first thought when I saw them poking at Shannon. Looked like they were making sport out of the locals."

"Could have been both," said Eoin. "Not the first time young warriors goofed off when they were meant to be doing a job."

"What was your impression of the rest of the squad?" Nolan asked

"The complete opposite. They moved like a unit should, worked together like they had been doing it for years. Throw in the anger from having three of their lads gutted and I wouldn't want to take them on alone."

"Why Shelter Bay though?" Eoin asked. "I made sure that town was as safe and far away from the conflict as I could get and still be within, reasonable, reach of the Grotto. How in the world did they know to poke around there? We don't get supplies there; we don't hunt in those waters. It's in our territory, but not an active section. So how?"

"I don't think we should discount dumb luck," Nolan replied. "For all we know they were prodding at all the coastal towns along the eastern shore. It could be coincidence they found one we were using."

"It would explain why they would send the rookies in first. To them the lass looked like a lone pup, and without her coat no less. More than likely she piqued their curiosity, but not their caution," Angus said, tipping his chair up onto two legs and balancing perfectly with little effort.

Eoin rubbed a hand over his face. "And we just confirmed we have holding there. Perfect."

Nolan leaned back in his chair, "We'll keep an eye on Shelter Bay so this mess doesn't touch the locals. Meantime, I want patrols increased along the entire border. If these skirmishes, both here and against our sister clans, are gearing up for a larger assault, I do not want to be caught sitting on our hands."

Eoin growled. "We've kept the squid at bay for five generations. They won't take our home now."

The other three men grunted in agreement. If the Nereids wanted to turn these sporadic battles into a full-scale war, then so be it. The Selkie can and would be ready. They would be waiting.

*M*andy sat on her porch, the cool evening air biting through her thick sweater. One knee tucked up close to her chest, while the other swung the bench swing back and forth, back and forth. The creak of the chains suspending the wooden seat a familiar comfort.

Her tears had long dried, leaving a spike pounding her head behind her eyes. The screen on her phone remained black in her hands. Tormenting her with its lack of news. Still, she could not seem to let the block of metal and glass out of her sight, for fear of missing the moment when it would light up and someone on the other end of the line would tell her that her friend, her sister, had been found, that she was safe. So, the device stayed clutched in her hand. Useless.

The screen door groaned as it swung open. Mandy did not bother to look as her parents came out to sit on either side of her. She would only start crying again if she saw the worry on their faces. She was so tired of crying.

Her dad's strong arm came around her shoulders and she leaned into his warmth, pulling in as steady a breath as she could manage. Her mom's hand smoothed over her knee, lending her own comfort as well.

Her father's voice rumbled against her cheek. "They'll find her, Baby Girl. One way or another, they'll find her."

"It's been three days," Mandy whimpered.

Her mother grasped her hand over the phone. "Shannon is strong, Honey. Whatever mess she found herself in, that girl is smart enough and resilient enough to get out of it again. And she has all kinds of people waiting to help her do that. We just have to see where she will need that help."

Her dad hugged her tighter. "And until then, we wait, we watch, and we pray. That is the biggest and greatest help we can give her right now." Mandy nodded and finally let herself look up at her parents giving them a tiny smile. Glancing around the rest of the porch, she noticed her two little brothers had come out as well. Standing silent vigil, lending support in their own quiet way.

The family sat and watched as the sky faded from blue, to brilliant red, to deep velvet black; one by one sparkling stars joined the soft quiet of the Luis family. Mandy heaved a heavy sigh. Shannon would be okay. And until she could wrap her arms around her sister herself, Mandy would give her worry to hands better equipped to handle it than her own.

Chapter Fifteen

$\mathcal{A}$ knock on Shannon's door brought her head up from the book she was reading. Miriam had been appalled that Shannon had never heard of the volume let alone read it. The book had promptly been thrust into her hands. Shannon still was unclear whether Miriam telling her to read the novel was more an endorsement, or an order. Either way Shannon was reading it and so far her cousin had been spot on.

Out of habit, Shannon beat her fist twice on the arm of the chair, in acknowledgement of the knock, before her brain caught up with the action. No one here would know that was her way of giving permission to enter. The door opened… No one except her father.

Eoin let the door swing wide so he was fully visible, but he remained in the doorway. For a few breaths, father and daughter just stared at each other. Both trying to convince themselves they were truly there.

Eoin raised his hand, "Hi sweetheart." Tears began to rim Shannon's eyes. Eoin took one hesitant step into the room. "Do you remember me?"

Shannon nodded. "Dad." It was now Eoin's turn to fight tears. Out of everything wrong with the way their situation had unfolded, Shannon not being able to remember him had been by far his biggest fear. She had been so young when he had left, so small. There was no way for him to know how much of her childhood she was able to recall. A small smile came despite the tears. Annie had kept her word. At the least, she knew who he was.

"May I come in? Can we talk?" he asked. A heartbeat passed, then two, then five, but eventually Shannon gave a slow nod. Eoin slowly released the breath he was holding so it wouldn't come out in a rush and sat at the foot of the bed. Eoin knew they needed to talk, clear the air, so to speak, but he didn't want to crowd her either. With so much time passed, they were practically strangers, especially from her point of view. Her last memories of him were when she was only six years old.

Running his fingers through his hair, he hesitated. Where were you supposed to start in a situation like this? "Are you settling in alright?" The basics work he supposed.

Shannon smiled slightly. "Yes. Everyone here has been very nice, for the most part."

"I'm glad. I had hoped you would get along with the clan." Silence pressed in on them both, neither of them knowing what to say next. When the awkwardness became too much, Shannon blew out a breath and asked the question she really wanted to know, or at least one of them. "Why did you never tell me? Why would you and Mama keep this from me? Being a Selkie is a part of who you are. A part of who I am. I feel like I don't know anything about you at all...And there wasn't much to know to begin with, beyond the stories Mama would tell me as a kid."

Eoin grimaced but resigned himself to those kinds of questions. "When you were born...Your mom and I knew we were going to have to make a choice between raising you as a human, or as a Selkie. At the time, things with the Nereids were tenuous at best. The former option seemed like the safer and more stable one. We were planning on telling you when you were older, sixteen, maybe eighteen. I was supposed to be back with you both by that time, so we could have told you together."

Eoin watched as emotions flashed across his daughter's face one after the other. He wondered if she would ask the question, he had opened the door for. It took a minute but eventually her hands moved. "Why? —Why did you never come back?" A few stray tears escaped only to be quickly swiped away. "I understand how the coat works. I know you had no choice to leave.

But your... Debt...should have been paid when I was what? Thirteen! So why did you not come back then?" The hurt and confusion he saw threatened to undo Eoin s own composure.

"At first, yes, it was the coat that kept me away. But when my time was up, and I tried to get back to you and Annie...I couldn't leave." Shannon glared, uncomprehending. "I would love to blame Nolan for the entire thing, and to an extent he is a huge part of why I stayed, but in truth, I could not leave. We were losing too much ground, losing our home, our only safe haven. The home and people I wanted to introduce you to were being picked off a bit at a time. The men needed me at the head of our forces. Nolan is a good leader, and a fine general, but he was spread far too thin. Had I returned to you the first chance I could, like I wanted to, within a year or two there would have been nothing left of my people." He paused. "Our people."

"I couldn't leave, Dear One," he said, pushing through the knot in his throat. "If there was another way, please believe me, there is nothing that would have stopped me from being with you and your mother. You girls are everything to me. Everything. But I...I couldn't. I'm so sorry lass. I'm so sor—"

He didn't get any further than that before Shannon throwing the covers off and flinging herself into her daddy's arms. Eoin clutched her like she would disappear if he allowed his grip to loosen.

How long they stayed like that, neither knew, neither cared.

A while later, Shannon leaned back so she could look Eoin in the eye. Then practiced fingers ran along her collar, finding a worn piece of leather. Shannon tugged the necklace over her head and laid it across Eoin's lap, and looked up at him, waiting.

Smiling, her dad removed his own necklace and gently placed it in her hands. Without a word the two began working the many knots running along pearl and shells alike. It was small. It was simple. But Shannon suddenly felt like that six-year-old on the beach again. A lot had happened to the both of them. They had a lot to learn about who they had become over the years. But in the silence, in the calm presence of her father sitting next to her, Shannon let herself believe the words he had told her so long ago.

"When I come back, we ll untie the knots together and it will be like time has not passed."

It was a start.

Tyrus was bored, mind numbingly bored. Of course, watching for a Skinner who may, or may not return to one of the most drab towns he had ever seen was not exactly the most exciting assignment. At least he did not have to deal with Atticus' temper while he was there.

How many days had he been up here? He had lost track a while ago. The humans kept time differently than the Nereids. This made it a bit more challenging to gauge how long he had been baking under the sun. He could almost feel his skin drying out as he sat on a bench across from the building displaying fish. The humans seemed to be fascinated with the creatures, especially the small, loud ones.

Tyrus had not spent much time around children, neither human ones, nor his own kind. As such, he was at a loss as to how to react to them. If nothing else, they were probably the most entertaining thing there was to watch while he waited for his prey. Their antics were ridiculous, confusing, and more often than not, life threatening. The most fascinating part of the situation were the adults in charge of the hollering beasts acting as though such behavior was normal. Herding them back when they strayed, quieting them when they finally got too loud for their tempered ears, answering the endless questions spilling out of them.

Studying them over the last few days gave Tyrus a much more profound appreciation for the men and women who had trained him at that age. Maker knows he was no angel, especially when his talent started to manifest.

Wailing younglings, and glassed in pets aside, Tyrus was going to go mad if something did not happen soon. It wasn't that he was battle hungry; more often he was one of the more levelheaded members of his squadron. However, he was unaccustomed to having so much time to do nothing. Even in peace times there was training, or, tides, he would take a swim past the reef at this point. Anything to keep his mind and body active. He hadn't been this restless since his first days of battle school. Suddenly, Tyrus felt an odd kinship with the tiny male who refused to stay in his teacher's line of sight.

Distracted by the chaos of the swarm of children, he did not notice Magnus until he was dropping down on the bench next to him. Annoyed at having to force himself not to jump off the bench in surprise, Tyrus turned and glared at his friend's wide grin. Magnus knew he had startled him. He was too polite to outright say it, but not enough to not enjoy it.

"Having fun, are we?" Magnus asked, still grinning. Tyrus scoffed and shook his head. It was nice to hear his birth tongue after so much time listening to human speech.

"Non-stop thrills up here," Tyrus replied. "The corner market was out of red russets for the third time this month so the ladies of St. Clements knitting circle had to make do with goldens for their annual luncheon; Tom's daughter, Charlotte... Coplen, not Redesdale... is in love with the son of a charter boat captain in the next town over and there is talk of her and the kid running off to get hitched. Tom is "none too thrilled" at the idea;

and that guppy," he pointed to a child who had, out of the sight of his teachers, climbed up onto the four-foot stone wall which separated the walkway from the drop to the rocky shoreline below, "is either suicidal, or the genius about to discover human flight." They would not get an answer to the final question, as the boy had at last caught the attention of his minder and was thoroughly scolded into coming down away from the ledge and his potential breakthrough in human mobility.

Magnus leaned back on the bench seat watching the show alongside Tyrus. "What's a red russet?" he asked.

"Tides if I know, but evidently they are essential to a decent potato salad,"

"You have spent far too much time here," Magnus observed with a laugh.

Tyrus scoffed and finally glanced over at his friend, "What news on your end?"

"The other three raids were successful. This was the only location with complications, let alone casualties." Magnus hooked his ankle over a knee and watched the people passing by.

Tyrus grunted in acknowledgement. "Technically, this was never an official target sight. Atticus made that call when we found the girl."

"All sport, until a Skinner shows up."

"True enough." Tyrus heaved a sigh and stretched out his long frame, a few joints popping in gratitude of the movement. "Atticus give any hint of letting me come back? I haven't seen a wisp of evidence pointing to them coming back. None."

Before Tyrus was done talking, Magnus was shaking his head. "The commander's got an urchin up his backside about that skinner. He's galled by the fact one of them took out three of ours. Not gonna let up until he gets retribution." he said the last word with as much disbelief as Tyrus felt himself.

He ran a hand roughly through his hair. Atticus's honor and pride had been wounded. Tyrus would be stuck on the dirt till the end of time if nothing changed soon.

For a while the pair just sat and talked about nothing of consequence, then sat and talked about nothing at all. They had known each other long enough conversation was not truly required.

Across the street the adults herded the tiny humans into the long, yellow contraptions to be carried off Tyrus did not care where. The wind changed direction, and he leaned his head back, pulling the salt of the sea into his lungs. Tides he needed to get back in the water. If only the darned Skinner would show up! The animals lived half on land anyway, why could he not do so here? The Selk was obviously familiar with the area. Why could he not be lured back?

Tyrus sat up straighter. Maybe he could be lured back. "Magnus?"

"Hum." Magnus grunted.

"If you had the female's scent from something up here, do you think you could track her in the ocean? Even in her seal form?" Tyrus asked, following the trail of thought.

"Probably," Magnus answered, only half paying attention, his face turned up to take in the sun's warmth. "It would be a challenge. But if I had a good starting point, I could likely distinguish her from the others as long as the lock on her scent was solid." Sensing his friend's growing enthusiasm Magnus straightened up himself and with a smirk asked, "Why?"

Tyrus rose from the bench and slapped his friend's shoulder. "Come on." He said his long strides eating up the distance between him and the Skinner's house. "I think I may have a way to speed things up."

Chapter Sixteen

The days turned into weeks, and Shannon settled into life at the Grotto. Her days were filled with spending time with Tristan or getting to know her cousins. Somehow Patty, the castle housekeeper, had become one of Shannon's closest companions. Repeatedly, the assiduous women graciously carved out time from her work for simple things like, teaching Shannon old recipes or sharing stories about when she grew up with Nolan and Eoin as children. Shannon found it fascinating learning about her father from someone who had known him for so long, but it was her conversations with the man himself that were the most precious.

He was a powerful, strong-willed individual...a leader, but incredibly kind and gentle with her and the rest of his family. As they moved through the Grotto, reacquainting themselves, Shannon could see how much this place and its people meant to him. How much the responsibility weighed on his shoulders.

However, from what she saw, it was a welcome weight. It gave him purpose and drive to be better than he already was, because so many lives depended on his competence. He loved his clan to the bone and as she watched, it gladdened her heart to see, it was a love returned.

While it did not take away the pain and loneliness of so many years without her father, it was a comfort knowing he was doing something worthy.

The clan did their best to make her feel as at home as possible, and to a degree they were successful. Like her father, Shannon fit in well with the Selkies. They were quickly becoming as much a part of her as her own family back on land. It was her loved ones on shore, which made it difficult to fully adapt to her new life. She missed her mother, her lively presence which filled a room with laughter and color. She missed Zeke's calm, comforting watchfulness that always made her feel safe. But most of all she missed Mandy.

The woman had helped make Shannon into the person she was today. Easy laugh, sharp wit, tongue that would just as easily slap you back into place as sooth an aching hurt. Shannon knew that if the roles were reversed, she would be going out of her mind with worry for Mandy. But as it stood there was nothing Shannon could do. Chief Nolan, she hadn't managed to think of him as her uncle yet, had unilaterally refused to send word to shore of her well-being. "I'm sorry lass," he replied, not unkindly each time she would ask, "But Shelter Bay is too exposed to the Nereids right now. Trying to contact your friends would only put them in more danger."

Miriam and Tristan tried to comfort Shannon, but they agreed with the chief. Nolan was the authority in the Grotto, and she *did* respect that. They all had more experience than she in what amounted to matters of war. She had to listen to their advice, or in Nolan's case, orders. It did not, however, make it any easier to be content with the decision.

Shannon would be patient. Sooner or later the nereids would grow tired of watching her sleepy little town and Shannon could then be with her family again. Even if it would be different than before. Much different.

Miriam and Shannon were making their way through the eastern tunnels chatting as they walked. Her time in the grotto had been productive in more ways than simply getting to know her clan. Over the weeks she had spent in the odd cavernous space, those she spent time with did their best to teach Shannon how to speak.

Shannon understood learning to talk as an adult would be a challenge, but she did not expect just how tedious it would be as well. She knew how the words were supposed to sound; she had listened to people talk all her life. Yet getting her mouth to mimic those same sounds was a trial of patience all to its own, repeating simple words over and over, playing with sounds until they sounded, somewhat, close to what she needed for speech. Half the time she sounded like a child, which Shannon supposed in this aspect, she was.

Frustrating would be a gross understatement of the task. Shannon still used ASL as her primary form of communication, a fact Miriam delighted in. She was fascinated with the manual language and constantly pestered her cousin with questions about words she wanted to know. At least she was not the only child learning to "talk".

Surprisingly, it was Tristan she found the easiest to talk with, either with signing or in her stunted, broken speech. He seemed to understand her no matter how she chose to converse. It took a significant amount of pressure off of her shoulders and just let her speak. They could talk about anything it seemed. Marine life, battle techniques, books they had read, Selkie history, foods they loved or despised, anything and everything came with an ease of years of friendship, achieved in a few short weeks. Shannon only hoped they could still find time to talk when he was reassigned to another position than her guard.

It was this subject Shannon and her cousin were discussing. Miriam pulled the edges of her coat a bit tighter against a gust of wind winding through the tunnel works. "I'm honestly surprised Da has kept him back this long. Eoghan says he's invaluable on the battlefield. He's chomping at the bit to put him in his own unit once he returns to the front line."

"Hee...k-kood?" Shannon forced out. She still had trouble with softer consonants. They seemed to come out harsher than she wanted. Miriam seemed to get the gist of what she was asking though. She nodded. "Yes, he's very good." Her accent seemed to get a bit thicker as she went on. "There are some that say he will be the next Lann once Uncle Eoin steps down. I think that's why so many people were confused at him being on the sidelines for so many years. I know some of the old goats think it was a waste of talent."

"If protecting me was a problem, why did Tristan stay for so many years? Mama and Daddy both say, he stayed longer than anyone else he assigned to be my guardian." Miriam narrowed her eyes, trying to focus on the signs in the dim light. Shannon smiled, appreciating her effort, and repeated herself, this time much slower.

The young Selkie had to ask her to spell out a few of the words before she understood what Shannon was trying to say, but eventually communication occurred.

Miriam shrugged as they entered the diving chamber. She waved a greeting to the Reid standing watch at the gate. "I doubt Tristan would describe his posting as a problem," she said grinning back over her shoulder. "But it did take him away from the main front. A few things had to be restructured in his absence. Still, if either he, or Uncle Eoin, or Da for that matter, thought it was a real issue having him on land, they would have ordered him home years ago. If anything, Tristan being your guard was a kind of peace agreement."

"Peace agreement?"

Miriam nodded and planted a hand on her hip. "For the first few years of Uncle Eoin being back at the Grotto, he and Da used to fight like cats and dogs. He was not happy being away from you and your ma." She hesitated, "I was never told this explicitly, so technically it's just my opinion but..." Shannon waved her hand for her to continue. Miriam sighed, "At one point they stopped fighting, and it was the same time you and Auntie Annie got your own guard."

Miriam threw her hands in the air and stepped into the pool. "Uncle Eoin stopped pitching so much of a fit about being back at the head of the army and you two got the very best we had to defend you on land. Tristan was and still is, one of our best. He's also incredibly loyal. You needed a protector. Tristan was given the post, and he was gonna do the job as best he could, for as long as he was needed. I asked him once if he wanted me to talk to Da to get him assigned somewhere else, somewhere more exciting. He flat out refused. Said he wasn't going to leave you without someone to watch your back."

Shannon smiled at this, at seeing yet another side of her new friend, or old companion depending on how you looked at it. Allowing the topic to come to its' natural end, Miriam gave her cousin a nudge and said, "Let's swim. I'm itching to stretch my flippers." Grinning, both women dove into the salt-tinged water.

For the next few hours they enjoyed the freedom of swimming out in the open sea or relaxing on the rocks as they pleased. They made a point of staying close to the Grotto for safety's sake, but it still felt marvelous to be outside the walls of the castle and even the canyon. Beautiful as the Grotto was, it was not in their nature to be closed in all the time.

Miriam had gone chasing a school of sardines, but Shannon was full from their earlier snack so she entertained herself by weaving in and out through the coral and rocks nearby. The colors were not as vibrant as they would have been further south in warmer waters, but the patterns, formations, and the many creatures who made the reef their home were more than sufficient to keep Shannon occupied.

Occupied yes, but also distracted.

The water shifted around Shannon, the wake of something large and fast rolled over her skin making her look up. The ambush from before bombarded her thoughts and adrenaline flooded her veins. Thrusting her flippers downward she glided above the coral to get an unobstructed view of her surroundings. Whether it was paranoia or not, Shannon felt the itch of eyes on her back, but no matter where she looked, she could not find their owner.

In the end, it did not matter. Their owner found her. A flash of color caught her periphery, but before she could turn to face the threat, a body slammed into her side, dragged her down into the reef, and pinned her to the rock and sand of the ocean floor. A startled bark escaped her throat. Not enough to attract any kind of help, but certainly enough for her attacker to press something sharp into her back. Her new skin was thick, tough, but the pain the threat caused did its job. Shannon lay perfectly still and slipped into silence.

Trapped as she was against the bottom she could not see much, but what she could glimpse, fear sharpened into vivid detail. Her initial thought of a stray shark coming after her disappeared when her eyes latched onto jet black scales streaked with bars of bright yellow and pearl white. The patterning mimicked the stripes she saw on the moor fish they had at the marine center. It was simply on a larger scale. A much larger scale.

"You are a much more troublesome thing than one would expect to look at you. They don't really leave you alone often do they, Skinner?" His voice was rich, and had a kind of musical quality, like he was half singing as he spoke. His words were crisp, clear, not garbled at all by the water engulfing them. In fact, the water warped the sound like he was speaking through metal or glass, still clear, but ringing.

The effect was amplified when he laughed, making it sound like a brass bell rang in her ear. "Now before your friends get concerned, pay attention little pup." He practically spat the last word. Could you spit underwater? Shannon mentally shook her head. Focus.

A gold pendant on a thin chain was dropped in front of her face. Shannon recognized it immediately. Her mother loved lilies. Shannon had found the simple piece in a flea market and gave it to her mama for Christmas several years ago. Anita adored the necklace, the only one she wore more often was the one her father had given her before he left. She would never let that pendent be taken if she could help it. "I see I have your attention. Good." The necklace disappeared. "I'm going to give you the benefit of the doubt and assume you are not completely stupid. You know who this belongs to. If you do not surrender yourself to us by sundown tomorrow, the pretty little owner of this pretty little trinket will die. Slowly. Painfully, and completely unnecessarily."

The necklace came into view again, the chain twined around dark scaled fingers. "Tell anyone about this and she will die all the same." The weight on her back increased, and his voice dropped to a whisper, taunting and biting. "See you soon, Skinner." Then the weight vanished.

Shannon tried to right herself quickly, but by the time she scraped herself off the floor her assailant was gone. Not even a wake to show he had been anything more than a daydream. A terrifying daydream.

Shoving the water behind her, Shannon shot up until her head broke the surface and she sucked in air. The wind lifted her fur, water dripped off her whiskers, her flippers easily kept her afloat, and her mind short circuited. *"Mama! Mama's been taken!"* The few weeks she had been with her clan had driven home the seriousness of the conflict the Selkies and Nereids had been in for generations. Shannon doubted the Nereids would take particularly good care of a human caught in the middle, especially one married to a Selk.

"I need to tell Daddy." Shannon thought, but then froze. How did the Nereid know where she would be, or even that she was the right Selkie to threaten with that necklace? If he could find that out, what other information could he find out? Was there a way for him to know she had told her father?

Shannon growled in frustration. She could not take that risk. Of all the Selkies that called the Grotto home, she was probably the one who posed the least amount of threat to their safety. She knew next to nothing of the Grotto's defenses or the soldiers defending their borders. If this was a trap, which was almost a certainty, at least she would be the only one caught up in it.

Decision made, Shannon dove back under the waves and with smooth easy strokes started swimming back to the mainland. Back to her mother. Back home.

Tristan was sitting with Kent listing to Angus describe a fight he had got into against three Nereids when he was young. The details were flamboyant, exciting and, of course, all in his mentor's favor. How much of the story was true only Angus and the Lord above knew, but the man certainly knew how to spin a tale.

Angus was describing his grappling work when Miriam burst in, white as a ghost. The flush of dried tears and the exertion of running were the only color worked into her cheeks. Her gaze zoned in on Tristan and she ran straight to him, dodging tables and people as she went, her hand slapping the table to stop her momentum once she reached him.

Tristan stood and put a hand on her shoulder to steady her. "What is it?" He demanded.

Breathing hard, Miriam gasped out, "She...She's gone! We went... swimming. I was gone for... a minute. I swear it was only a few minutes!" she said her tears pitching her voice, making it as frantic as her eyes. "I can't find her anywhere, Tristan! I searched for over an hour, but she's—She's just gone. I'm sorry! I can't find her." Her fingers snatched his shirt in a death grip, "You have to help me find her! You have t..."

"I will," he promised, cutting her off and prying her fingers off him. "I'll find her Miriam. I swear it." He gently handed her off to Angus, all levity had drained from the older man. "Take her to the chief and let him and the Lann know what has happened. I think I have a pretty good idea where she could be."

"You do?" Kent asked, rising to his feet as well. Tristan nodded. Kent grunted and downed the last of his drink. "I'm coming with you. Give you some support, if she's gotten herself into something more serious than just wondering off."

Tristan finished the thought, "An extra set of eyes would be helpful." The two men started for the door, but a call from behind stopped them. Miriam had disentangled herself from a surprised Angus and was stomping up to them. "I'm coming too," she declared.

"Like hell you are!" Kent exclaimed.

Miriam pointed at herself. "Shannon was with me; she was my responsibility to watch. I'm coming."

"No, you're not"

Tristan cut off his friends and despite his own worry made his voice remain calm. "It's fine, like I said, we could use the eyes. If Shannon is where I think she is, she won't be in much more danger than our reefs as long as we move quickly."

"Our reefs are not exactly what I would define as safe at the moment. There is a reason we have been increasing patrols." Angus chimed in helpfully.

Tristan ran his hands over his face in frustration. The longer they stood around discussing this the farther away Shannon got without any kind of protection. Jabbing a thumb at Miriam, Tristan asked, "Knowing her the way we do, do you honestly think if we try to leave her behind, she will stay put?" All three men swung their gazes to the woman in question, who was doing her best to look stern. "Besides," he continued, "Miriam knows how to handle herself." Tristan raised one eyebrow at Kent, "You certainly saw to that."

Kent growled, not caring for being ganged up on. He pointed at the chief's daughter and barked. "You stay glued to our tails. No going off half-cocked. And if things get violent you run as fast as you can in the opposite direction."

"Preferably with Shannon in tow." Tristan added.

Miriam, knowing she wouldn't get a better deal, nodded her head vigorously in acceptance of the terms.

Tristan looked back at his teacher. "Let them know we are headed to Shelter Bay. If you don't hear from us in three days, send backup."

"You want me to tell the chief that two of his best warriors and his daughter are skipping off to the mainland." Angus half growled, half chuckled at the absurdity of it.

"To bring back his niece. Yes." Tristan reasoned.

"Fine. Your funeral when you return kid." Angus groused in surrender. "

The trio took the dismissal and marched out the door. Kent still grumbling at Miriam to get her to stay behind. The woman bit back as good as she got and continued on. Their bickering left Tristan to his own thoughts. *"You are smarter than this, Shannon. You know how dangerous it is for you to be out on your own right now. So why would you take off without a word?"* Concern, determination and just plain curiosity warred for purchase in the man's mind. When they reached the water, Tristan forced his thoughts to focus on one task at a time.

One way or another, he would find out what was going on soon enough. He just had to get to her. *"She better have a darned good reason for this stunt when I do."*

Chapter Seventeen

Shannon waited until after dark before she allowed herself to come ashore along the small stretch of beach behind her house. It was getting easier to sense when the coat would release its hold on her. Her transition from flippers to feet was as smooth as slipping on a pair of favorite shoes. A few practiced actions and she was off and walking.

From the sand, she could only see the back side of her childhood home. The lofty deck wrapped around the second floor, splitting the structure in two. All of the windows were dark, turning the glass into a mirror, reflecting the moon back at itself. Shannon had never seen the building so vacant, empty of life. Without her and her mother there to add vibrance, the home was a skeleton of what it could and had been. Now it stood, hollowed out, nothing more than boards and glass. A time capsule of memory, instead of a living extension of the two women who had loved it for so many years.

It saddened Shannon to see the old girl in this light, but in an odd way it also gave her hope. A hope that she was moving on from her childhood. It was a scary thought, but a welcome one. Maybe this time she could step forward with her entire family.

To do that, she first had to find out what had happened to her mother.

Shaking off the nostalgia, Shannon shuffled her way up the beach to the steep staircase leading to the second floor. Mama always kept it locked up tight, yet that was only a deterrent if you did not know where the hide-a-key was stashed. Stepping across the deck, taking care to avoid the horrendously creaking boards, Shannon crouched down by a massive potted plant shaped like a fat, fluffy dog. Anita had always been terribly allergic to realistically, anything with fur. So poor, chipped and scratched Rufus was the closest they had ever come to a "family dog."

Reaching past his lolling ceramic tongue to a strip of painter's tape stuck to the roof of his mouth, securing the spare. Shannon shook her head remembering her mother's words when they had decided on the hiding spot, "Under a flowerpot is entirely too cliched and obvious. Rufus can defend the key to our house with his own teeth, like any good guard dog would." Her smile had been so proud at her weird thinking that Shannon didn't have the heart to argue. And too her credit, as far as they knew, no one besides them and similarly topsy-minded Mandy, knew where the Rowle's hide-a-key was kept.

The key turned smoothly in the lock, barely more than a click to announce her presence. Still, she winced at the small noise. Shannon could not know where the Nereids had gotten a hand on her mom, but if she was grabbed upon her return home, there was no way to tell until she was inside the house if they were still hanging around.

Stepping into her mom's studio, Shannon shut the door quietly before the wind could take it. This room at least proved as empty as it had appeared on the outside. Propped up against a nearby cabinet was a beautiful, maple baseball bat they kept close at hand for protection. Shannon would have preferred to have one of her grandfather's rifles, but those were down on the first floor; The bat was better than nothing, so, choking up on the grip, she started her survey.

Moving methodically, Shannon checked every room in the house, her heart doing its best to break her ribs with its pounding. Every blind corner, every cast shadow held an unseen intruder. But as each room came up vacant, her breathing steadied, and her muscles released their death grip on her shoulders.

Standing in the middle of the living room Shannon placed her hands on her hips and listened. Silence. Finally sighing, whether in relief or frustration at not finding anything, she could not tell.

Shannon wracked her brain. This was the most logical place for her mama to be taken, so why was there no one here waiting for her to come looking for her. It just did not make any sense.

Flipping the deadbolt on the front door, Shannon walked out onto the porch. The Nereids were aquatic creatures like her. Maybe they were waiting down by the...Shannon did not have time to finish the thought. A hand gripped her mouth, almost taking over half her face. She swung the bat as hard as she could, but the angle was all wrong and the improvised weapon was yanked out of her hands and thrown clear of her reach with a clatter of wood.

"So nice of you to join the fun, little Skinner." The man was huge. His voice floated somewhere high above her head. Shannon doubted she reached even halfway up his chest. His other arm wrapped around her, trapping her entire torso like a vice. There would be no wriggling out of the hold like last time. He barely allowed enough room for her chest to move to get air in to her lungs, let alone any kind of escape. Amusement threaded his voice as he spoke again. "Let's see if your guardian angel is as devoted as I think he is."

"*T*his is a cute little town. " Miriam said as she looked around at the quaint line of shops on Main Street. "Your descriptions did not really do it justice Tristan."

"You really think she came back here on her own?" Kent scanned the town too, but his eyes were more keen on searching out the slightest threat than taking in the town as a whole. Tristan's gaze was focused on locating a certain brunette. "Sure? No, but it is the most likely place she would have gone. I don't wish to dwell on the alternative reasons for her disappearance."

Kent grunted, "So where do we start then?"

Tristan pointed in the direction they were headed. His feet finding the route without him having to make a conscious effort. "Her first stop would have been to let Mandy know she was back. This time of day, she will be at work."

Miriam gripped his arm, a wide grin spreading over her face. "Does that mean we are going to the Marine Center?"

"We are going there to find Shannon and bring her home Miriam. Not to sight see." Kent growled from around Tristan's other side.

Miriam waved a hand in his direction, dismissing the comment. "Oh, I know that. But I've been hearing about the center, and Shelter Bay in general for years. Excuse me for getting exciting at being able to see everything with my own eyes."

Tense as he was with not knowing where Shannon had run off to, Miriam's idle chatter actually managed to calm him a bit. After a bit of thought, Tristan was not entirely sure if that was not her purpose for the comment in the first place. It was true, she was excited to be in Shelter Bay for the first time, but Miriam also had an uncanny sense of those around her. Relieving tension in a troublesome situation was instinct to her. It was probably a good thing she had chosen to tag along.

There were very few cars parked out front when they reached the Shelter Bay Marine Center. Swinging through the doors, the lobby was equally as sparse. A family making their way out of the insect wing, and a few teenagers goofing off by the shark tanks made up the bulk of the traffic in the lobby, most seemed to be winding down to head home. It must have been slow the entire day, because the only receptionist was a young woman who looked bored out of her mind. Walking up to her, Tristan smiled and asked, "Hi, you wouldn't know where Mandy Luis might be? We just got into town, and we wanted to surprise her." Not *entirely* a lie, they would be surprising her, and they did just arrive. The fact it sounded like they were already friends was simply convenient.

His excuse seemed to work on the girl; she pointed down the left hall, "I believe she's stationed at the manta ray tank right now."

"Thanks," he said, and headed in that direction. When he made a few turns without hesitation, Kent smirked, "You know your way around this place."

"You would too after six years," Tristan responded, taking the teasing in stride. A minute later, the wide, shallow tank populated with a dozen or so manta rays came into view. As advertised, Mandy stood behind a small podium, keeping an eye on the touch tank. On spotting her, Tristan's steps faltered. In all the time he had been stationed as Shannon's guardian he had never seen the woman so worn down. It struck home just how right Shannon had been about her friend's worry for her. Even at a distance, she looked weary. It was somewhat disturbing to see the normally spunky woman deflated.

At least one good thing would come out of this situation. With Shannon here, Mandy would at least know she was safe. That thought was quickly followed by another. If Shannon had come to see Mandy, why did she still look like someone had run over her dog. Dread sank his stomach, and he quickened his steps.

Hearing someone coming, Mandy straightened and painted a very convincing smile on her face. The transition was even more unsettling with how real it looked. Only her eyes gave any hint that something was wrong. "Well, hello!" she said her voice peppy and excited. "You guys came at a good time. The rays seem to be wanting to show off right now. Just be sure to only touch the tips of the wings when you pet them, not down the center." Her hands waved to mime where it was okay to touch the aquatic animals with dramatic flair. An Oscar worthy performance.

When her eyes finally rested on Tristan's face, the mask of professional cheer slipped, and her brow furrowed slightly in confusion. "You," she whispered, as if speaking out loud would help her brain place where she had seen him before. "You're the one who saved us that night." She stepped around the podium to stand in front of Tristan and his friends. He nodded, not sure how to start the conversation. As it turned out, he didn't need to.

Gripping his arm, Mandy's words were frantic. "Shannon, the friend I was with the night those goons attacked," her voice cracked but she continued, "She's been missing for weeks. Have you seen her anywhere? Do you know anything?"

Tristan's eyes dropped at the weight of what she was saying. "Then you haven't seen her?"

"Seen her? I just told you she has been missing. Why would I ask that if I had seen her?" She was babbling now, and Tristan did not blame her. His training was forcing his brain to stay sharp. He looked over his shoulder at Kent. "This just got more complicated. If she had left on her own, Mandy would have been her first stop."

"What about Aunt Anita? She would want to see her mother as well, maybe she went further inland." Miriam suggested, crossing her arms tightly over her chest.

Tristan shook his head. "Anita is safe, and she knows where Shannon has been. Mandy didn't, it was her and Zeke she was worried about. She's been asking all of us to take her to go se..." He was cut off by sharp nails digging into his arm even through the leather of his coat. He had always wondered why women would have their nails shaped like talons. He supposed the offensive power of the acrylic claws were one advantage. It was certainly a discomfort to the one on the receiving end.

Looking down at the one attached to the claws, Tristan saw Mandy's face had transitioned from worry, to pure, unchecked fury. Her words came out low and hissed. Mandy was nearly a full head shorter and human, but even he had to admit, the effect was...unsettling. "Where is she?"

"I don't kno... "

"Uh-uh. No! You...all of you, were talking as though you had seen her, talked to her in the last few days. And seeing as how I don't know you," she glanced at Kent and Miriam, "And I was barely introduced to you, I would very much like to know how that is possible. Did you take her? Where is she?"

Kent put a broad hand on the wrist clamped onto Tristan. "If we were her kidnappers, would confronting three of us be the best plan there, lass?" His words were gentle, calm, and completely ineffective. Mandy's eyes narrowed to slits on the warrior, exuding menace. Tristan found himself holding back a laugh at Kent's disconcerted expression, when she hissed, "I will head-butt you. Back up."

The surprise on Kent's face at her blatant threat, was too much for Tristan. A grin split his face as he chuckled, unapologetically. He was cut off however, when Mandy, and surprisingly Miriam, smacked him in the chest.

The unexpected ally made the irate blonde pause and look at the other woman. "It's not funny you clot!" Miriam slammed her hands on her hips.

"Her head-butting Kent is completely hilarious," he argued.

Miriam scoffed. "Fine. Maybe it is a tad funny, but this is hardly the time to be laughing," she claimed as her lips fought their own battle with a smile.

"The both of you just want to see me knocked on my backside by the sprite," Kent exclaimed, offended.

"Yes." Tristan and Miriam said in unison.

"Can we please get back on topic!" Mandy exclaimed, trying to focus on the trio. "Where is Shan..." Once again they were interrupted, this time by the young woman from the front desk, "Hey Mandy, Mrs. Lennot said that it was alright to close early since we are so slow. Once your guests leave, you can clear out. Dr. Timmons is still in the back if you need him," she said while walking ...toward ...the door.

Mandy rubbed the bridge of her nose. "That girl has no situational awareness."

Having calmed down, Tristan turned back to Shannon's friend, resigned. If Shannon was not here, then something else had happened to her. They needed to find her fast. Even if doing so meant cutting loose a few secrets, "Shannon was with us," Miriam and Kent's heads snapped to him, but he pressed on, "It was safer for her to get out of town after what happened to the two of you. That's where she has been for the last few weeks. But now she has disappeared. We thought...I thought she may have come to see you, but if you haven't seen her, then..." He trailed off, and Mandy shook her head.

"I haven't seen her at all. If she was planning on coming to see me, then she hasn't made it yet. Could you have just beat her here?"

Tristan shook his head. "She had nearly a full day's lead on us."

Mandy raked her fingers through her hair. "What is going on?"

"If they figured out who she is, they might have taken her as leverage," Miriam suggested tapping a finger on her hip in thought.

"Who's they?"

Tristan ignored the question. "How would they have known who she was? I'm not sure they even knew her name, let alone who her father is."

"But you were protecting her," Miriam noted, "Having a personal guard would send up a flare she was someone of importance."

Kent crossed his arms, "Let's not forget you killed three of their men. Would put a sour taste in our mouths if the roles were reversed."

Tristan tilted his head in acknowledgment of his point. Mandy was busy being stunned at the casual mention of the fall of the three attackers. "So, the question becomes, where would they hold her, and what do they want for her return?"

"If they went to this amount of trouble to get ahold of her, my guess is they will not waist time letting you know at least the latter of those things. The Nereids are efficient if nothing else." Miriam said.

"So ...what? Just wait for them to contact us with demands?" Kent blanched, not one for sitting still.

Tristan, fully accustomed to the practice, was a bit more open to the idea. "It is better than just wandering around the ocean looking for her without a starting point."

"Exactly. If they are looking for you specifically, Tristan, it might be simpler to just find a defensible position and wait for them to come to us." Miriam said, her hands dancing as she animated her point.

Tristan nodded and then they both looked to Kent. He threw his hands up, "Fine!" Huffing, he turned toward the front doors. "Let's go find a place to be sitting ducks." He grumbled, as the others fell into step behind him.

Mandy shook herself out of the semi-trance she had fallen into listening to the strange trio. "Wait!" she called, catching up to them right as they were pushing on the swinging glass. "Who are you people? Where is Shannon? Who took her?"

Miriam placed a hand on her shoulder trying to slow her progress. "You're safer here, lass."

"If you know who took Shannon, then I want to help." she tried to push forward but was not getting very far against Miriam. Still, it was wasting time they could not afford to lose. Tristan circled back to the spitfire and extracted her from Miriam's hold, "Mandy, you remember me from before?"

Mandy nodded, "You saved us."

"I protected the two of you before, you can trust me to protect Shannon now. However, I can't do that if I'm worried about you getting hurt as well. I know you want to help. I know you want answers. But I do not have time to stay and explain things right now. My priority has to be finding Shannon. Do you understand?"

Mandy pressed her lips together but nodded this time in resignation. "Okay. Just...bring her home safe... Please."

Tristan smiled, "I will. I gotta find her first."

"That might be easier than we thought," Kent called back to them. He was the only one facing the street and so was the only one to notice the towering figure. A small brunette stood trapped in his grip. Long barbs protruded from his forearms to graze against her throat. Her wide eyes locked with Tristan, and he felt his gut sink to the ground.

"Shannon!" Mandy screamed and started running for her friend. Kent snagged her around the waist and swung her behind him, putting his broad back between her and the Nereid.

Laughter traveled the distance between the hostage and her family. "You are more popular than expected. Oh well," he pressed the barbs harder, making her arch awkwardly away from the points, "three for the price of one, so to speak." His grin disappeared, anger twisting his mouth into a snarl.

Tristan strode forward, his accent growing thicker with his rage, "You really think you can take on all three of us by yourself?"

"You assume I am by myself."

It was Kent who laughed this time. "If you had any kind of support, they would be in front of us. Your honor, or what you parade as such, doesn't allow for hiding in the bushes." Kent squared off to the Nereid, still blocking Mandy from his view. "You're all by your lonesome."

"You're in our territory, fish, you have no claim to anything or anyone here. Release Shannon, and maybe we let you go back to your friends." Gone was the soft, easy way of speech Miriam had been using with her friends and Mandy. Now, steel threaded every word, every syllable, iron hardening her backbone to match her words. Here was the woman who had been trained since birth to help lead her people in a time of war.

Tristan gritted his teeth and forced himself not to contradict the chief's daughter. She could negotiate all she liked, if those spikes left even a scratch on Shannon, the man was dead. The Nereid did not seem to grasp the threat to his life properly.

The giant shook his head, calm and collected, as though they were having a disagreement about what to have for lunch. Either he was stupid, overestimating his skills, or a lot more powerful than they could see. None of those options were favorable. "No. No, I have a better idea. My new friend and I, Shannon did you say her name was, are going to head down to the shore, "he thrust his chin at Tristan, "You alone will follow. I release the girl, I kill you, everyone else gets to go home."

"You're daft!" Kent shouted.

"Possibly. But I have orders to see him," The Nereid jabbed a finger at Tristan's chest, "dead for killing our men. I would prefer not to shed blood unnecessarily. I am willing to let the rest of you go. Take the offer. It is the best one you will get."

"And if we kill you outright instead?" Tristan countered.

The Nereid sighed, as though disappointed, "Then this pretty little thing will be the first to die." His eyes bore into Tristan. "You Selks may be stronger, but we are much faster. Attack me before we get to the beach, any of your friends follow us, and I will slice her throat before you make it three steps." He dug the natural blades into Shannon's neck again, pulling a hiss through her teeth.

"Your choice, Skinner. I do not have a lot of patience left. Take too long and she will die all the same."

Tristan's gaze darted between his friends, but the Fish was right. There was no way for them to get to Shannon before blood was drawn. He growled in frustration. They were at a stalemate.

The Nereid realized this as well and blew out a breath once more. "Fine. Seems you need a bit more incentive." He looked down at his captive, and Shannon saw actual regret in his stare, but also iron determination.

He was going to kill her. Tristan was moving before he could think to do so, but just as the wretched fish had said, he was not fast enough. He was going to watch while his Shannon died, and he was helpless to stop it. But by the coat on his back, the squid would not live to taste the sea again.

The barbs flared, and his arm began to press in earnest to Shannon's neck, the first drops of blood ran down her throat.

A whistle split the air, followed quickly by a metallic "Bong!" The Nereid went slack, falling to the side while a dark hand snagged Shannon's arm and hauled her in the opposite direction of the lethal spines.

Tristan slowed his pace when he saw who had snatched the woman away from what should have been certain death. Dr. Zeke Timmons scowled down at the unconscious man. His dark skin and large stature gave the impression of a pissed off bear. Tucking Shannon protectively under an arm, he swung the shovel in his hand across his shoulders.

Turning his glare on the three Selkies, his drawl heavy, he bellowed across the parking lot. "Somebody better start telling me what the heck is going on!"

Chapter Eighteen

When Tyrus woke, he was pretty sure he had been stung by a dozen jellyfish then swam right into the side of a gorge. The way his skull was buzzing, it was the only explanation. The next thing he noticed was his head was the only thing hurting. His skin wasn't itching to the point of insanity; his joints no longer felt like they would collapse under his weight, and best of all, he could take a deep breath without it burning all the way through him.

His watch had kept him dirt-locked longer than any Nereid had any business being. Sure, they could walk just fine on land like their shoreside counterparts, but after a few days, the strain of being out of the water took its toll on a body. Even the mind started to grow a bit foggy if left dry too long. He tried to convince himself that was why he had been so monumentally stupid.

What was he thinking bringing the girl to the marine center? Had he simply left her tied to a chair at the house, he would have had a much stronger position to maneuver from. Or perhaps waited for Magnus to come back and support his attack. But no! He took one look at the three skinners walking through town clearly looking for the girl, rushed to get to them before they looked elsewhere, and botched the only chance he had to take the upper hand against them. It was something he might have done fresh out of the academy, but even then, he was not that foolish.

He blamed the dirt, the dry air, the addled thinking, which had landed him here...Where was here?

He focused on the water around him. It was cool but not uncomfortable. The current was nearly non-existent, and he could not hear or smell any large predators in the area. He couldn't really sense anything in the area. The oddity of this made him crack his eyes open and look around.

It was bright, so he couldn't be that far down. Rough rocks of varying shades of brown and black surrounded him jutting out from coarse sand. He frowned at the stones. He did not recognize the formations. And where were the Selks? There was no way they had just dumped him in the middle of nowhere, not after he had tried to kill their friend. He winced when he remembered the fear in the girl's eyes as his barbs grazed her throat. He shook himself. She is a Selk. Her fear should have no bearing on his actions.

With a smooth stroke of his tail fin, Tyrus glided through the boulders to try and get a better handle of the landscape and maybe figure out where in the riptides the Skinners and dropped him. A few seconds later the water ahead of him warped and curved like there was nothing there. The sand stopped, as though it hit a solid object, but there was nothing there.

Beyond the invisible barrier the ground was grey and Tyrus could make out...walls? Dread hit him like a bull shark. He surged forward. His hands collided with glass. "No, no, no, no!" Hands turned to fists, banging on the clear wall with a hollow 'thung."

Figures strode forward on the other side of the boundary, confirming his suspicion. The loathsome Selkies had put him in one of the human's large tanks they used to display the sea creatures they kept as pets!

Hissing, he shot upward. There had to be a way out. These were designed for fish and turtles and sharks, not anything with hands. Breaching the water at the top of the tank, Tyrus nearly collided with the thick metal grating spanning the length of the entire pool. The thick bars designed to support anyone walking would have been wide enough apart to fit through, were it not for the mesh running over the bars to provide a flat, uninterrupted surface for those above to work on. Only his fingers could slip between the gaps, and even that was uncomfortable.

Not wanting to waste his time with the steel, he dove back under the water. The figures he had seen before were easy to make out now that he was paying attention. One was the woman he had threatened, he believed they called her Shannon, and the other was only vaguely familiar. She was human, slightly taller than the Selkie woman and had hair the color of the sun streaming through water. She was not as awkward or fragile looking as humans tended to be, which intrigued him.

Nereids tended to leave the humans alone. They had no quarrel with them and would even, sometimes, help those who had gotten stranded in their waters. However, *this* human had helped to put him in a box and that was something he would not forgive quickly.

Gaining momentum from his dive, Tyrus tucked his body and slammed his tail into the glass. The impact created a much louder bang than last time, but the cursed material held firm. Swimming back and forth along the clear wall, he began testing various parts of it. Ramming his fist, striking his barbs along its smooth surface, anything to try and weaken the barrier. The blonde smirked at his inspection of the cage and walked over to the corner.

Curiosity peaked, Tyrus paused to watch her. Retrieving a black pole with a white box on top, she walked back and planted the stand in front of the tank dead center so he could see.

It took him a minute to decipher the blocky, human script, but when he did, rage flooded his brain, and he rammed his tail so hard into the glass it vibrated. The blonde laughed so hard she doubled over, which only served to stoke Tyrus's temper to greater heat.

The sign was a simple white sheet of stock paper set in the metal stand. On it was written two sentences. **"Please do not tap the glass. The fish do not like it."**

"I don't think he likes my joke," Mandy signed, still laughing.

"No, I don't think so," Shannon replied smiling herself, *"I'm going to go tell the others he's awake."* She squeezed her friend's shoulder and headed towards the front of the building where the others had settled in to figure out what to do next.

Having got control of herself, Mandy looked back at the tank, and the furious merman...Nereid, pacing the glass. Even with him right in front of her, she was still having a hard time believing all she had been told in the last hour.

Tristan, Kent, Miriam and Shannon had done their best to explain the basics of the situation, while she and Zeke had sat in stunned silence. At the beginning, Mandy thought her best friend had lost her mind and found a group of people just as delusional. That was until Shannon had said her name... actually spoke... out loud! It had, quite literally, knocked her on her backside. She did not know whether to scream, or laugh, or cry. It was a miracle she had never even thought to pray for. Shannon being mute was just a part of who she was. Why change a person she loved so dearly? But to hear her sister say something as simple as her name, was an incredible gift. One that gave more weight to the insanity the leather clad trio was spitting. Dumping Shannon's kidnapper into one of the shark tanks in limbo and watching him turn into...what he turned into, sank the crazy ship to the bottom of the ocean with all of them on board.

The creature...Nereid...man, whatever you called him, seemed to come to the conclusion that ramming the glass, while impressive, was not going to do much good. Those tanks were designed to take the charge of a great white shark if need be. While he seemed to be much stronger than his frame would suggest, he was not getting out of the tank until they wanted him to. If they wanted him to.

His movements smoothed out, became less agitated. Every twitch of muscle, turn of fin, even the tilt of his body to cut through the water was dynamic, fluid, completely effortless. It was mesmerizing watching him glide back and forth along the length of the tank. Mandy suddenly had a greater understanding of the old sailors' myths about the allure of mermaids. Deadly beauty.

His human frame was massive, only missing seven feet tall by a few inches. In this form, he was seven feet and then some. Dark blue and green scales ran over his tail in shades so similar you thought they were one color until the light shifted and the color would alter completely.

Unlike in the movies, his torso was also covered in scales, rather than skin, though the colors did become marginally lighter in tone. Gills flared every now and then at his sides along his ribs. Mandy wasn't sure how his arms did not interfere with his breathing, but he didn't seem to be struggling at all.

His face was so alien. Large eyes, with no white showing unless he shifted his gaze to the side. Vivid emerald fought with jet black pupils trying to compensate for the light in the tank. The green brought out the same shade in his scales, making them pop. His features were sharp. The darker scales created a natural contour that was down-right intimidating. Flashes of multiple canines tapered to points revealed themselves when he would growl or hiss in frustration. The sound bled through the glass sending shivers up her spine.

He was powerful, and clearly aggressive, but that same easy precision she had seen in his human form was magnified now. It was like watching the tiger sharks who normally inhabited the tank he was in now. Menace was as ingrained in him as the patterns in his scales. He could rip her apart if he wanted to, if she gave him half a chance.

"Note to self," Mandy thought. *"No cleaning the tank when the pissed off Nereid is in residence."*

Chapter Nineteen

Shannon walked into the break room to find the others in a heated discussion. Zeke was concerned about the Nereid being in one of the enclosures. The staff would be back in the morning, and while the tank they were using was not currently open to the public, it was not off limits to the employees. Explaining how an angry merman was swimming around in a tank that was supposed to be empty was not a conversation any of them wanted to have.

On the other hand, Kent and Miriam's plan to transport him back to the Grotto was not without its flaws as well. Tristan worried, given the distance between Shelter Bay and the Grotto, there was too much space and time for the Nereid to escape and find a way to strike at them again.

Thankfully, Shannon was able to get hold of her grandparents and learn that her mother was fine. They, at least, did not have to mount a second rescue mission. Understandably, Anita was...perturbed... that her daughter almost died less than an hour ago. It took a while but thankfully, they were able to convince her not to come charging back to retrieve Shannon. She was fine. They were all fine and would be heading back to the safety of the Grotto soon... they hoped.

Slapping her hand twice on her hip brought the conversation to a halt. *"He's awake."* Tristan nodded and he and Zeke started heading out the door while Miriam and Kent just looked confused. "A little context for the non-signers in the room, please?" Kent asked.

"The fish is awake," Tristan called over his shoulder, not bothering to stop his progress down the hall.

When the Selkies turned the corner, the Nereid stopped his pacing and released a sound somewhere between a shriek and a hiss. The fins along his forearms flared, the spines lengthening in hostile challenge.

"Yep," Zeke murmured, "he's awake alright." He crossed the open floor to the glass to get a better look at the creature. "It's completely fascinating. The fins on his arms must function as pectorals, while the ones running along the backside of the main body of the tail are dorsal fins. I've never seen a caudal fin that large before. I wonder how fast he can move?"

Mandy came to stand beside Zeke, "Don't know how fast he can go flat out, but he can turn on a dime."

Zeke hummed in thought, "The additional fins must allow for sharper turns. Larger eye orbits: I bet he has excellent night vision. If he has a collapsible ribcage, it might mean he is able to dive to...Ow! "

He was cut off as Shannon came up behind her friends and smacked them both in the arm, hard. *"He is not a research subject, or a rescue we get to play with."* she signed, glaring at them both. They had the decency to look a bit sheepish.

"Sorry, Shan. Hard to turn off that part of my brain," Zeke swung an arm at the tank, "You have to admit it's pretty cool though. This guy is something people have been telling stories about for centuries. Can't blame me for being a little excited."

"Fish-brain tried to kill Shannon. Hard to forget that one either," Tristan pointed out, staring down the Nereid. Zeke sobered and looked back at the tank himself. "You think he can hear us?" he asked. "Through the glass I mean?"

Miriam shrugged then stepped forward. "Let's find out." Pitching her voice up slightly, she asked, "Why did you kidnap Shannon?" No response. "Why was your squadron in our territory?" No response.

"Were those the best fighters you had, because that fight was over very quickly. It was pathetic really." Tristan jibed, and when the Nereid's hiss got louder, he smirked. "Well, he can hear us at least. Doubt he is going to answer any questions like you're throwing at him Miriam."

"Not without... incentive." Kent interjected.

Miriam shook her head, "That's not our call to make."

"He's our prisoner." he reasoned back, his tone almost business-like.

"We are not torturing him!" Mandy protested, horrified at the suggestion.

"It's nothing they haven't done to any number of our own soldiers." Tristan said, grimacing both at the idea of having to perform the task, and a memory, not as buried as he thought it was.

"Either way," Miriam said, taking back the conversation, "He is a prisoner of war. There are certain rules we have to follow for something like this."

"Like they have any mercy on us when the roles are reversed!" Kent bellowed. "We are not going to get anywhere with him unless he has a reason to cooperate."

"It doesn't matter. We will not sink to their level!" Miriam said adamantly, holding her ground. Seeing she wasn't going to budge, Kent threw his hands in the air in surrender.

The prisoner in question laughed and said something in that musical language of theirs. Despite the water, his voice was clear, his words crisp as anything said on land. There was an odd kind of echo around the words, like when someone spoke into a metal bowl.

It must have been insulting because a second later Kent growled and rammed a fist at the glass where the Nereid's face was. A resounding 'bong' rang on the pane. The Nereid flinched and clasped his hands over his ears against the noise. "Huh," Mandy said thoughtfully, "It really does scare the fish."

🌢

*T*heir attempts at getting information out of their prisoner proved fruitless. Not that anyone was truly surprised. Prisoners were not common due to the fact both sides were uncannily resilient. There simply was no point in taking them if their efforts were going to be wasted, which left them with a conundrum. What exactly were they supposed to do with the Nereid as he was proving just as helpful as any others in the past? Unless they were willing to revisit the option of torture, which, if they were honest, none of them were, they had found themselves at an impasse.

In the end, hunger forced everyone to retreat to the break room for food and to reevaluate their options. It was nothing special, just sandwiches they had thrown together from what supplies there were in the fridge. Simple, but it did the job.

The others were talking back and forth about what to do. Zeke would pipe in with a question every now and then. Despite the stress of the last few hours, the conversation was relaxed, easy, like they had known each other for years.

Mandy stared at her food in thought, mulling over the whole situation. They needed something, anything from the Nereid so they could see which step to take next. An idea popped into her head, and she sat up straighter. It was probably foolish and might put her at more risk than she was comfortable with, but if it gave them even a tidbit of information, it was more than they had now.

Going back to the fridge she quickly threw together another sandwich from what was left and slapped it on a paper plate. The others were still distracted so she just slipped out the door and headed for the back tunnels.

Mandy had always liked it back here. It was a side of the marine center that none of the guests ever got to see, like a backstage pass at a concert. This time however, who she was going to see was a lot scarier than a rock star.

Plate in one hand, Mandy snagged a bang stick as she climbed the stairs on the backside of the tank holding the Nereid captive. Three times she had to force her feet to keep climbing. Her heart felt like it was going to come out of her chest. She reached the top landing. A few steps in front of her was the latch to a trap door which, normally, would allow divers to enter and exit the tank. Now it was a possible escape route if she messed this up.

"This is so stupid," she told herself. Stupid or not, her hand grabbed the latch that held the door in place, lifted, and yanked it back with a scrape of metal on metal. When the bolt slid home, it clanged and Mandy winced. So much for subtle.

The door was too heavy for her to lift with just one hand, so she set the sandwich and pole on the floor then threaded her fingers through the grating. With a grunt, and almost falling on her backside for the second time today, she got the section of metal floor flipped open. As soon as she dropped the grate, she dove across to the other side, snatched the bang stick and brought it to bare at the gap in the floor.

Her heart was pumping so fast she could hear the blood rushing in her ears. "Bad idea, bad idea, bad idea." The words repeated in her head, mocking her foolishness. After a full minute when nothing appeared under the water, her grip on the pole loosened to something a bit less painful. "Maybe he doesn't know I'm up here?" She thought, just as something large and fast moved under the water across the opening in the floor.

Mandy squeaked and clutched her weapon in a vice grip as the shadow passed again. She was surprised she did not snap the pole in half when the man's scaled face at last peaked above the surface, wary of a trap. With the same ease someone else would sit in a chair, he placed his hands on either side of the door and hauled his upper body out of the water to sit on the edge of the gap.

The pigment in his scales seem a bit duller when he was not submerged. It was still disconcerting to see something...someone, who was so different from her. His wide eyes watched her, took in every detail, not missing a thing. Though what conclusions he drew from his observations, he kept locked tight.

Mandy fidgeted on her feet, well aware of how dangerous this man could be. But she had made this choice, she was going to stick with it. *"Stick isn't working,"* Mandy thought, *"then let's see how far a carrot will get us."* She straightened her spine and said. "I..." Nerves constricted her throat, clearing it, she tried again. "I thought you might be hungry." She nodded her head to the sandwich on the floor a few feet from his hand. His eyes darted to it then back at her. His gaze narrowed. "Do you...eat sandwiches?"

He remained quiet, staring her down. After a few beats Mandy sighed, "Well if you don't want it, I'll just" She went to pick up the sandwich, only for him to let out a loud hiss. This time she did fall on her backside. It was like she had stepped on the tail of a snake.

Instead of getting embarrassed, she got mad. "That is just rude! Hissing at me and all I wanted to do was bring you some food! You've been trapped in there for hours; I thought I would be nice. More than you did when you took my best friend, by the way, and that is how you are going to treat me?"

"What do you want, human?" his question startled her. More the fact he spoke than the question itself.

"What? I told you, I brought you food."

"I see this. You have said this. What do you want?"

Mandy bounced her heel, making the grating rattle. "One question," he raised a brow. She continued, "A fair trade. A sandwich for one, honest answer to one question."

He gave a humorless chuckle, "You and the Skinners think I would betray my people for so little." He moved to sink under the water again. She was losing him, Mandy stepped forward, urgency threading her voice. "Mine... isn't that kind of question," he paused. Curiosity flashing in his eyes, and maybe a bit of amusement.

"Shannon and the others don't even know I am up here. In fact, they will probably be mad when they find out I came here alone." she offered, "Will you at least consider answering my question? Truly consider it and the sandwich is yours." He tilted his head eyeing her, the bang stick, the path behind her, then the water below, clearly weighing his options.

When his gaze drifted to the plate, Mandy knew he was at least thinking about it. His back straightened like he was bracing for something, he leveled his glare on her and said, "Ask."

"What is your name?"

His brows shot up. Not what he had expected. "Why would you ask that?" he scoffed. "You could have asked me anything you wanted, and you inquire my name?" He sounded incredulous. His gaze swept her again, reassessing. Whether that would be in her favor or not, time would tell.

For now, Mandy nodded, "I don't like calling you the Nereid, or him, or the merman." He winced at the last one and Mandy found herself fighting a smirk. She squatted down and nudged the sandwich toward him. "My name is Amanda, but most call me Mandy." She laughed, "Not sure which of those I'd be comfortable with you using, but those are your options."

He smirked then reached for the sandwich. Until his fingers touched the plate, he watched her like a hawk, waiting to see what she would do. Mandy did nothing but watch, patient for her answer, if one was to come.

The Nereid ate in silence. By the time he was finished, Mandy's shoulders were slumped in defeat. Well, at least she had tried and now they didn't have to deal with a merman cranky with hunger. Rising to her feet, she waved the bang stick at the hole. Hopefully the sea creature knew what the thing was and would not make her use it.

He shoved the plate away, then stared at his impromptu waitress/prison guard. Her patients used up Mandy waved the pole again. "I don't want to hurt you, but I will if I have to. Please get back in the tank."

Still, he stared, not moving. She huffed. "Look would you please just... "

"Tyrus."

Mandy stalled. "What?"

"Tyrus, son on Cassius. That is my name hu-Amanda." He slid off the ledge, into the water, leaving a gob smacked woman up top. His head rose back above the water. "And thank you for the food." It was several heartbeats before Mandy got a hold of herself once more, and moved to close and latch the gate. That had...worked?

"Tyrus." She murmured a small smile tipping her lips. An odd name for an odd man.

Chapter Twenty

*T*he news of the Nereid's name came as more of a shock than expected. "Tyrus, son of Cassius?" Kent said dumbfounded. All three of the natural born selkies looked a bit put out. Shannon wasn't sure Miriam was breathing at the moment.

"You're sure he said Cassius?" Tristan asked, advancing on Mandy who had claimed one of the chairs in the corner. She nodded, not bothering to answer the question for the third time. Tristan went back to the pacing he had done since this conversation had started. There was something important he was missing here, if only his brain would locate the information he was looking for. Zeke crossed his arms. "What is so special about this Cassius guy? He seems to have all of you a bit jumpy."

"He's one of the five Legatos Legionis; a general of sorts." Miriam answered, raking her fingers through her hair.

"And an argument could be made of those five, he is by far the best," Kent grumbled, none too pleased.

Zeke spoke to the room as a whole rather than just one person. "How much crap are we in for snatching the son of a guy like that?"

Tristan didn't pause his stride as he spoke. The motion helped keep his brain clear to think rationally. "Not sure honestly. The Nereids aren't like us. They are an army, yes, and a powerful one, but they are not as tight knit as the clans. They have the advantage of numbers, but we fight like every member on the battlefield is a close family member." He looked at Shannon. "Because they are. It is simply the way we are. The Nereids...aren't like that."

Kent nodded. "They are brutal, efficient soldiers. Their individual units can sometimes be more loyal than others, but at the end of the day, they are still just soldiers to the army at large," he shrugged. "To them, a soldier can be replaced."

"But that's only common soldiers, right?" Zeke drawled. "This is the son of one of, according to you, their best generals. We can't assume he is not going to take issue with the fact his son is now in enemy hands."

"Doo...tey...know...wi...av im?" All eyes shot to Shannon.

"What'd you say, honey?" Zeke asked, focusing on her.

"Do they know we have him?" Tristan interpreted without thought. Shannon tapped her nose, letting everyone know he was dead on.

"Why wouldn't they?" Tristan asked and signed at the same time. His fluent sign, alongside his casual ease with which he understood Shannon still caught her two friends off guard.

"He was alone when he took me from home." Shannon answered, also taking his skill in stride. "Alone when he brought me to the Marine Center, and no one attacked us when we got the upper hand on him. The guy who told me my mom was kidnapped was different, but I haven't seen or heard from him since I came on shore. If they operate in units, where is the rest of his?"

Kent pointed at her when Mandy was done translating. "Lass has got a point."

"If Shannon is right and he's alone, it begs the question, why would they send someone of his influence without any back—" Tristan's eyes widened in realization, his mind finally knocking loose what had been dancing at the edge of his memory. With a curse he took off running for the tank. The others, confused, followed right on his heels.

Tyrus, for all the world, looked like he was lounging on the sand, hands behind his head, fins lazily flaring every now and then to keep him where he wanted. At their approach, he rose to his full length, eyeing each of them with suspicion.

Tristan marched up to the glass and glared up at the Nereid. "Are you the older or younger son of Cassius?" He growled. Tyrus grinned at the question, his pointed teeth making it even more threatening. Tristan cursed and struck the tank with such force the glass rippled.

"Both y'all need to stop beatin' up my tank before it shatters," Zeke berated.

Shannon ran up to Tristan and gently placed a hand on his arm. Reflexively he latched onto her arm as well, his thumb rubbing the inside of her wrist. He calmed, marginally. "What's wrong?" she asked.

Pulling in a deep breath through his nose, Tristan explained. "Cassius has two sons. Both are pretty well-known warriors." The Nereid chuckled at hearing this. Mandy pointed at him. "Don't you make this any worse," she ordered. Surprisingly, Tyrus focused on her instead of the Selkie talking.

"The older brother is a centurion. One of the best, and he commands their best, including him," he jabbed his unoccupied thumb at the man-fish. "The younger brother has built a reputation as one of the army's best single combat fighters, which may explain why they let him come on land on his own. They thought he could handle it. But that's not what has me concerned."

"What does?" Miriam asked. The question drew the attention of the Nereid, his grin, arrogant and knowing. He was fully aware of what had Tristan spun up, and was enjoying the show of watching the anvil drop.

Tristan's gaze left Shannon and locked on Kent's. "Rumor is that Cassius's youngest son is a Wader."

It was Kent's turn to loose a string of choice words. "We have to move him now," he shouted over his shoulder as he sprinted to the back of the tank. Tristan moved to join him; the man would need help if they were going to get the enemy soldier out of the tank without killing him, but Mandy snagged his arm. "Darn it! What is a Wader?"

"A telepath," the answer came from Tyrus, amusement lacing his words as he watched the Selkies scramble to adapt to the new development. "Those with talent are able to communicate with our comrades from miles away," his tone blatantly implied he was numbered among the 'talented."

Mandy paled. "How long do you think we have?"

"There is no way to tell. We don't know his range or how many fish are in the area." Tristan growled. "He's been awake for hours. It could be hours yet before his support shows up, or minutes. There is no way to know for certain. The only advantage we have at the moment is Shelter Bay is well within Selkie borders. If we're lucky, he's out of his range." Tristan looked back at the prisoner. The grin plastered on his face did not bode well for that faint hope. "We'll take care of it," he signed to Shannon, squeezed her shoulder in reassurance, then chased after Kent.

Shannon watched him go. her brain working overtime. *"Where can we take him that is more secure than here?"* she asked rubbing a hand over her brow, turning the problem over.

Zeke's thick drawl sounded from over Shannon's head, but he spoke to Miriam, "What is the average range of a Wader?"

She shrugged, "No clue. We only know they exist, not how the ability works."

"Alright," he said stepping closer to the tank, "Let's be generous to be on the safe side, and say, ten miles or so." He gestured toward the back hall. "Tristan said the town falls in your territory." Miriam nodded confirmation. Zeke went on, more talking to himself than the rest of the group. "They are sea creatures. Logically, if one was taken out of his natural environment his abilities would diminish."

The big man looked up at the captive Nereid, the grin he previously sported was nowhere to be seen now. Zeke chuckled. "I'm right, aren't I?" Zeke tilted his head to the side. "How long can a Nereid survive out of water?" Tyrus bared his teeth, but Zeke continued, unfazed by the threat, "Best you answer that question truthfully, man. Wouldn't want to accidentally kill you in transport."

Tyrus's gaze flicked to everyone remaining in the viewing area before colliding back with the marine biologist. "Three days. Four is the longest I have ever heard of anyone making it. If you call a blistered, half mad husk surviving."

"Are you euryhaline?"

Confusion flashed across Tyrus's face. "Salt and fresh water," Dr. Timmons explained.

"Yes," he bit out, starting to see what his near future was going to look like.

Zeke smiled and went to seek out the other men. "Now that, I can work with."

Chapter Twenty-One

Tristan was loathe to admit how long it took Kent, Zeke and him to get the Nereid out of the tank. Honestly, if Zeke had not thought to grab the net they used to capture resistant sharks, they probably would still be floundering in that tank with the slippery eel. None of them could say they escaped unscathed by the experience, but at least none of them were seriously injured.

Kent and Tristan were forced to shift into their sea lion forms, as they were stronger in the water that way. Unfortunately, they were now stuck in the skin until their clock ran out. A predicament that was solved when he learned Shannon's longtime friend drove a massive truck as it was the only vehicle that fit his linebacker frame.

Once the Nereid, or Tyrus as they now knew him, was securely bound he was promptly tossed in the bed of the truck with Tristan and Kent following behind to lay across his legs and upper torso. Their weight did most of the work of keeping the enemy soldier from squirming too much, not that it stopped him from trying.

All three men were probably on par with each other as far as military skill and experience. With the Nereid's natural advantage of speed neutralized by pure Selkie bulk, Tyrus, after a few unsuccessful attempts to throw his captors off, decided it was wiser to conserve his energy for when circumstances were more in his favor. He dropped his head to the floor of the bed with a thunk, and resigned himself to the unpleasant ride.

As Tristan looked over the edge of the truck, he saw Shannon doing her best not to laugh. The three of them must have made quite the sight. Two massive sea lions, chilling out in the back of a truck laying on top of a man that, had he been human, would have been squashed into an unsightly pancake. He grunted in amusement at the mental image.

With Tyrus quite literally under them, they did not bother to blindfold him as the girls piled into the cab of the truck and Zeke drove off further into town. Tristan and Kent ducked down as far as they could, so as to draw less attention to themselves.

Twenty minutes later, after many unnecessary turns to confuse their captive, Zeke pulled into his own driveway. It was well past dark by this point, so the motley group did not have any trouble getting into the house unseen. Even Tyrus behaved himself as he was ushered inside.

"Sarah is down south with her sister for a baby shower." Zeke said as he flicked the lights on for the hall and front room. "She'll be gone for the rest of the week." He sat Tyrus into one of the plush living room chairs and secured his bonds so if he tried to make a break for it, he would be taking the furniture with him. Tyrus's brows rose slightly, surprised at how comfortable his new seat was. On second thought, it may just be preferable to having the Selkies making him their chair. "*Everything in context,*" he thought.

Tristan trotted over to sit a few feet from the Nereid. His teeth were positioned to be in easy reach of Tyrus's throat should he try anything. Tyrus seemed to notice this as well and narrowed his gaze at the Selk. Kent stayed by the door, the massive sea lion, barring the main exit. The women chose to flop down on the couch.

For a while they all sat in silence. It was Miriam who first broke the silence. "Tristan, I think it is time for me to head back to the Grotto." Kent growled from the door. Miriam rolled her eyes, "I don't want to hear it. Da and Uncle Eoin need to know what is going on." Tyrus's head snapped to her at the name Eoin. Tristan growled bringing his attention back to him and away from the Chief's daughter. So, the fish did not know who they were specifically. He had originally assumed he had gone after Shannon because of her connection to the Lann. However, as Tristan thought back to the incident which had dropped them in this mess, Tyrus had blatantly stated he was only interested in killing him for the death of his men.

"It's too late to do anything now. We are all exhausted and need some sleep," Zeke said standing, his knots checked and rechecked. Tristan flashed images at Miriam. She glanced at him then back at Zeke, "Tristan says he'll take the first watch." Zeke nodded then had the girls follow him to the get them set up for the night.

It was going to be a long one.

*T*he morning brought with it the joyful noise of Kent and Miriam bickering back and forth about her going back to the clan on her own to update the Chief and Lann. Feeding off each other, both their accents got so thick that those who did not grow up listening to it could not understand half of what they were saying. Not that it mattered much. Most of the arguments were the same as the ones brought up the day before. And like yesterday, neither could agree on the best course of action. Tristan knew it was going to come down to one just making the choice no matter what the other said. His bet was on Miriam. Kent was stubborn like no one else, but Miriam had been trained by her mother,

Fiona. Tristan doubted there was anyone who could deter that woman. She had long ago passed the baton to her daughter. Poor Kent did not stand a chance.

Tyrus was still strapped to the chair, the hours had turned what had once been a comfortable seat into a plush nightmare. A body as long as his was not meant to stay in a confined position for so long. His only consolation was at least he was no longer in a box. He would take his victories where he could. Shannon, trying to stay out of the way of the two combatants, sank down onto the opposite loveseat to him.

When he saw the faint red mark on her throat, Tyrus made an internal wince. Selkie or not, he hated the thought of hurting a woman. They were supposed to be protected, not dragged into violence. He held back a grimace. He was the one who had asked Magnus to lure her here in the first place. Tides, he was tired of this crap.

"Your..." Shannon looked up at his voice. Despite how foolish he knew it was, he pressed on, "Your neck, is it bad?" he asked, his words barely more than a mumble. Her hands raised out of habit, until she realized the Nereid would have no clue what she was saying. Instead she smiled tentatively and said, "Jus a scatch."

Tyrus's brows furrowed in confusion. "What?"

Shannon took a deep breath, focused on the shape of the words, and tried again. "It juh a scatch."

The confusion did not abate. "I don't know what in the riptides you are saying," he leaned back in the chair. "It almost sounds like you're simple, but I- "

He was cut off by a fist plowing into his scull like a battering ram. Fingers snatched the longer strands of his hair and yanked his head up to face an incredibly angry Tristan. "No one talks to Shannon like that, especially the whale piss that tried to kill her." he released his grip on Tyrus's hair with a sharp flick of the wrist, snapping his head to the side. Tyrus hid a wince at the mild whiplash of the recoil. "Next time I break your jaw."

"Skinner brute," Tyrus mumbled trying to stop the ringing in his head. Tristan had been moving to sit next to Shannon on the couch, but at the Nereid's comment he turned back around, one brow arching up. "Oh, I'm the brute?" He waved a hand at him as though he was gesturing to something disgusting. "This coming from the one who kidnapped my charge, threatened to slit her throat in front of me if I did not allow myself to be killed, and then gave the threat an all fire try when I didn't move fast enough for your liking."

"You killed three of my men." Tyrus surged forward, his bindings the only thing keeping him from laying into the Selkie. Good grief that human knew how to tie knots.

"I saw their bodies. You blindsided them! They did not have a chance in the world to defend themselves."

"They were caught off guard, because they were trying to take Shannon away. I would have done nothing more than scare those boys for being in our territory if it had not been for that. Their deaths are on your head for giving the order to take one of mine!"

Tristan was seething now, the dam of the last few days finally breaking free. "Our peoples have been at war for near five generations, but we have never gone after your civilians. We attack only soldiers. Your women and children have always been safe from us. I thought the Nereids at least had the decency to uphold that standard, and until this month, you did."

He leaned down, looming over the restrained fish, his words taking on a distinct growl. "I killed soldiers. You were the one who made it personal," he stabbed a finger into Tyrus's chest, "you, changed the tempo of a war near a century old, and you will bear the blame of what happens as a result."

When Tristan was done, Tyrus sat silent. As much as he hated to admit it, the Selkie was correct, more than he knew. It was Tyrus who had told his brother he had found Shannon on land, with no coat, and seemingly, no protection, a stranded pup from her pod. Had he kept his mouth shut, none of this mess would be happening now. At the same time, it was his duty. He had to report her... Right? Tyrus let out a mild hiss. Even to his own mind that excuse was weak.

A soft voice from the corner caught the attention of both verbal combatants. "Why are you guys at war?"

Looking over to the source of the noise, they saw their fight had gained the attention of the remaining occupants in the house. It was Mandy who had posed the question, her arms crossed over her chest as though to comfort herself against the intensity of the two enemies in her friend's living room. "How did the war start?" she asked again, "Why do you fight?"

"We didn't always," Tyrus said locking eyes with the young woman.

She shook her head, "I didn't ask how long you have been fighting," she said, "I asked why." She raised her brows in question, looking between the two of them. Shannon leaned forward on the couch, *"It's a good question."*

Tristan signed and spoke at the same time. "War tends to break out when one nation attacks the other out of the blue." His stare would drill holes in the Nereid if it could. "We have tried to make peace multiple times through the years, but they refuse."

"The Selkies are the ones who refuse to bend."

"Bend? Why would we bend when the only thing you have asked for is completely unreasonable? Something you had no right asking for in the first place."

"Whoa, whoa." Zeke placated, trying to head off another screaming match. "Tristan, what exactly did the Nereids ask for in the last negotiation?"

Tristan scoffed, "Our home." He plopped down on the couch next to Shannon. Being near her seemed to settle him, slightly, and he could use a dash of calm right now. Shannon's shoulders loosened as well. He continued, "The ambassadors, demanded the Selkies abandon every one of our ancestral homes, or they would rip us from them by force," he shot Tyrus a savage grin. "A task that has proved more challenging than they thought."

"That seems a bit extreme," Mandy commented, coming to sit between the two men on the floor. Crossing her legs she got comfortable for what she suspected would be a long debate. She looked at Tyrus, hoping he would explain.

Tyrus sighed, then answered her unspoken question. What was the harm at this point. They had never tried to hide their motives for fighting the Selks, and for some reason he wanted her to understand. "The Selkies can move onto land. We can't." He tried to adjust against the ropes to get more comfortable. He was only marginally successful. "Skinners have taken control of every single protected site that could possibly shelter us, and still give us access to the sea. It is only reasonable that the ones who have the greater need should have the sites."

Mandy tilted her head at his answer. "Need does not justify taking what is not yours."

"Thank you!" Tristan exclaimed, pointing at her.

Miriam chimed into the conversation. "Selkies have lived in the Grottos for centuries. We did not take them, we found them as they were, and built them, and our society into what they are now." She eyed Tyrus. "The Nereids did not have any complaints until the turn of Twentieth Century. Before that, we were...neighbors, who didn't really speak to each other."

"What changed?" Mandy asked, looking again at Tyrus. He was more than a bit outnumbered in the room, and she wanted to hear both sides of the argument. He looked her square in the eye and said bluntly, "You did."

It was Mandy's turn to look confused. Zeke was following however, "You mean humans." he stated.

Tyrus nodded. "Humans, in the span of a few decades, became more advanced than we thought possible. You started exploring in depths you had never reached before. Finding things that you thought were myth. In the past, humans have reacted to things they didn't understand in one of two ways," he looked between the two humans in the room, "Either awe and wonder, or fear and hate; there doesn't seem to be a middle ground for such things. And when one of our outlying villages was discovered, the humans in question chose the latter." He bowed his head at the retelling of his history. "Those that were taken were torn apart. Experimented on to see how we were fit together."

Zeke's voice was gentler than Tyrus had heard since he had met the man. "If that is the case, why fight the selkies instead of the humans?"

Tyrus laughed. "Despite how weak you are on an individual level, we would have no chance fighting against your numbers," he shrugged. "Besides you all were shredding each other to bits at the time."

"Turn of the century. Oh gosh!" Mandy exclaimed. "World War One. That was the first war where submarines were a major component of war." She looked at all the mythical creatures around the room. "All of you would have been caught in the crossfire."

Kent shrugged. "No more than the humans. My grandfather fought in the Great War for the British Navy right alongside the Humans."

"We had no idea what was going on above," Tyrus said. "All we knew was the humans had finally ventured into our territory, were stealing our people, and we had no way of combatting the numbers we would face if we retaliated in a head on collision. So we did the next best thing."

"You came after us." Tristan finished for him; his tone dry.

Tyrus took the tale back with a glare, "The humans were only going to get bolder, pushing further into our waters. We had to keep as many of our people safe as we could. Our cities are far too exposed to their technology. We'd be on display for anyone who chose to search the right area," his voice rose in agitation.

"You blame us for your ancestors not thinking ahead to possible attacks from above. We offered to help you fortify."

"No amount of fortification will help cities built on the ocean floor! You people took every, single one of the protected sights. There are none left!" The ropes strained against the pull of his wrists, his anger lending him strength, his barbs tried to lift from his skin, but they too were pinned down. "You refused to give us anything, that might be useful in protecting our people. You had to keep your precious, ancestral lands while my people were dying. So yes, in lieu of you giving us even *one* of the protected sites, we could and will take them all."

"Why do you call them protected sites?" Mandy asked softly. Hesitant to voice the question in the face of his blatant rage, but the phrase kept sticking in her mind and she thought it was important.

The Nereid soldier looked down at Mandy, fear in the face of his temper lay in the back of her eyes, but the emotion was tamped back. She was not letting it sway her. Seeing this, he took a deep breath and tried to answer her questions. "The Nereids have known for years the Selkie homelands are protected against any outsiders looking at them. It's a unique magic to those locations. When the humans get near, they see nothing but an ordinary island. They move on by, none the wiser of anything strange living there. That is why they are called protected sites. Anyone the Selks do not wish to see their home, does not. That kind of magic could save my people, both now and future generations. But the Selkies took all the land with this kind of magic attached to it."

The room was dead quiet. The three Selkies who were born in the Grotto, rapidly looked between each other, in silent communication. Finally, annoyed with being left out, Shannon tapped her thigh twice. "What is it? What did he say that has you three riled up?"

Tristan hesitated, then looked at Miriam. As the chief's daughter she had the most authority in the room. She studied Tyrus. He was the embodiment of a loyal soldier in the Nereid army. She could tell he believed every word he was saying. If she was honest, had the roles been reversed she was not sure if the Selks would not have done the same thing. But, there was one fatal flaw in his reasoning. One that could be corrected easily, yet it also would require hot to reveal something that is not talked about openly even among the clans. Should she tell a Nereid of all people? A nation who had tried to destroy her clan, her race, for as long as she could remember. In the wrong light, what she was considering could be considered treason.

But, if it brought about the opportunity for peace, lasting peace, it was worth the risk. This man was one of the Nereid's best warriors. His father was one of their generals. If he spoke on their behalf, his words would have weight. She had to take the chance and hope her father agreed with her judgement. Her gaze left Tyrus and locked with Tristan, patiently waiting for her decision. She nodded her assent.

Tristan looked aside at Shannon then to Tyrus who was watching him like a hawk. He could not believe he was about to do this, but nevertheless, he opened his mouth and voiced a sentence that shifted the foundation of the Nereid's whole world. "The land we chose to make our homes is not the reason we are sheltered from the world."

Chapter Twenty-Two

If Tyrus had not been tied to a chair you might have been able to push him over with a gentle breeze. There was no possible way what the Selkie was saying could be true. "What do you mean?" he asked, incredulous. "Of course, the sites protect you."

But before he was finished speaking, Tristan was shaking his head. "No, our homes themselves do not provide any additional protection beyond natural camouflage. Anything more is done by the clan Weaver."

"Lyra's mother?" Shannon asked.

"Yes," Tristan said. Tyrus looked between the two of them not understanding the exchange, but impatient for the Skinner to continue his insanity. He did not have to wait long.

Keeping a handle on his temper Tristan tried to explain where the Nereid was wrong in his thinking. "Everything you just described about how we keep out of the public eye of the modern world is due to the work of the Weaver, not the land we chose to make our home centuries ago." He leaned forward to rest his elbows on his knees. His temper and resentment towards the Nereid reseeding as he settled into an instructor's mindset.

"A Weaver is a person similar in theory to a Wader. It is a someone with an...extra set of talent or abilities that are not necessarily specific to the Selkies. In fact, there are several races who have Weavers in their clans." He waved a hand dismissing the rabbit trail. "The Weaver's job is to weave a barrier of magic around a location to misdirect attention away from what is at the center of the weft. In this case, the Grotto. Every clan has a dedicated Weaver for each fief."

"The land has nothing to do with it at all?" Tyrus asked his voice hollow.

All three clan-born Selkies shook their heads. "None at all," Tristan said with finality.

Tyrus leaned his head back against the chair staring at the ceiling. *"All these years, so much death and pain, and they were fighting for the wrong thing."* His mind whirled trying to reconcile this new information. But then, something Tristan had said at the beginning of the impromptu lesson circled back to the forefront of his thoughts. He lifted his head, "You said that other races use these...Weavers as well, to hide their people?"

"Absolutely. The Lycanrai, the Drake and the Cahtoy, to name a few. I'm sure there are others."

"So it is possible that one of my people could..." Tyrus trailed off.

Tristan seeing where he was going, answered the unfinished question, "Possible... yes. With the right training."

Everyone stayed quiet while they let Tyrus absorb the information. Mandy scooted forward on her knees and started working on the knots at his ankles. Kent, seeing this, began to protest, but Miriam raised a hand to stay him. It was clear to see they had knocked the wind out of the soldier's sails. He was not going anywhere until he had learned all he could. Why not loose his bonds, gain a bit of trust.

Mandy finished with his feet, and when she had finally worked her fingers through the restraints at his hands, Tyrus pulled them free and rubbed his wrists trying to get the blood to flow back into the deprived extremities. "Thank you," he muttered softly down at Mandy. The peace and kindness in her eyes as she smiled gently up at him, calmed his own nerves. Humans were odd creatures, this one especially. She was fire hot enough to scorch bone one minute, balm to soothe a startled babe the next. Internally he shook his head, a mystery for another time.

Raising his head, Tyrus looked into the face of the man he had been taught his whole life to hate, to kill and drive back at all costs. Yet now, this same man was offering a hope his people had been searching for centuries to find. A part of him said it was too good to be true, that it was not possible for it to be that easy. The other part of him asked the question, what part of the situation was easy? If what these Skin...these Selkies were telling him was true, he would have to not only find someone among his own kind who could become this 'Weaver', but he would have to convince his leaders that having a Weaver meant that the fighting could stop.

War was such a large part of their lives; he was positive there would be many that would not accept this solution purely because it was not the way they had done things in the past. But the way they had done things so far had gained them nothing but death, pain and endless fighting. He may be a fool for believing them, but if the Selkies were going to offer a real solution to the conflict, one where his people would be safe, he owed it to his people, to himself, to try and make that hope a reality.

So when next he spoke, his words were clear, firm, and with a lot of effort, devoid of animosity. "I would assume, like Waders, not just anyone can be a Weaver." The Selkies all nodded. "What is required for a person to become one?"

"Ailis told me once it is more a matter of temperament, than talent," Miriam said, thinking back to the long-ago conversation. "A Weaver needs to be a calm, level-headed personality, but also someone who will not crumble under pressure. They are extremely detail oriented, to the point of obsession, but relaxed enough to let the weave work on its own when needed. Most of all, they have to be willing and able to listen to the people and environment around them, to adapt the weave to any situation that may arise." Miriam smirked, "She called it a symphony of contradictions. She said the person capable of becoming a Weaver, represented the weft and the weave itself."

Shannon scoffed. "Why in the world does Lyra think she was going to take over for her mother if those are the requirements? She is as uptight as a person can become and not explode." Those who knew the prissy woman chuckled at the comment.

Miriam focused back on Tyrus. "Do you know anyone who fits that description?"

Tyrus was dumbstruck. There was no way. There was...just...no...possible way it could be so simple. A soft hand rested on his, and he looked down at Miriam. "Who?" she asked, knowing already he had a person in mind. "My...My sister." He croaked.

This seemed to surprise the others in the room as well. "You're having a gaff," Kent barked, half laughing at the concept. "You're telling us your family has a Wader and now a possible Weaver as well. No way."

Tyrus pointed a hand at Miriam. "She just described my sister to a tee. Hadriana is a meticulous musician. It frustrates her when she gets a single note wrong even if the rest of the piece is perfect, but when she focuses and performs well, she loses herself in the music." It had been a long time since he had seen his sister, he smiled slightly thinking of the young woman. "She is one of the kindest people I have ever met in my life, but push her the wrong way, and she is more stubborn than a bull shark." he chuckled. He swept his gaze around the room.

"Everything you mentioned can be applied to my sister. The only thing that could be a problem is..." He hesitated, not wanting to reveal a weakness in his family, but he needed to know if it would be a problem. "How much physical strength is needed for the work?"

Miriam's gaze softened at the buried worry she saw in the Nereid's eyes. He cared for his sister, that much at least was clear. "Not much at all. It is a power of the mind and will, not the body. Why?"

Tyrus waved her off. "It does not matter. She can do it," he said with certainty. "With training, she can do it." He turned to face Tristan again, determination straightening his spine. "If a Weaver is what protects your clans, and you are willing to train one of ours to do the same for our cities?" Tristan nodded his assent, and Tyrus felt his resolve solidify. "Then I can speak with our leaders about a ceasefire. A future where our people are safe is all we have ever wanted. If that can be achieved without more bloodshed, then there will be many who will dive for the chance."

"You hope." Kent mumbled under his breath. Tyrus chose to ignore the commentary.

"We have a deal? You train our Weaver and stop the raids, and we in turn will stop attacking your fiefs."

Tristans voice was level. "You can get your Senate to agree to that?"

Tyrus grimaced. "The Senate I have no sway in." He held up a finger. "But the generals are another matter. I have known those men all my life and have gained their respect in battle. They will listen to me. The Senate in turn will listen to them."

Tristan stood from the couch and placed his hands on his hips. "Miriam, it's been a while since I have spent a long period of time at the Grotto. You think your Da will go for this?"

Miriam only took a second to consider before nodding in agreement. "Yes. Especially since all he is asking for now is training. That should be an easy price to pay for peace. I don't believe the Chiefs will have any issue with the idea, beyond them having to work with Nereids."

At her words Tristan stuck out his hand. "You've got yourself a deal, fish." Tyrus gripped the offered hand. That quickly the history of two proud peoples turned on its head, moving away from a slow death for both involved, toward a path of peace. Maybe even friendship.

Shannon tilted her head at the tension still clearly visible in both men. "Perhaps civility was a better place to start," she thought.

The decision was made for Kent to escort Miriam back to the Grotto to inform Chief Nolan and Eoin that they had not only found their missing family member, but may have also found a way to halt a century-long war. After Tyrus had admitted there were no reinforcements coming to his rescue, the closest Nereid was well out of range of his mind, the Reidh had finally relented on her leaving the group as long as he was the one to take her back. Shannon thought it was cute the way he doted on her.

The problem came when it was time for the rest of the waterborne to leave to retrieve the unwitting soul who held the fragile peace of two races in her hands. Shannan certainly hoped Tyrus was right about his sister, otherwise, this was going to get very messy, very quickly.

Mandy had disappeared for a while into Shannon's house while everyone else made plans on where to meet up after everything was settled. She returned just as Miriam and Kent transformed and ducked below the waves, wearing her sleek, black and blue wet suit. Dropping a pair of flippers and goggles on the ground she planted her feet, jammed her hands on her hips, and braced for the fight she knew was coming.

Zeke and Shannon lifted a single eyebrow, and at the same time uttered the same word; one in sign, one aloud, but the same nonetheless. "Why?"

Mandy firmed her shoulders. "I'm going with you," she stated, like it should be obvious.

"No, you're not." Zeke and Shannon looked sideways at each other when they spoke in stereo again.

Before they could regroup Mandy tried to defend her position. "I am not sitting on my hands while you galivant off for who knows how long. I'm not going to drive myself crazy wondering if you are okay or not. Not again, Shan." She shook her head at the thought. "So, I'm going with you."

"What are you gonna do Mandy? Dive into the Atlantic and hope you don't freeze," Zeke asked, getting louder than he intended. He loved his friend, but there were times when he was uncertain whether or not she was sane.

Mandy gestured to the rest of her body. "Wet suit."

Confirmed. She was crazy. Shannon stepped forward to take a shot. "You won't be able to keep up with us. We are too fast. If we have to dive, you will either run out of air or be crushed by the water. I'm sorry sweetie, but you can't come with us."

Mandy raised a skeptical brow, and pointed to the two men who had yet to weigh into the conversation. "He turns into a fish." She waved at a properly affronted Tyrus, then pointed to Tristan, "And he turns into a seal."

"Sea lion." Tristan corrected.

"Whatever." Mandy dismissed. "You really, think that between the two of our mythical little friends here, we cannot come up with a way for me to come along?"

Tyrus looked down at the, from his vantage point at least, petite woman and smirked. "Little?"

Mandy's fist found her hip and she glared up at him. "That's what you're contending right now Sasquatch?"

The smirk fell. Now Tyrus was lost. "What is Sasquatch?" No one bothered to answer him.

Shannon looked at Tristan in question. He knew more about the ins and outs of the Selks than she did. However, with a chuckle, he too was shaking his head. "Sorry lass. If there was a way for Selkies to bring humans down with us, Eoin would have brought Shannon and her Mum to the Grotto years ago."

Mandy looked distraught. "But..."

"No," Tristan said firmly. "There just isn't a way to do it."

"Not for the Selks maybe," Tyrus said smugly, and now every eye swung to him. With all of the attention on him, Tyrus was beginning to question the wisdom of speaking up in this particular conversation.

Mandy was a bit slower to react than she would have liked. If she were honest, she was not sure what she wanted was possible, even with magical friends, but now that there was even the slightest of chances for her to join her friend, she dug her teeth in further. Stepping to the side to stand next to the towering man, Mandy crossed her arms and said "He can do it. I'm going."

Tyrus was a bit speechless at the gall of the blonde spitfire. Her tenacity had him actually considering fulfilling her request. "We have to go into Nereid territory to get his sister. It's too dangerous. You can't come." Tristan said, trying to recover from the blindside Tyrus just threw them.

Mandy just stared at him not budging.

"No," he tried again. Same response. He looked at Tyrus, irritated he had to crane his neck to do so. Why were Nereids always so tall? "You're going along with this?"

Tyrus shrugged. "She's been told the risks. If she wants to stick her hand in the eel pit, that is her choice."

Mandy peered up at him. "You just admitted your hometown is an eel pit."

He looked down at her. "You want to anger the only one who can take you down safely?" he asked, the smirk which quirked his lips an outright challenge.

Mandy grinned a little too brightly and turned on her tour guide voice. "I love eel pits."

Tyrus chuckled and shook his head. A strange woman indeed, but entertaining. He swung back to a very angry Tristan and Zeke. "You can't let her do this,"

Rumbled the bear of a man, his fists making hammers of themselves.

At this declaration Tyrus outright laughed, making the others jolt back at the surprisingly pleasant sound, like a deep reed flute. "The fact that this annoys you all is only making me want to help her more. Besides, on this particular trip the danger should be minimal. If you are so worried about her safety, she can stay with you and Shannon on the outskirts while I go in to retrieve my sister." The sarcastic grin broke the spell his laugh created, and the irritation came back in force.

Zeke was about to dive into another argument, but before he had a chance, the Nereid rolled his eyes, snagged Mandy's hand and started pulling her toward the waves. He was done debating. The lot of them were wasting time. Mandy leaned down and managed to snatch her swimming gear as the large, lithe man towed her into the surf.

The Spring water was frigid as she stepped in, but soon her wet suit did its job and she adjusted. Looking over at her impromptu ally, Mandy had to force her jaw to stay where it was as Tyrus's transformation rushed over him. Scales emerged from tanned skin like someone had poured paint over his body until he was completely covered. His irises flooded his eyes until all she could see was brilliant emerald contrasted with the pitch black of his pupil. The contented smile as he eased back into his natural habitat flashed his razor-sharp canines. Mandy had never been more unnerved yet fascinated before in her life. She had not realized the two emotions could coexist so well. But here she was, thoroughly ensnared with both, as she followed the living breathing myth.

He kept his head above water with little effort, and when her own feet left the sandy bottom, he placed his large hands under her elbows and helped her stay in breathable air as he pushed them further from shore. Two splashes from where they had come told Mandy, Shannon and Tristan had come after them.

Mandy tilted her head up to Tyrus. He was still intimidating, but whether from their fragile truce giving her comfort, or she was simply getting used to the way he looked, she was no longer terrified. "So," she said, her voice only wavering slightly. "How does this work? What do I do?"

Tyrus eyed her. Too late now to back down. "You do nothing." he said, matter-of-factly.

Mandy frowned. "But..."

Tyrus shook his head. "No, just relax and don't fight the air."

Mandy was even more confused now. Tyrus started to tilt his head forward but stopped in mid movement and glared at her in warning. "If you bite me, I will leave you down there."

"What? Why would I bi-" She was cut off as his lips melded with hers. On instinct she tried to push him away, but his arms were iron around her back and neck holding her in place. Shannon's bark of panic was the last thing she heard before Tyrus, still holding her tight, dove them both under the waves

Chapter Twenty-Three

Down, down, down they dove, until there was no way for Mandy to reach the surface on her own. When they had reached a depth that Tyrus thought was safe he stopped and let them float in the void of the open sea. Lips still sealed to hers he gently blew into her, forcing her lungs to expand with his own air.

As soon as the first taste of cool air hit her lungs Mandy, remembering what Tyrus had said at the beginning, made herself relax and allow the oxygen to sooth her panicked lungs. The feeling was surprisingly pleasant. It was like walking along the beach in winter, fridged and clean, like the air was cleansing her from the inside out until she felt completely refreshed. Tyrus released her and the feeling remained. Her eyes stung from the salt in the water as they widened to saucers.

Tyrus tried his best not to laugh as she kept her lips clamped shut, whether in fear of breathing in the water, or him kissing her again, he did not know. He would not blame her if either were true. Still, she could not stay like that the entire time they were down here.

Cupping her face in his hands, his amusement poorly concealed he said, "It's alright. You don't have to hold your bre-hhhhhff" Just as he was about to say the word, his own breath was knocked out of him, by a full-grown sea lion slamming into him on a full charge.

Turning the force of the blow into his own momentum Tyrus whipped around and shrieked his anger at Tristan, who had placed himself between the two women, bellowing his own fury. Shannon glided in slightly behind Tristan, putting another body between him and the human.

Tyrus flared his spines. "What in all the tides was that for Skinner?" He was practically vibrating from the effort of not ripping apart his new, reluctant ally. Tristan tilted his head at Mandy, then growled again. Instantly Tyrus understood and scoffed in disgust. "She's the one who wanted to come with us." He reasoned, pointing at the troublesome human, her hand now clasped over her mouth to force herself not to take in water.

Alarm flooded Tyrus when he saw the crimson tint on her face grow into an even deeper shade. Pushing his muscles for every ounce of speed he could, he whipped around the two Selks to reach her side again.

Mandy's head pounded against the back of her eyes, to the point her oxygen deprived brain thought they may pop out of her scull entirely. But that pain was nothing compared to the screaming of her lungs. Some kind of creature had been loosed inside them and was trying to claw their way out. Black began to edge her vision. She was going to die. She was ready for that outcome, but was peeved at herself for being stupid enough to put herself in this situation.

Then Tyrus was there. His strange face contorted in fear. Fear for her? That did not make sense. He was the one who had dragged her down here to drown. Right? He was trying to say something, but her ears were no longer working. His hands were on her face again, tighter than before. With him holding her up, Mandy focused in on his lips, trying to read what he was saying. B..ee..t? Ee...oay? Bree? Urg! Why could she not hear him?

Apparently Tyrus got tired of trying to communicate with her, because he hands suddenly left her face. One dug into her wrist and yanked her hand away from her mouth, while the other swung lower and swatted just below her ribs, forcing her diaphragm to contract. Mandy, with nothing preventing her mouth from opening, gasped and water rushed into her lungs.

Instantly her head stopped throbbing and the burning in her lungs eased. Her breathing smoothed out into an even cadence. Wait. Her eyes locked on the relieved face of her, previously believed, murderer. Mandy purposely sucked in a massive breath, allowing her lungs to expand fully. Paying attention to exactly what her body was doing she became further confused.

The air Tyrus had pressed into her lungs when they first dove below the surface could still be felt in her chest where it had settled. Mandy could feel the cool internal wind surrounding the water she was breathing and turning into air her body recognized and knew what to do with. It actually kind of tickled.

Mandy noticed she was starting to sink further down and snagged Tyrus's shoulder to keep her stationary. "How?" she gasped, less surprised that her words were intelligible than she ought to be. After everything she had experienced that day, speaking clearly was not landing high on her list of 'odd things that need explanations, right, the heck, now'.

Tyrus had transitioned from relief, to irritation. "Are you trying to kill yourself?" he barked at her. "I told you I could make it so you could come down here. Why in the great waters were you holding your breath?"

Before she could answer his obvious question, a dark fuzzy head with large, worried, brown eyes nudged him out of the way so she could look her friend over for herself. Without hesitation Mandy raised her hand and scratched Shannon's fur behind her ear. "I'm okay Shan. I don't know how," she said, lifting a brow at Tyrus before turning back, "but I'm okay."

A rumble from her other side drew her attention. Tristan was growling at Tyrus again, trying to make the man keep his distance. Kicking free of Shannon's inspection, Mandy glided up to the Selkie and placed a hand on his back. "It's alright." Swimming to where Tyrus had chosen to tread, his tail swaying back and forth without conscious effort, she kept her movement's steady, unhurried so she would not tire herself out.

"Whatever you did, thank you." Some of the tension in the Nereid's shoulders loosened. "What exactly did you do?" Mandy hedged. A small smile tipped the corner of Tyrus's mouth as he explained. "Ever heard the old wives tale "A kiss from a mermaid will save a sailor from drowning?"" Mandy nodded and out of the corner of her eye caught Shannon doing the same. "Well, you're experiencing the basis of that myth."

Tyrus swam closer. "It's called Mirroring. Every Nereid can do it as far as I know." he shrugged. "Not many get the chance to try though. As long as my breath is in your lungs, you will be able to survive what I can survive."

"How long does it last?" Mandy asked, her words sounding tinny in the water.

"Until you surface again, or I die I suppose, whichever comes first," he shrugged. "It's why I had to dive so far, so fast. If you made a dash for the surface we would have had to start this process over again." Looking around them like he had not just warped reality, he addressed the group as a whole. "We should get moving." He stared at a slightly calmer Tristan. "We are deep in your territory. I would rather not be gutted by enthusiastic pups trying to make a name for themselves in taking down the lone Nereid."

Tristan made a chuffing sound which Tyrus assumed was meant to be a laugh. Huh, he had never heard that sound from a Selkie before. Shaking off the thought he kicked his tail and led the rag-tag lot in the direction of home.

After about ten minutes of swimming, he looked over his shoulders and noticed that Mandy, goggles and flippers in place, was severely lagging behind the other more natural born swimmers. Flaring his dorsals and letting his tail fin curve, he smoothly flipped over the heads of the two Selkies and maneuvered to glide beside the struggling human. One look and he knew she was not going to be able to keep the pace he needed to set.

They did not have time to go back and drop her back off on land so he snagged one of her ankles on an upstroke, eliciting a yelp, and unclipped her first flipper. Before she could mount a proper protest, he had the other cumbersome piece of plastic off and was slinging her onto his back, careful not to let his spines scrape her. "You're too slow. Hang on." With a few strokes he was back in the lead and setting a much faster clip than before. Apparently, even he had slowed down for her without realizing it, and yet, he could not bring himself to regret having her along. It would keep the female Selkie in check and in turn the male. Or at least, that was what he told himself.

*I*t took several hours before the four of them were able to reach the heart of the Nereid territory. More than once they had to take cover from one patrol or another from both sides of the conflict. Until the alliance was made official, Tristan and Tyrus were in rare consensus that it would be wise to keep out of sight of both parties, so as not to cause further strife before the idea of peace was even broached.

The Selkie lands, logically, were situated closer to land than their scaled counter parts. Islands and various rock formations allowed them to function and defend their territory in their sea lion forms. There was plenty of fishing and shelter, and should the need ever arise, they were close enough to land for them to take advantage of the unfavorable environment for the Nereids, either for an offensive platform, or a place to retreat to that the enemy could not follow without a great deal of planning.

The Nereids, by contrast, preferred large reefs, and open ocean where their speed and agility could be used to greater advantage. Underwater trenches and caverns provided a few more secluded places of refuge, but it was not the first choice for the majority of the mer-folk. It did, however, mean that when they crossed the border with two Selkies and a human in tow, they were diving for cover much more frequently with the increased patrol units protecting the border and outer waters. Tyrus did not care to think of what they would have to contend with when they did reach the city.

He would have to stash the Skinners some-where. A series of caves he used to play in as a boy were his first choice. They would be out of the way but could easily escape through the canyons if need be. Maker willing, it would be an over-precaution.

The human would be odd, but would not start a... complete panic. If he was careful, and avoided the more populated squares, he should be able to reach his home without drawing too much attention. Tides, this was turning into a headache.

For Tristan's part, he was wound tighter than a spring the further they swam into enemy territory. He did not like the idea of being left behind while the Nereid had the opportunity to do whatever he pleased on his home turf. But at the same time, there was no way for him to accompany Tyrus and not draw the attention of the entire city. He supposed it was the first test of trust this fledgling alliance was going to face. Would Tyrus be true to his word and only go into the city to retrieve his sister, or would he come back with the rest of his squadron and imprison the daughter of the Lann and her guard?

As foreign as the concept was, Tristan, to his immense surprise, did trust Tyrus, son of Cassius. The pure, unabashed hope that had come over the seasoned soldier's face was not a look easily faked. He was still livid at his attempt to kill Shannon and would watch the man like a hawk whenever he was in proximity to any of his family. However, for now, he believed he would come through for them. Time would tell if his instincts were correct.

With fond memories, and practiced ease, Tyrus funneled his 'guests' into his childhood playground. "You should be safe in here while you wait," he said as they passed him to move deeper into the cave. "This place never failed to hide me when I was trying to duck my tutors. There is only one other person who knows about this place, and he has no reason to come down this way now" He pointed a finger towards the ceiling, dozens of stalactites pointed back at him. "If you need to go up for air, swim straight up hugging the side of the trench. There is about a thirty-foot gap between the top of the trench and the surface, there is no cover between those two points, so I would suggest you make that track as few times as possible.

Tristan nodded his head in acknowledgment. It was sound reasoning. Fortunately, they had surfaced not long before they came to the caves so Shannon and him should not have too much trouble staying down for a few hours. With any luck, they would be long gone back down the road to the Grotto before the issue of air would come into play.

Tyrus clenched and flexed his fingers, trying to rid himself of pent-up tension. The idea of working with his lifelong enemy was still sinking in. The unease was, oddly, a comfort, assuring him he had not completely lost his mind. "If things go well, I should be back in a little over an hour. You need to be ready to move out as soon as I get back."

An image flashed in his mind of Tyrus coming to the edge of the cave with the vague figure of a female Nereid in tow. In the vision, two selkies emerged from the cave and swam off into the distance. The image faded and Tyrus jerked back. He suddenly had a greater sympathy for his brother's discomfort for him Wading into his mind. He was used to being the one doing the diving, not having it done to him. The images were so vivid, he could hear the meaning behind them, even though no words had passed between them. Tristan would have them ready when he returned.

Was this how the Selkies communicated? No wonder they were able to coordinate so well in battle, if every one of them was the equivalent of a Wader. If they could match them in range...the thought was unsettling.

"I...I'll be back," he said, shaking off the unpleasantness of the moment, and swam for the opening, slinging Mandy onto his back like she weighed nothing more than a backpack. She clung as tight as a youngling as they sped for the city.

The capital city of Sitaltna rested at the bottom of an abyssal plain between three hills on the edge of a trench that stretched for miles to the north and south. These formations were the only natural defensive structures the city could boast of. The lack of light at this depth also helped to conceal the thriving metropolis.

The city was laid out in wide rings, descending in size as you moved closer to the center. Buildings of white or grey granite, varied in shape from squat, open space, columned structures, to towering spires like manmade stalagmites, to domed concert halls. The ridged lines of the architecture were both beautiful and intimidating. It was as though a stoic engineer and a free flow artist had been put in charge of the design. Neither could figure out who was in charge, and this was the compromise.

Where the buildings themselves lacked color, the people who made Sitaltna their home made up for it in spades. Nereids of every combination of color and scale pattern weaved in and out of the swim-ways like living May Day ribbons. Whatever source of light they were using only added to the glamour of the scene.

Holding tight to Mandy's arms Tyrus followed the rim of the gorge until he reached the eastern edge of the city. This section of town was not as heavily guarded as the rest for its proximity to the trench. The thinking was that anyone trying to breach the defenses from the trench would have to first contend with the many patrols in order to even have a chance of getting this close. The fact this was exactly what Tyrus, Mandy and the Selks had done was not lost on him. But this time at least, he was willing to let the matter go as it served his purposes. However, he did make a mental note to speak to his friend on the outer reach squadrons about the hole in their security when this mess was over.

The Eastside was not the best section of town due to the lack of guard presence. Add the fact Tyrus had a human remora latched onto his back and he made sure to stick to the back routes and out of the way passages as they wove their way inward. It took much longer to get where he wanted to go, but since they reached the home of Legatus Legionis Cassius without bumping into sentries or criminals alike, his efforts were well worth the extra time.

His childhood home, blessedly, was on the second most outer ring of Sitaltna, so they did not have much terrain to weave through in order to make it there. His father had gained enough station in his long career to merit a decent sized estate and space from his neighbors. Cassius was a very private man. The latter perk was what had finally made him except the manor a few years after his youngest son was born. Tyrus had spent the bulk of his life, before he went into full military service, within those walls, and when the sporadic leave time was granted to him, he still returned.

With Atticus living either with his squad alongside Tyrus or with the other officers, the estate was currently the permanent home of only two souls. The general himself, and his only daughter, Hadriana. The last he had heard from his father, the Legatus had been harassing the Selks in the eastern oceans. If they could avoid the staff, they would be golden.

The manor grounds were expansive. A grove of pristine seaweed grew evenly around the whole estate. Decorative coral and carved stone were strategically placed around the grounds to catch the eye of any passersby. The native fish and crustaceans scampered around, but the poor creatures that wandered into the house would soon become dinner.

The walls of the manor were rectangular, but all the edges were smooth and slightly rounded, so there were very few right angles. This gave the impression the entire building was made from one solid piece of stone. Wide, with two stories, like it's master, the house imposed on as much territory as it could on the ocean floor, but cared little for reaching towards the surface. Lamps were set at regular intervals to allow for light and to showcase the workmanship of the artisans who had made the tiny palace.

"Wow." Mandy said in awe. "You lived here?" Tyrus nodded, not feeling the question needed more of an answer than that. Readjusting his grip on her arms twined around his neck, he said. "Come on. Hadi's rooms are around the rear of the manor. If she is in her rooms, we should be able to get in through her balcony."

Mandy frowned. "Why not just go through the front door, if this is your house too?"

Tyrus chuckled as he kicked his tail, swimming for the back gardens, doing his best to keep to the shadows. "I am meant to be stationed with Atticus along the border. It is probably best to not have my father find out I was here at all until we find out for sure that my sister can be this Weaver person."

"You don't believe Tristan?"

"I trust a Selk about as much as a bull shark."

"Then why go through all this trouble?"

Tyrus paused for a moment before answering. "Because I am tired of killing and seeing my friends killed. Even if it is a long shot, I'll take any chance I can get at this point."

Tyrus ducked them behind a line of coral to watch for the guards he knew his father would post for Hadriana in his absence. Seeing his caution Mandy purposefully kept her voice low. "Tristan said you were one of the Nereid army's best warriors."

Tyrus smirked at the comment. "Just because I'm good at something does not mean I want it to be necessary my whole life, as it has been for my father, and his father, and his father. Soldiers will never be obsolete, but I do hope for the day when we are no longer a dire need."

He pointed up at the wide balcony spanning the length of the house between the two floors. "See the lights in the windows on the right?" he asked. Mandy bobbed her head. "That's Hadi's suite." He swung his companion from his back to his front, her flaxen hair trailing behind her, then flaring out around her, framing her face with gold. Tyrus shook off the unexpected distraction. "I have to move fast before any guards sweep by on their patrols. I need you to hold tight, so we will be as streamlined as possible."

Mandy grinned. "You got it, Flounder."

Tyrus raised a brow. "Flounder? You know what, never mind, just hold on tight." Wrapping his arms around her back and tucking her head into his neck, he took one last glance around the yard and surged up and across the yard. He was through the balcony doors with barely more than a ripple of a wake at his passing. First hurdle down. Turning around to the adjoining room, he faced his next challenge. At least this one greeted him with a smile.

Chapter Twenty-Four

$\mathcal{H}$adriana, daughter of Luciana, had been curled up in her swing-seat looking over her latest lap harp piece, there was something off in the second bridge that was bothering her, but she could not seem to put her finger on, when her brother decided to dive over her balcony and into her rooms at top speed. It was a pleasant surprise, but a surprise, nonetheless. The thin, strung together reeds of carved music tumbled off her lap in a clatter and she jolted from her favorite lounge nook.

Her heart felt like it was going to beat out of her chest in fear of a man suddenly in her rooms, where in the low currents were her guards! She was about to call out for them when her intruder released the strange looking person holding onto him, and she finally got a glimpse of his face. Fear turned to joy in an instant. "Tyrus!" she exclaimed racing forward to throw her arms around his neck laughing. His deep chuckle at her enthusiasm helped her believe he was actually here, instead of her conjuring him in a doze as she was prone to when tucked in her lounger.

"What are you doing here?" she asked, not at all angry at the turn her day had taken. She looked to the side and got a better look at the person, or rather woman, who had stormed the castle with him. Her appearance was incredibly odd. Her scales were a stark contrast of black, blue and pale cream. But they were so smooth it almost seemed as though she did not have scales at all. Perhaps the poor girl was sick like her. Glancing further down her body only solidified this deduction further. Her tail was split in two! At the sight she yelped, threw her hands over her mouth, and gave a few backward strokes to gain some distance. "Seaweed and sand-dollars, what happened to your tail?"

The woman gave a confused frown, then looked at her brother. Tyrus said something in a choppy language, and the girl laughed and said something back. Hadriana darted her eyes between the pair. The words were strange but a few of them did sound familiar. "Tyrus what is going on? Who is this woman? I thought you were not due back home for moons yet."

Tyrus swam forward and placed a hand on her shoulder to calm her. "It's alright Hadi. This is a...friend of mine, Amanda. Mandy this is my sister Hadriana." He spoke in Nereidite, but the yellow haired woman seemed to understand his meaning and smiled. Hadriana tilted her head. Strange as her appearance was, her smile lit up her face, accentuating her best features. She was quite lovely, in the bizarre way a lionfish was lovely, but pretty all the same. Hadi glanced sideways at her brother, suspicious, before spreading her tail fin to show off the multihued threads of color and gave a slight bow. If she was her brother's guest, she would be the picture of politeness, despite her poor start to their introduction.

Gesturing to the carved lounges padded with thick sponge and bound with vibrant cloth, Hadriana did her best to recover her bearings as hostess. She forced herself not to squeak when Mandy took her split tail, spread them further apart on a bend and then bringing them together again straight. Her arms followed a similar motion, to get her moving in the direction she wanted. The ends of her tail then fluttered until she swung her hips down onto the settee, her hands pushing the water to hold her down. The wide grin on Mandy's face at her accomplishment instantly endeared the strange woman to Hadriana. Anyone who could take joy in something as little as sitting down, was someone she wanted to know more.

Gathering the reed sheets she had dropped; she placed them in a thick hollow tube to protect them from damage. When they were safely back on her shelf she turned back to her brother. "I'll ask Kalani to bring us some sweets." She was about to knock on the gong that would summon her maid, when Tyrus's hand clenched around her wrist.

"No." he said, his voice devoid of the happiness that had lightened it a minute ago when he came through the door. "I don't want the servants to know I am here Hadi. I came to talk to you."

Hadriana's eyes widened. Following her brother's tugging she swam back to the half circle of seats and sat in her previous perch. The seriousness in his tone, sharpened her own words when she asked, "What's going on Tyrus? Are you in trouble?"

Tyrus tilted his head in thought as he sat next to Mandy. "No. Well...Not yet anyway."

Hadi narrowed her gaze. "That's not helpful, Ty." She was starting to get irritated at his avoiding the subject.

"I need your help, Hadi."

"With?"

"Ending the war." he said bluntly. Hadriana laughed. He could not be serious. She was the last person that belonged in a battle.

"If I was capable of fighting, I would have joined the war medics years ago. We both know that is far beyond my capabilities." She was honestly a little insulted he would bring this up to her. Tyrus knew how much it irritated her that she could not venture much farther than the local market without being too weary to do anything for hours afterward. She had made her peace with her health a long time ago. There was no changing it now.

But Tyrus was shaking his head. "I would never ask you to fight, but I have discovered something that you may be suited for that would aid our people far more than another spear ever could."

This intrigued Hadi. She motioned for him to continue. Poor Mandy was so out of the loop all she could do was glance between the two siblings, like a tennis match being commentated on in Chinese.

For his part Tyrus did his best to explain what had happened in the last few days. Everything from the death of his squad-mates, his posting on land, the confrontation with the Selkies, his capture by them and the humans, to the possibly the greatest discovery to have happened in decades.

Hadriana sat quietly and listened, only interrupting for clarification on one point or another. When Tyrus seemed to come to a stop in his tale, she ran her fingers through her black hair, not caring that it tangled the braids keeping it out of her face. "So many years at war, for the wrong purpose." Lifting her head, she met her brother's tense eyes. "Have you told Father?"

"No." he said definitively. "You know he would never except something like this without proof."

"Well, how do we prove it to him then? There must be a way. If this is true than our men, and the Selks for that matter, are dying for no reason other than it is what we have done for generations."

It was here Tyrus hesitated. He was not sure how his sister was going to react to what he had to say next. Sensing his dilemma, Mandy rested a hand on his scaled forearm and with a confident smile, gave him a nod of encouragement. Taking a deep breath Tyrus forced himself to plunge into the reason he had risked coming into the heart of the city.

"Hadriana." She sat up straighter. Tyrus did not use her full name unless he was truly serious about something. "I had the Selks explain who would be best suited to be trained as one of these Weavers. The description of the ideal pupil fit you exactly."

Hadriana blanched. "Me?" Seeing her start to get spooked, Tyrus held up a hand to stay her.

"It's why I came to Sitaltna. I want you to come back with me Hadi."

"Leave the manor!" She was ashamed to admit it but fear shot through the young Nereid woman. "I...I can't Ty. I can't my heart... "

"Would not be an issue." he interrupted. "According to Miriam, being a Weaver is more about mental strength than physical. And you are one of the smartest people I know Hadriana." Rising from his seat he put his hands on her shoulders. A small whimper escaped her as the weight settled. "If I could do it myself Hadi, I would, but I'm not suited. You are smart, kind, stubborn as crab." That was rewarded with a strangled laugh. Tyrus grew serious once more. "But most importantly you care about people more than anything," he tipped her chin up. "Even the Selkies."

"I have never heard you utter one harsh word against them, despite Atticus and I spouting our mouths off. You are a mediator. I can think of no one else better suited for this." Gripping her arms tighter, his voice strained at the fervor of his words. "I have seen how much it pains you not being able to help our people because of your body betraying you. This is your chance to help not only our own kind, but to bring peace between an old enemy. Please, I know you can do this Hadi. Please help. Say you'll try."

Hadriana felt the weight of his words. Her breathing became labored and she suddenly felt slightly woozy. It was like her body was taunting her for even considering doing something so outrageous. It was Tyrus's next words which quenched her resolve to iron. They were words she would remember for years to come. "The Maker has a habit of drawing his most prominent warriors, from the weakest of souls. If you do not believe in your own strength, then trust in His."

Hadriana straightened. Determination blazed in her eyes. She did not know how, but if this was what was being asked of her then she would face it with her head held high. Her breathing still shaky, her voice still small she asked, "When do we leave?"

Chapter Twenty-Five

Mandy had sat in silence while Tyrus explained things to his sister. She had not understood a word of the exchange beyond a few names she recognized popping up here and there, but she did not mind much. Listening to the two of them talk was like listening to an acapella performance. The words had the shape similar to Italian, but the way they were pronounced was like they were partially singing. Whether the tone of the word changed the meaning or not, she did not know. She made a mental note to ask Tyrus later.

A stray thought had Mandy pushing down a chuckle. The musical sway of the conversation had a mesmerizing effect. Her mood rose and dipped slightly on their inflection the same way a song in her own language was capable of doing. It made her wonder what kind of conversation overheard by ancient sailors had born the myth of sirens luring men to their death. Based on what she was hearing, it was quite possible some innocent Nereid woman could have been talking about a new hairstyle, or what they were making for dinner and accidentally enthralled the workmen of a passing ship. Imagining a besotted seaman launching himself overboard at the unsuspecting woman, in love with their words on the price of sea cucumbers, and Mandy was swallowing a howl of giggles. A truly unfortunate misunderstanding indeed.

"Good gracious I'm tired, if this is what I'm entertaining myself with," she thought, then made a mental shrug. Who was she kidding? Her thoughts would be just as bizarre and random on a fully rested brain. Mandy tried to get her mind to focus on the matter at hand. Not an easy task when you could not follow the conversation beyond the facial expressions. She tried anyway.

Glancing between the two Nereids she tried to see the family resemblance. Mandy studied them closely, and saw they had the same eyes, bright green, and like her brother, the color brought the emerald shades in Hadriana's scales to the forefront. Their smiles were similar as well, wide and unabashed. Mandy had been startled when she saw the expression on Tyrus's face when he reunited with his sister. It was a good smile. Made him seem less likely to tear someone apart with his bare hands.

Once their midnight black hair was taken into account, there was not much else that hinted at their shared parentage. Tyrus was all sharp angles, cutting ridges, bound together with a whiplike strength.

Hadriana on the other hand had a rounder, heart shaped face, a pert nose, full lips comfortable with her gentle smile, and wide eyes just shy of being too big for her face. With her raven hair flowing around her face and down her back, Hadi looked like an artist's perfect picture of a mermaid.

Like her brother her scales were blue and green, but where Tyrus's were sapphires in a shadowed forest, Hadriana's were spring grass and bluebells. Bright, clean...happy. Even her fins were soft and delicate, like someone had draped chiffon to frame her perfectly. A similar, lightweight material twined around her torso, folded so as not to interfere with her gills along her ribs. Tiny, flower-like stitches were embroidered halfway down her waist and then added sporadically down as the fabric split into four tails down the vest like dress. The soft fabric only added to the ethereal image of the mythical creature she was.

The conversation seemed to be coming to a close. The expression on the young woman's face was immovable, almost stern. *"So the flower had a few thorns,"* Mandy thought. Good, she might need them before this little adventure was done.

Hadriana began flitting around her room gathering things she would need for a journey. Tyrus swam back over to where Mandy was sitting. She was glad she had remembered to grab a weight belt. Otherwise, her buoyant self would be floating all around the room, with her flapping her arms like a crazed bird trying to stay in the general area of where she wanted.

"I take it she agreed?" Mandy asked, as he took the seat next to her. He nodded. "Yes. Once she gathers what she needs, we will head back to the others and then onto the Selkie lands." His fingers clawed at his hair, and Mandy saw his barbs lift slightly in his frustration.

"You're doing the right thing," she stated, trying to reassure him of that fact. He only nodded and watched his sister buzz around in her hurry. She could tell he was worried. Deciding it was better to change the subject, she asked, "Does your sister not speak English?" Snorting, Tyrus looked at her sideways.

"You have a habit of asking the most out of-the-dark questions, at random."

"What?" She exclaimed, "You speak English perfectly. I assumed it was common for you to learn it in case you ran into humans." He laughed at her reasoning, drawing Hadi's attention before she went back to her work.

"The human language that is most common in the land closest to our territory, in this case English, is taught in schools from a very young age. But unless you are in a position that takes you on land often, not many Nereids get a chance to use it, so..." He held his hands in a shrug.

"Use it or lose it." Mandy said flatly. "That's what my high school Spanish teacher told me. He was right of course. That is somewhat comforting to know I am not the only one who did not retain something I studied for four years."

Tyrus bumped her shoulder with his. "You seem to get by with that finger thing you do with your friend."

"ASL?" she asked.

"Is that what this is called." He waved his fingers in random patterns as he said this. Mandy threw a hand over her mouth to contain the snicker when he accidentally formed a *very* rude word. Noticing her expression Tyrus asked suspiciously. "What?"

"Oh nothing," she said innocently. "You should use that sign the next time you see Zeke. He will love it."

"Is that so?"

Mandy nodded solemnly, the tips of her mouth twitching upward. "Oh yes. It is a wonderful greeting."

"Really? Well then, I shall have to greet the Skinner when I get back to the caves." He countered raising an eyebrow. Mandy lost it, nearly falling off the settee. Only the water baring most of her weight kept her from spiraling on the floor. "Not if you want to keep your hands. Shannon will think it is funny, but I'm not sure Tristan is ready to pass up the excuse to pummel you."

Tyrus shrugged one shoulder and put some distance between them. "I would probably do the same if the roles were reversed." He turned his head to look her in the eye and said seriously. "I am surprised you are not as angry as he is."

The smile dropped from Mandy's face. She suddenly found her hands very interesting. "I am. But I am trying not to be."

"Why make the effort?" he asked, genuinely curious about her answer.

"For the same reason you are working with your lifetime enemy. Peace. If the Nereids and Selkies can find a way to work together instead of tearing each other apart, then there would be no reason for Shannon to be sequestered in the Grotto." She clenched her fingers together until her knuckles were white. "Maybe...I wouldn't have to lose my sister."

Tyrus opened his mouth to reply, but was stalled by Hadriana, bag slung across her back, swimming up to the pair and declaring., "I am ready." Her expression was entirely serious, however her soft face looked so innocent it had the same impact of a five-year-old telling his mother he was going to brave kindergarten. Mandy could not help but smile at the woman. She was quickly growing to like Tyrus's sister.

You could see a physical change come over Tyrus as he shifted into the mindset of a soldier. It was a harsh reminder that was exactly what he was. Studying his frame, Mandy was suddenly extremely glad that, at least for the moment, they were allies. If she had anything to say on the matter, it would stay that way.

"Are we going out the same way we came in?" Mandy asked, rising to float between the two Nereids. Holding a hand up to stay them, Tyrus moved to the door of the balcony to survey the back gardens. He was not thrilled with what he saw.

When he and Mandy had first come through it must have been during a shift change in the guard post. What before had been an abandoned array of various aquatic shrubbery was now manned by not one but two armed soldiers from Cassius's estate. It had been many years since he had lived in the manor, so he was not familiar with these specific guards. However, knowing his father they would be well trained and not evaded without some sort of plan. That was not taking into the fact he had Mandy and his sister in tow. Neither of which would be able to swim very fast.

Holding back a growl of frustration, Tyrus turned back to the two women. It was his responsibility to get them out safely. It would be tricky, but he would find a way to make it happen. He had to. "The garden is no longer an option," he said with no room for argument. "How many staff are inside the house today, do you know?"

Hadriana's brow furrowed in thought. "We are not expecting any guests and with just me in the house right now, those working are at a bare minimum. I believe it is just the kitchen staff, a handful of maids, the two grounds keepers, the four stable hands, three soldiers on the interior and the housekeeper." She ticked off her fingers going over the count in her mind. She snapped as she realized who she was missing. "The messenger relays should be wandering somewhere below, if the housekeeper has not put them to work. They tend to get into mischief if they get too bored," she said with an amused grin. Hadriana mentally went down her list again, then nodded in satisfaction. "Yes, that's everyone in the house. It may even be fewer than that. It is market day, so some may have gone into town for the weeks' previsions."

Tyrus nodded, running through the layout of the manor in his mind. If his sister was correct, and on these details, she always was, then they should be able to manage getting out without too much trouble as long as they could avoid the servants who were going about their chores.

"Alright," he stated making his decision, "I say we make for the library. We can head out one of the side windows. There should be fewer guards on that side of the house, but we have to move quickly. Hadi has been on her own for a while now, and I would rather not run into someone trying to check on..."

He was stopped mid-sentence by an all-to-familiar voice. "Hadriana!" Hadi's eyes went wide as she heard her name called. Mandy looked between the siblings, not liking the sudden apprehension flooding both of their faces. "Who is that?" She whispered to Tyrus.

His eyes darted to the door as the call came again, this time closer, then around the room for any hiding place that would not be glaringly obvious. He only partially heard Mandy's question, answering her automatically, while his mind was busy elsewhere. "It's Atticus. My brother, and squadron commander." Now Mandy's eyes were saucers.

"Why is he here?" Hadi squeaked. "I thought he was posted on the eastern border..." She waved her hand frantically up and down his frame. "With you!"

"I have been stuck on land the last few weeks, how am I supposed to know that? But he cannot find out I am here."

Hadriana bobbed her head so quickly Mandy was surprised it did not pop off its hinge. The Nereid woman gripped both their shoulders and shoved them towards the corner. Child's play where Mandy was concerned, but a more difficult task with her brother who was more than a head taller than her. Her point was made, however, and reenforced by her hissing through clenched teeth. "Get in the wardrobe! I'll find a way to get rid of him so you can slip out. With any luck I will follow shortly after."

While not the most original hiding place, it was readily available. Tyrus and Mandy crammed themselves in and shut the door behind them just as a heavy fist pounded on the door to the suite. Atticus, not the most patient individual on the best of days, did not wait for his sister to answer his hammering, but simply bouldered his way in.

"Here you are Sister. Did you not hear me calling?" His voice carried well through the wardrobe door, hardly muffled at all. Hadriana's bell chime tone answered her eldest brother's crashing cymbals. "I believe the entire manor heard you Atticus. I just did not see the point in wearing myself out shouting back to you when you were obviously seeking me out." She swam forward and gave him a hug. "Not that I mind the surprise, but what are you doing here? I thought it would be moons yet before you could come home."

Atticus dropped the smile that had sprouted on his face when greeting his sister. "I lost three of my men. We were recalled so they could... be replaced." His tone left no doubt as to his opinion of them trading out the men he had lost.

Hadriana's reply was soft with sympathy. "I am so sorry Atticus. That is awful. How is Tyrus taking it? Is he with you?" Tyrus's eyebrows rose, he wondered how long his sister had been so good an actress. She was good, but his brother was no fool. He only hoped it would be enough to escape without have to confront the man.

"I ordered Tyrus to stay behind on land. He will return when he has dealt with the skinner who butchered our men."

"I'm sure he will perform his duty with excellence as always. With three men gone, you here, and

Tyrus on land, you must be spread pretty thin. Who did you have stay with him?"

Atticus looked a bit uncomfortable as he went to one of the tables to snag one of the snacks a maid had placed there earlier in the morning. "Tyrus is perfectly capable of handling one Selkie dog on his own."

Hadriana let her mouth drop. "Atticus! You left him up there, on land, by himself? Why in the great tides would you leave him without any aid."

Atticus, instead of admitting his shortsighted-ness, got angry. "It is one skinner Hadriana. Have a little faith in our brother, he will be fine."

"A Selkie who can best Damien is hardly someone to take lightly." Atticus froze, but Hadriana did not notice. "You could have at least let Magnus stay with him. He would have done it in a heartbeat, had you allowed him to." Hadriana crossed her arms and flicked the end of her tail in irritation. Even though she knew Tyrus was, technically safe, she did not approve of Atticus leaving him out to hang like he had.

Atticus's next words were low, a gravelly hiss tingeing the edge. "How did you know Damien was among the dead?"

Hadriana stilled. Her mind raced to cover the mistake. "He was missing from the group when you arrived at the manor." She hedged, but the centurion was already shaking his head. "The men went straight to the barracks, and I came in through the front entrance. You would have had no way to see my men at all, let alone known who was missing from our ranks." One stroke of his tail and he was looming over the smaller woman, his eyes narrowed in suspicion. "How did you know Damien was among the dead, Hadriana?" he asked again.

Hadi had never seen her brother in this light. Sure he was grouchy, and he had a temper, but she had never been afraid of the man before. Her knowledge of where their brother was and what he was doing in actuality, only added to her apprehension. "I... I," she stammered her mind going utterly blank. Instinctively, she maneuvered so her body was blocking the path to the wardrobe.

It was probably the worst thing she could have done in the situation. Atticus saw the movement and followed the line back to the offending piece of furniture. Shouldering his sister aside he charged at the wardrobe, yanked open the door, and watched in bewildered shock as his little brother came tumbling out with...a human. Why in the world was a human here? How did she get inside the walls? Why was Tyrus hiding her? Why was he here himself in the first place when he was meant to be hunting down the Selkie scum?

Tyrus righted himself immediately and placed himself in front of Mandy, blocking his brother's view of her. He knew Atticus had already seen her, but there was no use making him dwell on her for a moment longer than necessary. His efforts didn't seem to matter much. Atticus's gaze flicked between him and the human. Gone was his elder brother, in his place the stern, brutal centurion emerged.

"I will address you disobeying orders and abandoning your post later Tyrus. First, why is there a human in our sister's rooms?" He did not shout, he did not growl; he spoke clearly, and evenly. That, more than anything, unnerved Tyrus. An irate Atticus was unsettling, a calm and quiet Atticus was down-right terrifying.

Tyrus squared his shoulders. He was already waist deep in this mess, might as well dive in fully. "I have found a way to stop all this Atticus, ad way to protect our people and not have to fight the Selkies. They are willing to teach us how to protect ourselves from the human world." Atticus's gills flared wide as he sucked in a sharp breath at his brother's words. Fire simmered in his eyes. Tyrus saw this and his heart sank. This was the very situation he had been hoping to avoid. Out of all of them, Atticus was the most like their father, and like their father, Tyrus knew his brother would not listen, not without proof. He had to try though. "We don't have to fight them," he insisted. "We had it wrong, this whole time it wasn't the..."

With every word Atticus' expression twisted, horror, confusion, betrayal...rage, until finally he had heard enough. "You are working...with...the Skinners." Tyrus winced at the slur. He had heard his brother say it thousands of times, he had used it himself just as often. But hearing it now, knowing what he did, it rang differently this time. Did he sound that full of hatred when he spoke of the Selks? How long had that bitterness been festering? Had he ever not sounded like that? Important questions, and ones he intended to answer, but now was not the time.

His commander, now that he had locked onto the fact he was consorting with Selkies, would be deaf to anything else that came out of his mouth. Already he could see the fury and hatred Atticus held for the Selks blazing over him and lashing out at Tyrus. They had to get out of here, out of the city. Right now.

His eyes darted over his brother's shoulder and locked on Hadi. She looked so small in the face of Atticus's anger. Clutching her bag to her chest, twisting the rope in her grip. He doubted she had ever seen Atticus like this, and he hoped she never had to again.

Putting a palm on her stomach, Tyrus pushed Mandy back toward the balcony doors as he spoke to his sister. "Hadi, take Mandy and get out of the city. She knows where to go." he said firmly, his stare honing in on Atticus, on his opponent. "I'll catch up when I can."

"But..." Hadi chirped.

"Go, Hadi." He barked at the same time Atticus ordered. "Don't move Hadriana!"

For a few heartbeats Hadi was frozen with indecision as to which brother she should listen to, but in the end, she knew what her choice would be. It was the only one she could make. Swimming high toward the ceiling she arced over the two men and then glided for the doors. Mandy was already moving, letting her body fall into the current of the water so she didn't have to fight so hard. For a human, the woman was an excellent swimmer and was going to make darn sure she was not the one to slow them down.

As feet and tail disappeared over the balcony edge, Atticus let out a war cry that no doubt was heard in every corner of the house, "Traitor!" he roared, and launched at his brother. Tyrus was ready. With a twitch of a fin and a tilt of his body, he angled just right so his brother's momentum carried him past, the blow not anywhere near making connection. Keeping his barbs flat, Tyrus twisted, and unleashed a brutal combination on his brothers kidneys, ribs and the edge of his gills. His scales protected him to a certain degree, but not entirely.

Staggering from the blows, Atticus whipped his tail around, the barbs in the end of the navy-blue fin barely missing Tyrus's face, but nicking the edge of his hip. A thin stream of blood floated into the water. The salt stinging the wound and bringing Tyrus's mind into focus. He had been holding back so far, not wanting to truly bring harm to his brother. He knew why Atticus was doing this, he even respected his desire to punish...a traitor. But he made a vital mistake with that last strike.

The barb-strike had been aimed at his face and neck. Had he not moved when he did, Tyrus would be dead right now. Atticus was in the unwavering grip of his temper, and he was angling for the kill. If that was the way his brother was going to play, fully conscious or not, then he could not afford to do anything but match his effort. Not if he was going to survive to help his sister and, much as he hated to admit it, the Selkies as well. There was no other choice. Tyrus gritted his teeth, and flared his barbs.

He was playing for keeps.

Chapter Twenty-Six

Grabbing the edge of Hadriana's small table he hurled the lightweight piece of furniture end over end at his brother. The resistance of the water against the flat surface stalled its progress, until the momentum from the spin of the edge caught up with it. Atticus, thrown off by the erratic flight of the table, misjudged where it was going to go and ended up with it slamming into his right side.

With furniture flying about the room it gave Tyrus time to drift back a few strokes, gaining some distance from his brother. Using the time he had bought himself, he reached over his shoulder to the back side of his armor. Pulling out the narrow silver rod from the concealed sheath, Tyrus flicked his wrist and brought his weapon to bare.

When released the metal staff expanded from something barely longer than his forearm to a span of over six feet. The length of it was not smooth but rippled with textures, like a stone cast in silver, so as to provide grip from anywhere. The end was slightly thicker than the rest of the staff with three woven rings providing a blunter edge in contrast to the opposite end of the staff. Three prongs, slim but sturdy carved to tapered points. These points, unlike the rest of the weapon were glassy smooth, meant to slice clean through armor, body and bone alike, then withdraw with rapid speed.

The trident had long been associated with the merfolk, and for good reason. It was one of the few weapons that could operate in water without the current being a hinderance. As such, most soldiers were taught from day one of training how to use one. Some had more talent with the weapon than others. Both of Cassius's sons fell into that category. He had taught them both well, but unfortunately for Atticus...Tyrus had been the better student.

Before he lost the advantage of his brother's vision being blocked Tyrus surged upward then cut immediately down at a harsh angle. Letting his dive carry him down and around his opponent, when he was mere feet from the centurion, Tyrus thrust the head of the trident at Atticus's shoulder. The clang of metal on metal rang through the room. Though slowed by surprise, Atticus had also used the momentary cover to draw his own trident from his back. He was not fast enough to strike out, but he did manage to bring the shaft to bear on the cross piece of the thorns and redirect the blow backward. He then tried to bring the butt end down on an intercepting arc to Tyrus's dive, aiming for his head. Tyrus, ready for this parry, slithered through the space between Atticus and the floor like an eel.

Coming around to the front, Tyrus spun and lashed out at Atticus's torso, when contact was not made, he whipped the shaft back to defend against the next onslaught of blows from his brother. They had spent hours, days, years sparing with each other. They knew the others' patterns nearly as well as they did their own. The clash and ring of the fight was like church bells and battle drums colliding in one room: dreadful music. But unlike when they practiced their trade as children, or in the ranks of the army as men, today, Tyrus could not afford to delay any longer than he had to.

So, on his brother's next forward thrust, Tyrus instead of deflecting as was the safer and frankly smarter choice, he tipped the trident until it was vertical, spreading his hands wide, he caught the middle of his staff in the thorns striking at his chest. Before Atticus could react, he yanked his staff around a full circle, taking the locked trident with him, and drove his weapon into the ground, burying the head.

Using the jammed trident as a fulcrum, Tyrus whipped his entire body around to slam his tail, barbs flared into his brother's side. Atticus went flying across the room at the impact and crashed into the frame of

Hadriana's bed with a groan. Blood pooled more heavily in the water. Tyrus had struck true.

He watched as Atticus tried to rise, to engage again, but his wounds proved to be too much even for the colossal Nereid. Seeing his brother brought so low...by his own hand...flooded Tyrus with guilt, remorse and more anger than he cared to admit. It should never have come to this! They should be fighting together, as they had their whole lives, not thrashing each other until one was bleeding and could not move. It was not right.

However, amongst all the pain, and anger, and confusion, there was one feeling which permeated them all and allowed Tyrus to turn for the doors and his escape. Conviction. Despite his brother's reaction, Tyrus knew he was doing the right thing, for him, for his family, for his people. If he was the only one that understood that for now, well, it was a place to start.

"I have not betrayed our people, Atticus." he said over his shoulder and prayed his brother would remember his words when his head was cooler. "I am trying to save them, same as you. The only difference is the way we are going about it. I hope you will understand. One day." With one last look behind him he shot out the doors and over the balcony. Now that he was on his own, the sentries in the garden were little more of a challenge than children with big sticks.

Putting on as much speed as he could, Tyrus followed the path he thought was the most likely one his sister would take to get out of the city. His lips tipped up when he spotted the figures of two women, one Nereid, one Human. He knew his sister a bit too well. Mandy did not have fins, and Hadriana had never been in good enough health to ever become an especially skilled swimmer, so they were not making as much progress as he was comfortable with.

Grabbing Mandy around the waist and his sister under the arm, he began towing them as best he could to get some more speed. "The guards will find Atticus in no time; we have to move faster."

"Is he...?" Hadriana's words choked off at the end, not finishing the question she desperately needed to know, but could not make herself ask. Fortunately, Tyrus could assuage her fears. "He's alive," he said firmly, "Which is exactly why we need to get out of the city, before he can get anybody organized. Reassured, Hadriana nodded then redoubled her efforts.

They wove in and out of the various homes and businesses, dodging people going about their normal day, soldiers and wild sea life. When the homes and buildings began to thin out into open ocean and then the rock formations of the trench, Tyrus's heart lightened. They were going to make it. They were going to be able to escape without him having to harm any more of his brethren. That faint hope was dashed when a painfully familiar silhouette rose from behind an outcropping. To make a bad situation worse, the Selks, having seen him from their vantage point in the cave, had swum out to meet the trio.

Magnus stood like living lightning, yellow and white scales running in jagged strips through jet black, his trident fully extended and at the ready. His eyes darted between Tyrus and Hadriana, the human, and finally the Selkies. Confusion warred with violence in the gaze he leveled on Tyrus. His voice was cold when he finally spoke. "I was going to ask why I would have been ordered to capture you at any cost, even death. I thought Atticus had lost his mind... finally snapped, because that was the only reason he would be spouting the nonsense he was." He swung back and forth between Tyrus and the Selkies once more. "I guess you were the one who has lost it. Selkies Ty? Really?"

Moving in front of the women Tyrus held up a hand in placation. "Please, Magnus. I know how bad this looks; you have to trust me. I have a good reason, but there is no time to explain right now. The city guard will be right on our tails, and I have to get them out of here."

Magnus gripped his trident tighter, preparing to bar the way. Tristan began moving to engage the Nereid, but Tyrus jabbed a finger at him and shouted. "Don't touch him!" He was not going to watch another of his family be hurt today.

Magnus sneered. "Not going to give your new friend permission to kill me, Ty?"

Tyrus glared at his friend. "I would kill anyone who tried to hurt you Magnus. You are my friend, my brother. That has not changed."

"Hard to believe when Atticus, your brother, was found swimming in his own blood."

Tyrus swiped a hand at the accusation, "Atticus started that fight not me! I would have left in peace had he allowed it, but you know how stubborn he is. There was no way he was going to listen to anybody once he had made his mind up that I was a traitor."

"Aren't you?" Magnus hissed, "From the looks of things, that is exactly what you are."

"You know me better than that Magnus. You know *me*. I would never do anything to harm our people. I am trying to save them from war. From a useless war."

"Useless! You are the first to tell me we fight for the Nereids surviv-"

"Magnus!" His friend blanched at the bite to his voice, but Tyrus pressed on. "I promise, I will explain everything if you give me the chance. But now is, not...the...time. Trust me Magnus. I am no traitor. I am still the same man I was when we met last. I know what I am doing." He dared to swim closer. It seemed his friend was just as hesitant to fight him as he was. Tyrus gripped Magnus's shoulder and looked him square in the eye, letting him see the certainty there. "Trust me," he pleaded, his voice low enough so only Magnus could hear.

Magnus's lips pressed tight together, his brows so furrowed they almost touched. At last he released his tension and jerked his head behind him to the rest of the trench. "Go. I'll redirect anyone coming this way."

Tyrus could have sunk to the floor in relief, but he could not afford to lose the advantage his friend was offering. He squeezed his shoulder. Words strained with checked emotion he said, "Thank you."

"I expect that explanation, Ty."

Tyrus grinned and nodded. Magnus tipped his head again. "Get out of here before I become sane again."

Laughing more with an excess of built-up stress than any humor, he waved the two women forward and got the Selkies moving away from Sitaltna. It gave him comfort knowing he had one friend remaining at his back at least.

●

*T*he mismatched group of five swam in silence for hours. What was there to say? Their actions were changing the course of two cultures, of history itself. It was a burden not one of them was certain they could carry, but they would do their best to shoulder it with the respect it deserved.

Shannon could not believe it was only a few weeks ago that the most she had to worry about was dropping the trays of fish when pulling out breakfast for the animals at the Marine Center. Her life had been drastically normal. Normal, but good. She had a Mama she adored, friends who were more like family, and work she enjoyed doing every day. Now, while her life was different, radically different, upon quiet reflection she realized she would not change a single thing.

Closing her eyes, she tipped her flipper making her body spin in a graceful twirl, loving the feel of the water surrounding her. As much turmoil as she knew was ahead of her, Shannon was at peace. She was exactly where she was supposed to be, doing exactly what she was called to do, alongside the people, old and new, who meant the world to her.

The moment Shannon had slipped into her coat; she found a piece of herself that had been missing for so long. Her life had tipped completely upside down, yet there are times in life where it is necessary for things to be turned on their end, when the status quo must be challenged, if not overthrown.

Yes, she had a good life in Shelter Bay. Yes, had things stayed the same, she could have been happy. But, it was also true she would not have the answers she had been searching for the majority of her normal life. Her father would have remained a distant memory. Miriam, Kent, her Clan, faces she would call precious now, would never have had the chance to even become strangers.

Her gaze drifted to the Selkie who swam beside her, Tristan, strong, steady, honorable Tristan. Shannon had no doubt he would have continued to guard her as he did now, making that normal life possible. However, without her putting on her coat, without this change of course, she would never have known the remarkable man who had willingly taken up that mantel. The one who put in the effort to learn her language even if he never got to use it. The one who could make her laugh when she was about to cry. The one who defended her right for knowledge of her past, and her future.

Now, Shannon and her companions swam toward the edge of yet another change in the current. As somewhat of an outsider, the sting was less harsh for Shannon than it was for the others. As it will be for those that awaited them at the Grotto. It would not be easy. It would likely take longer and demand more pain and effort than any of them knew. But, like the day she had first slipped her arm in that fitted sleeve, this was a change that was necessary. A change which brought with it a chance for peace, where there was none before.

Crossing the border into Selkie territory, Shannon truly understood, for the first time, the choice her dad had made when he stayed behind to protect their people. There are some things in life that are worth the sacrifice. All wanted what was best for their people, and if this fragile deal they struck with a man, who had initially meant her harm, could bring about a reality where her worlds were one and the same; that was a crusade Shannon would happily enter. That was effort and sacrifice Shannon would take on without complaint. As far as she was concerned, it was just another cost of the coat.

One, she would gladly pay.

Pronunciation Guide

*A*ilis *C*allaghan: (A-lish) (Selkie) Weaver of the Eastern Atlantic clan, and mother of Lyra.

*A*manda *L*uis: (Human) Known as Mandy. She is Shannon's best friend.

*A*ngus *H*arrok: (Selkie) Commander of the Bacainn, mentor of Tristan and father of Kent.

*A*nita *R*owle: (Human) Eoin's wife and Shannon's mother.

*A*tticus son of *C*assius: (Nereid) Centurion. Brother of both Tyrus and Hadriana.

*B*acainn: (Bah-Cane) Gaelic word which means "barrier" or "obstruction". A title for the elite warriors among the Selkies.

*C*assius son of *C*ato: (Nereid) Legatos Legionis for the Nereids. Father of Atticus, Hadriana and Tyrus

$\mathcal{E}$ion $\mathcal{R}$owle: (Eee-on) (Selkie) Father of Shannon, brother of Chief Nolan, and Lann of the East Atlantic clan.

$\mathcal{E}$oghan $\mathcal{R}$owle: (Oh-when) (Selkie) Son of Chief Nolan and Lady Fiona, brother of Miriam, cousin of Shannon, and heir to the clan.

$\mathcal{E}$zekiel $\mathcal{T}$immons: (Human) Known as Zeke. Marine biologist at the Shelter Bay Marine Center, and self-appointed big brother of both Shannon and Mandy.

$\mathcal{F}$iona $\mathcal{R}$owle: (Selkie) Wife of Chief Nolan, mother of Miriam and Eoghan, Aunt of Shannon, and Lady of the Grotto.

$\mathcal{H}$adriana daughter of $\mathcal{L}$uciana: (Had-Ree-Ana) (Nereid) Noble-woman of the Nereids, Daughter of Cassius, sister to Atticus and Tyrus.

$\mathcal{K}$ent $\mathcal{H}$arrok: (Selkie) Member of the Reidh, son of Angus and best friend of Tristan.

$\mathcal{L}$ann: (Lawn) Gaelic word meaning "blade" A title given to the greatest warrior in a Selkie clan.

$\mathcal{L}$egatos $\mathcal{L}$egionis: The rank of general in the Nereid army.

$\mathcal{L}$yra $\mathcal{C}$allaghan: (Selkie) Daughter of the clan Weaver.

$\mathcal{M}$agnus son of $\mathcal{R}$emus: (Nereid) Best friend of Tyrus

*M*iriam *R*owle: (Selkie) Daughter of Chief Nolan and Lady Fiona, sister of Eoghan and cousin of Shannon.

Nolan Rowle: Chief of the East Atlantic clan, husband of Fiona, father of Eoghan and Miriam, brother of Eion, and uncle of Shannon.

*N*ereid: (Near-Add) Fully scaled from head to tail, these ancient creatures are the basis for the mermaid myth. When in their natural environment Nereids have long tails ending in powerful fins, while their upper body is more humanoid in appearance. Gills along their sides allow them to stay underwater for as long as they desire. When they choose to, they have the ability to shed their scales and appear human when walking on land. Nereids tend to be much taller than their soil-bound counterparts. As ocean dwelling creatures, they are only able to tolerate a short amount of time on shore. Most can stand approximately three days before it becomes too painful, and they must return to the ocean. After they have recovered sufficiently, they may return to land if they wish. However, the majority choose to spend their lives below the waves.

*R*alph *H*enesey: (Human) Husband of Rosemary, father of Anita and Grandfather of Shannon.

*R*eidh: (Ray-D) Gaelic word meaning "Ready". A title for the Selkie warriors who choose to remain in their seal form the majority of the time. This enables them to shift back and forth with as little time as possible.

Rosemary **H**enesey: (Human) Wife of Ralph, mother of Anita, and grandmother of Shannon.

Selkie: A person who possesses the ability to put on the coat of a seal, and when entering the water they turn into a seal. These individuals are bound in a balance of two worlds. Whatever time they spend on land, must be given back to the ocean in equal measure. A maximum of seven years may pass before the coat forces the selkie back to the water in order to repay the Debt. The only exception to this is when their coat is forcibly taken. In this instance they lose the ability to shift, their strength and speed are drastically diminished, and they are incapable of speech. Only the retrieval of the selkie's coat allows them to gain the full range of their abilities again.

Shannon **R**owle: (Selkie) Daughter of Eion and Anita Rowel.

Sitaltna: (Sí-talt-na) The capital city of the Nereids in the Atlantic Ocean.

Tristan **M**cKenny: (Selkie) Member of the Bacainn, and Shannon's guardian.

Tyrus son of **C**assius: (Tie-Russ) (Nereid) Wader. Brother of Atticus and Hadriana.

Wader: A title given to those who are able to project their thoughts across great distances. Range is determined by the strength of the individual. This talent is most often found in the Nereids.

*W*eaver: A title given to those with the ability to weave an energy shield around a person or area to conceal whatever is within the shield. Size and effectiveness are determined by the individual's talent and training. The ability is not confined to any one species; however, it is most used among the Selkies in order to hide their homes from outside eyes.

Author's Note

Dear Reader,

It has finally happened! You have, in your hands, the solid form of a dream that began when I was a kid. Proof that God is faithful even to the prayers you thought were nothing more than the fantasy of a child.

I cannot tell you how much it means that you have chosen to come with me on an adventure within the pages of this book. It has been many years and a lot of trial and error to bring this story to you. But, at last, it is time for you to meet the wonderful personalities of Shannon, Tristan, Tyrus and Mandy, as they tackle questions about honor, duty, and where you must draw the line to do what is right.

So many people have helped me along the way to bring this book to you now. From brainstorming, and problem solving; to providing spackle for the many plot holes of my first draft and polishing my final manuscript until it appeared I had a grasp on English grammar; to pushing me to stride forward and not give up on making this childhood dream of mine a reality.

Mike, your work on the cover was beyond what I could have hoped for. You gave my book a beautiful piece of art I am proud to have represent my story. A superb job, thank you.

Mama and Daddy, thank you so much for your constant support, as well as your technical expertise. Because of you I might convince a few people I am a professional writer. Go figure that!

Grady, your fine tuning allowed me to make a fantasy story fall into the realm of somewhat believable. Your ribbing kept me grounded and smiling, thank you.

Ben, without your utter belief in my ability and relentless kicks to the backside, I more than likely would not have had the courage to move forward with publishing, thank you.

Most of all, thank you Lord for allowing me this opportunity to chase this dream. A dream I had given up on, but You decided to grant anyway. May your name ever be greater than mine.

Finally, dear Reader, thank you for taking a chance on this novel of mine. I sincerely hope you enjoy reading it as much as I did writing it.

All my love, your humble bard,

Darbie Hamilton

About the Author

*B*orn into a proud military family, Darbie Hamilton grew up moving all around the United States; each station bringing new sights, new people, and new stories to capture her attention.

Encouraged by her clan of bookworms, Darbie fell in love with the written word. Rarely was she seen without a book nearby. At the age of twelve she decided to dive into the world of imagination, painting pictures with words using paper and ink. Over the years her work transformed from two-page tales into sweeping stories of adventure, trials, and wonder.

Now settled in the hills of Tennessee, she still finds that wonder all around her. In the mountains, in the family and friends she treasures, and in the numerous blessings she has found in her life. From that wonder, she carries on writing; creating new worlds, meeting new characters, and diving into new adventures every day, both on and off the page.